SORRY, HUMANS

(Especially Greg)

Other Books by Splinter Press

Mere Mortal by A.J. Stevens
The Dissection and Reassembly of Cohen Hoard by Elesa Hagberg
Splinter's Edge by Boydell Bown

SORRY, HUMANS (ESPECIALLY GREG)

by Faralee Pozo

SPLINTER PRESS

Sorry, Humans (Especially Greg)
by Faralee Pozo

Cover:

Running Couple by Kevin Keele
Comic Book Explosion by Antipathique

Published by:

Splinter Press
Spanish Fork, Utah

splinterpress.com

ISBN-13: 978-1-960108-12-8

For Charlie, who for some reason doesn't seem to mind being married to an alien (or at least doesn't complain about it too much).

$[01]$ Sorry, humans.

Well, firstly, thank you.

You shared your world with us, and we are more grateful than you know. We have seen enough of the universe to realize how rare your generosity is. It is why we came to you in the first place (well, eleventh place). Earth is truly a beautiful planet: so colorful, so varied, its people so warm and passionate. So, thank you very much.

And secondly: again, we are very, very sorry. We lied. A lot. Oh, and also, sorry for exploding your planet. It was not at all intentional, not a reflection of how we feel about your lovely world. We liked it very much, and we feel so sad. ☹

We are sorry, though the destruction was not entirely our fault. Some of the blame should lie with all those rules and stipulations you put into the Occupational Accord nine years ago. You remember, those 94,537 regulations that your UN presented to us on Arrival,[1] mainly repetitions about keeping ourselves separate from the "general public ignorant to our presence."[2] We thought you simply liked trivial rules

---

[1]   We like the term *Arrival* better than *invasion*, if you are interested in the politically correct phrasing.

[2]   Number 1: Do not reveal yourself to the general public ignorant to your presence; number 3,027: Do not become a drain on the resources needed for the general public ignorant to your presence; number 21,001: Share every and all technologies with specified persons only, and no technologies are to be used against humankind, knowledgeable or ignorant to your presence, etc., etc.

and high numbers, so we did not take them as seriously as we should have at first.[3] Which was maybe why you kept us locked deep underground in a special Compound guarded by bazooka-wielding peacekeepers—so we did not even have the choice to break the rules.

I still managed to break one or two anyway.

I should be clear. Most of the blame does lie with us, not you. Thus: this very long apology. But more specifically, the blame lies with *me*. I should not include all of my people in the blame, as most of them had nothing to do with it.

And also, at least 22 to 24 percent of the fault lies with Greg.

I know you are probably thinking:[4] What is a Greg? Greg who? Or maybe: What does my brother-in-law/uncle/neighbor/uncle's neighbor have to do with this anyway? Depending on your origins, I understand Gregs can be common.

Well, *this* Greg is different.

Ah. Sweet, sweet Greg.

Anyway, I am not making excuses, but I would like to explain myself. I cannot return your planet unscathed to you, but I do think you deserve to know the whole story. Let me start at the beginning. No, not that far—let me start a year ago, before any of this happened, when the Earth was still whole and shiny.

I was attending a political gala in Washington DC in

---

3   Now that we know you better, we realize a love of high numbers and being 100 percent serious about every trivial rule are not mutually exclusive.

4   Do not worry, I do not actually know what you are thinking. I am not that kind of alien.

October. Once a year on the anniversary of the Arrival, a friend and I would sneak out of the Compound and attend an event, one event of our choosing, incognito. We had an annual "females' night out" as I think you call it.

We went in disguise as humans, and never told anyone we were aliens. I would not call this a lie. I simply do not think I need to share everything about myself with strangers. By the way, do you know how often you humans introduce yourselves by saying, "Hello, I am Barbara and I am a human"? Never. Even the ones named Barbara.

But more to the point, since it is literally rule number one in the Accord that said we were not allowed to reveal ourselves to the "ignorant general public" (which constituted 99.999999 percent of the total population), I tended to be silent on the subject. Should not my keeping this rule count for something?

True, rule number one *also* prohibits leaving the Compound, which rule we did not keep and which carried with it the consequence of possible planetary expulsion by catapult. You made this sound very scary. We did not want this consequence to be enacted much, so, we tried to be careful and discreet. But also, since our excursions were so rare, we tried to make them count.

Once, my friend and I went to a street soccer event in Africa, and once a high school swim meet in Chile. Two years in a row, we attended the swing dance night at the Springdale Community Center in South Carolina. That excursion was my favorite. With each outing, we spent an hour or two learning about you (with no ulterior or nefarious motives), collected needed supplies, and then we went back to the Compound in Alaska, back to our people, and none of you humans even noticed our presence—or, at least, not until a year ago when we attended the gala.

This particular gala was shaping up to be a boring disappointment, and I was ready to leave early.

I wore a jaw-dropping, eye-popping dress with a low back, red silk contrasting my dark human skin, my silver tentacles safely disguised as silver hair. Looking human, and amazing. It did not help.

Being on a giant, fancy yacht, the Lady Blue, should have been interesting, but that did not help either. And there was music, but the exact wrong tempo for dancing.

It was my friend's fault we were there in the first place. Political events, even human ones, are not my idea of fun. My friend kept trying to convince me that observing these boring United States representatives and senators while they did not dance was better than attending a commencement at the charter high school down the street (*my* first choice for the evening). I told her that this gala was a waste of an excursion. She won the argument by using her signature move—a particularly stern look—and I had just stormed away, when I saw *him*.

Greg.

Not your brother-in-law/uncle/neighbor. The other one. *That* one.

Midtwenties,[5] tall, light skin, blondish-brown hair—he

---

5   In case you are curious, no, we do not track age or time the same way you do. So while I may be slightly younger than Greg in terms of the passage of time relatively speaking, I am 398 planets' passing in our age measurement. Which is a bigger number.

wore a tux, but I could not tell by the outfit if he was government or staff. He had confidence, but it was not the *I am the smartest and most important person in the room* kind of confidence most government humans there had; it was more like he was comfortable with himself. His nose was a bit big for a human, and his eyes a bit small, with a few too many laugh lines to be taken seriously. His suit was a bit loose, though only barely long enough at the wrists and ankles for his tall frame.

And he was the most beautiful thing I had ever seen.

Booger.[6]

He locked eyes with me, smiled, and then approached without hesitation or embarrassment. He introduced himself, but all I heard was romantic music wafting through my brain like red *snorsgrass* ink through white clothes in the wash.

"*Booger*," I said aloud, tipping my head to the side and shaking it to get the music out and the feeling back into my brain. "I mean, very nice to meet you and what do you want?"

"What was that?" he asked, his mouth quirked in an annoyingly adorable half smile.

"I am sorry, what I meant was, I did not catch that, who are you and who do you represent?"[7]

He grinned. "I'm Greg, who I work for is top secret, so if I told you I'd have to kill you, and uh . . . who are you?"

---

6   This may look like your word for nose excretion, but it is actually a word in my language that is much too rude to translate.

7   I believe I am normally much better at this. I have no evidence I can offer to prove that, however.

Booger. It was exactly the sort of inane thing any average human would say. He was perfect.

"Booger," I said aloud again.

"That's not your name, is it?" Greg chuckled, a low rumbling I felt in my toes.

Stupid Greg.

For those Human Survivors reading this, I am not sure what your clearance level is. Perhaps you are one of the two or three dozen humans who were *read in* on the Arrival from the start, but more likely you were part of the general public ignorant to the reality of aliens, on your planet or otherwise. Either way, I should probably explain: among the many stipulations in the Accord,[8] it was specified that there was to be no "fraternization"[9] with humans, *aware or ignorant* of our presence (Accord 499a). Well, so far, this was a rule we had made no attempt to subvert in the slightest. Considering that we rarely saw humans at all, it was barely worth mentioning anyway. Also, the rule seemed to be mainly about sanitation, and we believe in good hygiene.

Greg was clearly human, one of the general public "ignorant to our presence" like the rest of the 99.999999 percent of the planet, and therefore had no right to be so exquisitely dreamy.

I looked over at my friend Penny. She stood to one side

---

8   Such as: follow the laws of the land, though we had no vote (number 7,342), leave virtually no footprint unless it was for improvements that helped the planet (27), keep quiet when it is dark (which is always because we are underground) to avoid flustering the wildlife, etc.

9   And several other unnecessary euphemisms. We may be aliens, but we knew what you were talking about. There was no need to pussyfoot.

next to a long table with drinks and empty glasses on top. She frowned at me, which was normal for her, to be honest. Her bluish-black, shoulder-length human hair framed her face like curtains around a stage, and I could tell looking at her stage-face that there was going to be trouble. I looked back at Greg again even though looking at him brought me physical pain.

"You're not going to tell me your name?" he was asking, since I'd only continued to stare and swear at him.

"Did I not?"

He smiled. "Will I have to guess?"

I let out a breath of relief. "Oh, would you? That would help me quite a lot."

Greg chuckled again. Then Penny was there, stepping in front of me.

"Goodbye,"[10] she said in her heavily accented English. She pushed me away toward a refreshment table draped in dark blue.

Greg could not be so easily dissuaded. "Is this your friend?" he asked as he caught up to walk beside me.

I nodded. "This is Penny," were the words that popped out.

"Nice to meet you. Where are you from, Penny?"

She gave him a fiery glare which he countered with open friendliness. She may have been a head shorter than his two-meter height, but with her small black eyes, she had a stare that could frighten mother *grogoolas*, and I had

---

10   It is basically the only word she knows how to say in any Earth language, though she understands everything much more than I do without my royal Speak-Easy translator technology.

not seen many people from any planet stand up to it. Greg simply smiled.

"We are from Booshlaboo," I found myself answering as we approached an overflowing food table.

Penny looked at me like I had lost my faculties, her severe eyes bulging.

"Is that in Europe?" asked Greg.

I closed my mouth.

Apparently taking this as confirmation, he continued. "You both are? You too?"

I nodded and shook my head at the same time.

"Wow, your English is unbelievable. You don't even have an accent," he said to me.

"Yes. Or thank you. It comes with the job."

"What do you do?" he continued, grabbing a tiny clear-glass plate from a pile on the table.

I picked up a plate too. "I am the seventh daughter of Morr, Keeper of the Sacred Sponge, heir to the Fallen Branches of Bough . . ." What was wrong with me? I truly was not trying to spill all of my very important and classified alien secrets, but spill I did. If you knew Greg, you would understand.

He grinned. "What was that?"

"Keeper of the Sacred Sponge—" I started again, seemingly incapable of holding my tongue.

"Like . . . you wash dishes?" He was piling tiny food onto his tiny plate now.

". . . Uh, yes. Well . . . I mean, those titles are sort of honorary," I lied, piling food onto my plate too.

He smiled but only with half his mouth. "So you're an *honorary* dishwasher?"

I puffed my cheeks up and nodded again. Penny's head was on the verge of splitting open.[11]

"Wow. I have no response to that. So you can tell me your job, but not your name?"

I opened my mouth, my eyes bouncing over to Penny's scorching glare. I tried to close my mouth, but instead my name flew out. "Aria."[12]

"It's a pleasure to meet you, Aria, beautiful honorary dishwasher and arranger of fallen branches. You are not at all what I expected when I saw you across the room."

"You were looking at me across the room?"

"Absolutely," he replied without a hint of shame.

We started walking in a circle around the edge of the large ballroom, Penny stomping along behind us.

"Almost everyone here is exactly what you expect," Greg said. "They're talking about the same things they always talk about: taxes, politics, other people's secrets. Have you met anyone interesting here? Besides me, of course." He actually winked.[13]

---

11   Not literally, of course. That only happens once every few years during her "cycle."

12   In case you are wondering, my name and Penny's are fairly accurate translations—not transliterations. In other words, Penny's name means *very small denomination*, and my name means *melodic solo*. I would tell you the transliteration, but I am told that both sound like we are saying very obnoxious Earth phrases. I will only say that Penny's name starts with what sounds like, "Moist musical beans" and then just gets worse from there.

13   This is a signal we also have on my planet, though the meaning is different. Luckily, I had been apprised of your human slightly-less-aggressive meaning to a wink, so there were no intergalactic incidents over it, this time.

I may have twittered like a sniveling *borshwat*. He looked sideways at me, the half smile making me sure he was X-raying my brain, and I turned away, trying to look like I was examining a swath of gauzy drapery with tiny lights under it on the wall. "Um . . . " I tried to remember his question. "The South African diplomat told a pretty good story."

"Oh, was it the one about the toilet brush and the basket of dragon fruit?" he asked, his half smile breaking into a full grin. "That's a good one. He's a nice guy."

I took a bite of something orange on a toothpick from my tiny plate (some kind of your cheese, I think) and tried to remember if there had been anyone else worth talking to over the course of the night. "That waiter over there recently lost their electric bass player to a 'rival band' and has tryouts for a new player on Sunday. I am thinking of going for it."

"Do you play the bass?" he asked, raising his eyebrows.

"Well, no, but I play the didgeridoo."

"You play the . . . I don't think those are interchangeable."

I contemplated this. "Okay. I will learn the bass too, then. How hard could it be? What is a bass?"

He laughed out loud. I could not tell if he was laughing *at* me or not, but if so, this human's laugh made me want to keep saying the wrong thing forever just to hear it again.

Penny finally managed to get me away from Greg when another human started talking to him. She pulled me to the other side of the room, hissing chastisements that I only half heard, urging me to go back to observing humans not named Greg.

"I know, I know," I responded in order to stem the stream of hushed yelling. "Time to get boring again."

I tried to stay away from Greg after that. Sort of. And maybe if I had succeeded, none of that whole exploding/destruction/screaming-in-the-streets thing would have happened. I tried to focus elsewhere, but my eyes kept straying over to Greg. Every time I started up a conversation with some senator or congressperson or king or janitor, Greg was in the background, smiling and making it look like his end of the room was so much more interesting than mine. I kept trailing off in the middle of conversations, my feet walking toward him of their own accord. Penny stepped in front me as I subconsciously started walking in his direction again.

"No," she said in our language.[14]

"What? No, it is fine, I am only—"

"No."

"But, Penny, I am *not*—"

"*No*. I see your eyes looking at him. I see you, and I am telling you, that is a very bad idea."

I scoffed. "Some wingman you are turning out to be."

"I am not your *wingman*,[15] I am not your friend, I am your adviser and I am telling you, Aria, Seventh Daughter of Morr, Keeper of the Sacred Sponge, Heir to the Fallen Branches of

---

14   Booshplubooverimelibarristan is the transliteration for what our language is called. But that is too long to say, even in our language, so we call it Booshy. Are you not glad you looked at this footnote?

15   Our word for this is translated more like branching leaf buddy. Which is very interesting. That is why I am telling you.

Bough, Final Monarch of the Thirteenth Planet of LifeStar, *Your Majesty*, do not pursue that human."

Oh. Um, yes. I do not think I have mentioned it.

I am the monarch of the Brooshaloo people. I am the alien queen.

$[02]$ Yes, it was me. I was the one to say "take me to your leader" nine years ago.

By the way, we already knew before we arrived that you would make the Accord, and what kind of stipulations you might include, though we did not predict there would be so many. We studied you from afar for years before we ~~invaded~~ approached. And then, we became what we believed you wanted. We became desperate refugees (which we actually were anyway).[1] We hid our weapons and power. We showed ourselves to be weak but not too weak, and similar but not too similar.

We also revealed ourselves to be green skinned and bald, with giant bug eyes. But that is not what we truly look like, of course. Other than our silvery skin and completely-black almond eyes and tentacle hair and pointy teeth and biolumi-nescence, we actually look exactly like you.

I am sorry I did not specify my royal title to you sooner, but I thought the term *alien queen* might be misleading.[2] And also it sounds super dumb. I had only recently inherited

---

1   Which was why we did not tell your leaders that I was the queen, just a temporarily chosen representative. Most refugee groups I know do not include monarchs.

2   Based on my research into your culture, I am guessing Alien Queen makes you think of something like this: me lazily sitting around all day, sucking out brains or laying eggs in people. It sounds boring. But also, I only wish I had that kind of free time.

my title from the previous queen (my aunt Sonata) when we started our journey through space, making the Arrival my very first act as queen, and I have done almost nothing you would consider queenly since. I do not lead or govern, per se, though I do wave and smile sometimes for my people, and I receive and (occasionally) read reports from my advisers. Even as I say that, it sounds embarrassingly silly and useless. So, quite a bit like the role of your US president, come to think of it.

Traditionally, the queen is supposed to be more like a buffer than anything else. We do not want our innocents to come up against the hostile aliens directly (which is you, by the way), so the queen is gifted with the technology to communicate with strangers (you, again) on their behalf. I use this technology to speak every Earth language with almost no accent. I can also change my appearance[3] and that of anyone in the close vicinity with a clap of my hands (or two if it needs a jump start). But not counting the initial Arrival, I have not had much cause to use these gifts, in an official capacity at least. After the Accord was created, we were locked into the Compound, and no one said a word to us ever again. No one fun, anyway.

At least you can be comforted in the fact that Penny and I were the only ones to ever break out of the Compound, it was only once a year,[4] and I think *I* was the only one to enjoy it.

---

3   Actually, we did not change our facial structure much. That way we were still recognizable to each other at a glance, and when Penny and I went out, she would not try to tackle me to the ground and break my thumbs for getting too close like she might one of you.

4   And we left the compound for a very good reason. The galas and graduations and dances were just a side benefit.

But despite Penny and my differing opinion on fun, she does keep me in line, and I make an effort to listen to her, as my royal adviser.[5] When Penny told me to stop talking to Greg at the gala, I did. I did not even say goodbye to him when we left. I may have gazed longingly at his back and broad shoulders, but for this you would not fault me if you had seen the faint outline of his shoulder blades. They were magnificent.

Penny and I hid in a broom closet that smelled like *ash-mell* dust, activated our gravitator, and transported away.

We did not return to the Compound directly, of course. Even with the assistance of our transporting gravitator technology, Washington DC is a long way from the mountains of Alaska, in case you do not know your geography. (Sorry, I am sure you do, no insult intended.)[6] So to break up the trip, avoid suspicion, and save on precious energy, we gravitated two or three blocks away and stayed overnight at one of our many prepared secret places of safety—a safehouse you might say. It was a one-room condo we secretly owned[7] in the neighborhood. A safecondo.

That night, after removing our human disguises (and the 'green alien' disguise layer we always wear underneath) with a clap of my hands, I lay resting on the very soft bed

---

5   Her actual title translates to something like Royal Backseat Driver. Many of our titles are metaphor. We consider this more straightforward.

6   And if you do not know your geography you will have to take my word for it since there is no way for you to look it up anymore to my knowledge. Oopsie.

7   Yes, we had a very large amount of your money, and yes, we stole all the money we had from you. But before you feel too indignant, keep in mind that it is just a lot of useless paper that neither of us have any use for now.

between a fluffy comforter and a fluffier mattress[8] and tried not to replay every word of my conversation with Greg. Could anyone be that perfectly imperfectly human? I'd always been fascinated by you and your varied cultures, but never on such a singular level. I realized he'd never told me anything about himself or his profession, only that he would have to kill me if he told me. Could that be a joke? Was *he* a joke someone was playing on me?

The next morning my thoughts were still full of gray laughing eyes and light-brown, wavy hair. Penny was scowling in the morning, but that is her resting face, so I ignored her. I got up, fluffed my head tentacles, sharpened my teeth, and got re-humanned up for the day using the facebender tech so we could take the train. The train would take us to the waypoint where we would gravitate the rest of the way to the Compound.

"Maybe we should leave early," said Penny as she picked through her array of all-black clothing[9] hanging in the tiny closet. "You absorbed enough zest last night, right? So, we have no other reason to stay. The sooner we get back, the better."

"Yes, I got the zest, but what is the hurry?" I asked.

---

8   Much softer than the hammock beds we had in the Compound. By the way, we do not sleep the same way as you, nor as often. But we did usually rest like this during the night when we were among you, to avoid suspicion and conserve energy.

9   I have no idea why she only wears black. She says it is to blend in, but blend in with what? Haunted houses? Black panthers? Where the asphalt meets the night sky?

"No hurry." She put her hands on her hips, watching me. "Can't you move any faster?"

I sat on the edge of the bed to put my socks on. "Penny, everything is fine. I got the zest from the senator of Texas, so the zest gauge is completely full. Does not that make you happy?" I looked down at the charm on my necklace, my Royal Everything Device[10]: full zest, and two hundred eighty power units, which was still enough for anything we might need. I looked back up at Penny's face. She was staring me down.

I sighed and started on my other sock. "Yes, I know I went 'off script,' last night, and spoke too long to . . . that human, but no real harm was done, right?"

She clenched her fists. "Not yet, no. Ready?"

I nodded, but then I just sat there on the bed.

Penny watched me a few moments, then she sat next to me, her voice dropping low. "You know that whole thing would never have worked out, right? Even if we don't consider Accord law—which I know you try to never do—you have responsibilities to us and our future. And you know the future of our people could never involve a *fling* with some *thing* that lives out here."

I chafed at her use of the word *fling* and *thing* (despite the fact that it was a very good rhyme), but I did not try to deny

---

10 This device includes the zest and power gauges, emergency shield, gravitator, air enhancement, and facebender disguise technology all in one sleek silver necklace. Penny also wears an air enhancement necklace, but it is much simpler, more like a thin metal chain. By the way, the royal Speak-Easy translator technology is a small chip embedded in my brain.

it. She was usually right. It was her talent. And my talent was forgiving her for how annoying it was.

We were silent as we left the safecondo, walking toward the train station. We had only gone a few steps when I slowed to a stop again. While the thought of riding your human trains normally entices me, knowing we were then gravitating back to the Compound again for another year—back underground to our tiny, curtained spaces, to the hundred thousand Accord stipulations and the ten thousand expectant faces—I could not put a single foot in front of the other.

Instead, I started walking the other direction. Penny called after me, but when I did not stop, she followed me, swearing.

Yes, Penny was right, but this was not about Greg—or even so much about a reluctance to face my responsibilities—as it was a reticence to crease the amazing jeans I was wearing. Why, on the once-beautiful Earth, did we bother to go shopping, find that adorable pink sweater, the perfect human jeans, and those stompy boots simply to get onto a train and go back to a crowded Compound to wear a sheet toga? Sometimes an outfit is so adorable, it calls for exciting things to happen while you wear it. I think this is something every species in the universe can understand.

So we walked. I smiled and Penny glowered, a constant stream of creative swear words spewing from Penny's lips that luckily no passing human understood.

I picked a flower growing beside the sidewalk, its many petals frail and yellow. I do not think you realize how fascinating it is: a living thing sending a smell to attract bees for its own benefit and humans by accident, without doing any damage to either.[11] My own planet had something similar, but of course our plant life is also sentient and evil and much larger. And the only plants that put out a smell also put out spores, killing you dead before you could say thanks for the flowers.

So this was nice.

I found my steps being drawn to a small farmers market, booths of more flowers than I knew the name of, fruits and vegetables that were so plump and colorful and fragrant they competed with the flowers for beauty. We were not allowed fresh food in the Compound. If we wanted any fruits or vegetables, we had to get them chopped up into tiny pieces, then frozen and smuggled in. Sounds violent, does it not? Our dietary needs are very similar to yours, but I had very rarely eaten a fresh *anything* from your planet.

I took one bite of a big pink peach, a sample given to me by a tall man with white hair and no shirt under his overalls. I felt the peach juice squish down my chin.

And then I guess I went a bit . . . wild.

I ran, stumbling from booth to booth, snagging green melons, colorful citrus, earthy roots, and berries of every color, taking bites willy-nilly while Penny ran back and forth behind me, throwing paper money at the stunned vendors.

I was just getting my teeth into a small round water-melon—refreshing on the inside, but difficult to bite into without completely unhinging my jaw, which I did not like to

---

11   I am not sure why I am explaining flowers to you, I am assuming you have seen one before the destruction of your planet. If not, this description is unlikely to do much for you anyway.

do in public. I was sort of gnawing on the rind,[12] some water-
melon pulp mixing with all the other juices on my cheeks and
chin, when I looked up to see someone blocking my path.

Greg.

See? He seemed innocuous, but he had the worst knack
for turning up at the wrong time and place. It was like he was
pulled out of my treasonous hopes and dreams and placed
there as a temptation right when I was at my least dignified.

I swallowed my bite of mangled fruit pulp, but there was
not a lot I could do about my bouquet of half-eaten fruits and
vegetables, or the mess I'd likely made of my makeup, not to
mention my adorable pink sweater that was probably ruined
under all the fruit I held. I smiled weakly at Greg.

"Aria, isn't it? Do you remember me? Greg? From the
gala?" He looked me up and down, a mixture of confusion and
amusement in his expression.

"No," I lied. Penny caught up to me and slid to a stop. I
could not see her face because the watermelon and pumpkin
in my arms blocked that side, and also my sight was locked
on Greg.

His eyes bounced between all the produce I held, and I
tried to gracefully put it all into a basket I spotted on the
ground. Some of it rolled out to trip other farmers-market
shoppers.

---

12   I have since learned that you humans do not eat the outside of a water-
melon, but honestly, I cannot keep track of all your fruits. Some you say
should be eaten with the rind and others you peel, but there seems to be
no system telling which is which. Anyway, you are wrong about some
of them. Durian, for instance, is way better with the spiky outside. Still
completely gross though.

"Finish this up for me, will you, Penny?" I said in English, in my most regal, unflustered voice,[13] motioning to the mess with a sweep of my arm.

"Is that a *Royal Command*?" she muttered under her breath in Booshy. I tried to glare at her as she scrambled around to get the fruit and then left to find another basket. We both knew my request to help with the fruit was not a command—she did not *have* to obey—but we also both knew she would do it anyway.

"Uh," Greg said, still taking in my fruity and flustered state. "Don't you have fruit in . . . where did you say you were from, again?"

"Brooshaloo."

"Right."

We both paused while I decided whether to answer about the fruit or wipe the juice from my chin. I settled on both. "Well, yes we did have fruit there, but it had to be picked before it ripened, before it could develop venom or deadly pollens or spores, so the flavor was not great."

"Ah," he said, a little dazed. By the ghost of his smile, he might have thought I was joking, or crazy. At least he was not having me arrested. Or catapulted off the planet. I should have said simply yes or no to his questions, but somehow, almost every time I opened my mouth in this man's presence, the truth fell out.

Penny was suddenly by my side again, her black human

---

13   I am pretty good at this. But only when I am unflustered and in a comfortable situation unlike this one.

hair swinging in her face, with two baskets full of my colorful produce mushed and mangled beyond recognizability.

"Hey, Penny," Greg said, eyes still locked on mine.

She swore at him, which, by his broadening wry smile, he somehow seemed to be able to understand despite it not being in his language.

"So, assuming there is any of it left, I'm here for some fruit, too. Care to . . . walk around the market with me, Aria?"

Penny side-knocked me so hard I squeaked. I tried to mask it with what I hoped was a girlish human giggle. "Um, no. No, we already have all we can carry here, so . . ."

"Right." He nodded and moved to walk past us. "Well, if you change your mind and want to join me later—"

"Okay," I said, turning around and hopping over to step beside him.

Greg raised his eyebrows and chuckled. I tried to muster up some shame, but could not quite manage it. Penny trailed along behind us, growling, which I had not heard her do since youthschool when BigThroat sniffed her tentacles.

"So," I said in the awkward silence of having to now face all the vendors I had practically stolen from a few moments ago. "Do you live here in Washington DC?"

Greg smiled. "Sort of. I'm just here for work. But I'm originally from a town a few miles away from here." We stepped up to one of the booths, and Greg started filling a bag with fruit.

I nodded. "And you love apples?" I pointed at the red, yellow, and green apples filling his bag.

He looked down at the bag. "Oh. We have a big meeting tonight before we leave, and my boss wants to have a bowl of fruit on the table. Make it feel homey or something. I thought apples would be easy and colorful? I'm supposed to get flowers too." He looked over at me. "You, um, you have some pulp on your . . ." He touched my cheek, but the juice had become sticky, so he pulled his finger away and wiped it on his pants.

I tried to wipe any remnants from my face with my sleeve. I got a glimpse of Penny's murderous expression as she followed behind us, and I quickly looked back at Greg.

"Do you know anything about flowers?" he asked. He paid and we moved on from the apple booth, wandering through the narrow aisle.

"I do, but where I am from, our flowers are more . . . carnivorous," I answered.

"Like Venus fly traps?"

"Sure."

"Like your fruit, too, then?"

"Well, all plants really." I shrugged.

He laughed. "Cool. Maybe something like that might be fun for the meeting?" We had moved from the fruit to the flower area now.

"No," I said, cutting in before he got too excited about that idea. "Trust me, I speak from experience. A carnivorous plant might look good for business meetings, but you would change your mind when your secretary is halfway down its throat in the middle of a slideshow on workplace safety."

He laughed again, a comfortable sound like an old engine. As we wandered, we found some already prepared bouquets at one of the flower booths. Greg bought one, paid the smiling woman, then pulled a flower out of the bouquet and handed it to me with a little bow.

The woman smiled wider, her face like sunshine to match her yellow dress. As we walked away, I heard her say quietly, "That's a hibiscus. It's edible, you know."[14]

Hibiscus, I repeated to myself, smelling the flower. When Greg turned his head, I took a giant bite of the hibiscus, trying to chew and swallow before he turned back around.

"*So . . .*" Greg said, drawing out the word like it was a sentence. He turned around to face me, and I hid the flower stem behind my back. We'd reached the end of the small market. Beside us was parked an orange truck vehicle that looked like it could be a hundred of your years old, all curves and gradients of rust color. Greg opened the door to the truck, and I fought off a wave of panic, knowing he was about to drive off and Penny was going to squeeze me back into the Compound and I would never see Greg again (unless I could somehow steal one of your satellites and direct it at him later).[15]

"Do you wanna get something to eat with me after my meeting tonight?" Greg asked, one of his hands resting on the truck door.

I gulped. "Eat?"

"I have to fly back home tonight, but my flight isn't until like four in the morning, so I'll just be lounging around somewhere. Will you still be in town? Do you already have plans? If

---

14   An edible flower? After all the people I have known that were eaten by our flowers, eating one back makes the taste *oh* so sweet.

15   And I really did not want to have to do that again.

not, you could be my date for dinner. Uh . . . maybe without your bodyguard?" He looked back at Penny.

For a moment I thought we'd been *made*, as your undercover operatives say, but then I realized calling Penny a bodyguard was meant to be ironic.

A date? I tried very hard to look into those sweet, sincere gray eyes and tell him it could never happen, but judging by his responding smile, whatever came out of my mouth must have sounded like *yes*.

[·03] It only took maybe an hour to convince Penny to let me go—that one more night could not hurt, that this was no treasonous and dangerous human fling, but a closer observation of humans.[1] Or well, of *a* human, but the logic still held.

And then, while I switched to a blue cotton top and denim skirt, I told her she was welcome to join us as long as joining us meant eating at a different table with a different face. She never exactly agreed, but she did not stop me when I walked to the nearby café on The Wharf that night.

The café was perfect. Outdoor tables sat under a pergola-style roof, happy[2] red flowers dangled from hanging planters at each column, and sweet and bready smells hovered like a blanket. Lanterns on each table provided the only light, the nearby dark water reflecting the lights back at us.

And there was Greg, leaning his shoulder against a column with his feet crossed, a green shirt that made his eyes look greener, a pair of dark jeans, and his attention and thumbs on the telephone device in his hand. His angles and colors were like a painting, like he was a model in a catalog with the caption, "regular, adorable human." Looking at him,

---

1   That is a lie. It only took Penny about *three* of your hours to get tired of yelling at me. But sometimes it is better just to let her tire herself out.

2   I have been trained and am very good at reading flowers (or at least the giant, sentient Booshy counterpart). So trust me on this. The flowers were happy.

I could almost forget about my masked alien physiology, about Penny hiding somewhere behind me, about my responsibilities, and simply pretend I was a human girl, nervous but excited for a night out.

Almost.

"Hi," I said breathily when I was a meter away. The ambient noise of the café was mild even with the other people there chatting at the outdoor tables, and Greg looked up, smiling and stowing his phone.

"I was worried you weren't coming." He stepped a little closer.

"Oh, am I late?"

"Not at all, but since you wouldn't give me your phone number, I was worried maybe you might stand me up and I would never see you again."

We gazed at each other for a moment, and then Greg motioned toward a little table, bowing with a playful hand flourish, and pulled out my chair.

We sat at the wrought iron table, and someone brought us large paper menus. "How was your meeting?" I asked a few blissfully awkward moments later.

"Great. Long. The flowers and fruit were a hit." He smiled and laid his menu down, leaning his arms on the table. "Did you like the hibiscus? I've never eaten one before."

So he *had* seen. I twittered and tried to redirect the conversation back to him as he took a drink of water. "Where do you work? I think you said something about having to kill me if you told me? If that is true, please do not tell me, I do not think it will be worth it."

He coughed into his water, but came up smiling once he

could breathe again. "Um, yes, *ha*, just a—just a joke. I forget English isn't your native language. I'm an aide for the Alaskan senator, Gwyn Kilcher?"

To which I thought, *Booger. Alaska*.

Gwyn Kilcher[3] was one of *my* senators—or, at least, my Compound was in her state, so she *would* have been my senator if I had been human with rights and a vote. I had never met her personally,[4] but I had been led to believe that the two Alaskan senators were among those elite few who knew about our existence, since we were (sort of) their constituents. Was it possible Greg knew about us too since he worked for her, knew what we were? And if so, did he suspect me of being an alien? Was he toying with me?

I asked/said none of this. "Do you like it? Your job working with a senator?"

"Sure, yeah. Gwyn's great."

"What is your favorite part?" I asked, eager to keep the conversation on him, and also genuinely interested.

"The sticky notes," he responded without hesitation or artifice.

"Sticky? Notes?"

"Yeah, you know, the little square note paper with a sticky back," he held his fingers up in a square. "Post-Its?"

"Ooh," I responded, leaning forward in my chair.

"Yeah, I used to have to buy them myself. Even though

---

3   Gwyn Kilcher. Very nice person. Long black hair, dark eyes, six foot one. Dead, now.

4   I had never really met *anyone* except the initial UN contacts and a handful of the same few soldiers, stinky with fear-sweat, wielding guns that would not have pierced our exoskeletons. Also dead now.

they don't cost much, you'd be surprised how quickly that adds up, but now I get as many sticky notes of as many types and colors as I want. I don't even have to reorder them myself—they're automatically refilled for me whenever I get low. Did you know there are waterproof sticky notes?"

"Waterproof?"

"Yeah, so I can spill stuff on them, write on them with a permanent marker, paint on them." He rubbed his hands together, genuinely excited by the prospect.

I giggled with secondary enjoyment. "Wow. I had no idea."

"Yep. I have access to all kinds of great office supplies: all thicknesses of paper and notebooks, ballpoint pens that write smoothly for days, and remind me to show you my collection of folder tabs, it's incredible. But yeah, the sticky notes are my favorite part." He sat back, sighing contentedly.

"Sticky notes," I said reverently.

His eyes crinkled. "Does that make me the most boring person in the world?"

"Not at all." Sticky notes sounded like the most interesting thing on *any* planet, but I was afraid admitting that might make me sound too alien. "So, you live there in Alaska when you are not here, then?" I asked.

"Yep, I just got a house there. They only brought me on staff about nine months ago, so I'm still getting settled. Usually I stay with my parents when I come to DC, but I'm staying at a hotel right now." He pursed his lips, watching me. "So, tell me, how does a dishwasher, even an honorary one, get invited to a big DC government soiree like the one last night?"

I coughed. "Well, I was not *strictly* invited. Penny and I sort of sneaked in."

Greg chuckled. "Of course you did." He waved his hand and a black–and–white suited waiter approached. Greg nodded at me. "Know what you want?"

I punched my finger randomly at the menu and hoped.

"The tilapia? Great choice. What vegetables?" asked the waiter, a younger man that seemed too tall for the size of his head.

"Whatever you have that is fresh," I responded, which made Greg laugh again.

He glanced up at the waiter. "She uh . . . she doesn't get a lot of fresh fruits or vegetables where she's from."

"Oh, where are you from?" the waiter asked.

I paused, looking at Greg. "Originally?" I had already told Greg the truth. Could I lie now?

Greg smiled. "I don't know how to say it. Is it Booshlaboo?"

I blew out a puff of air and nodded.

"Oh, yeah. Cool," said the waiter like he knew what we were talking about.

My people had been told that those who knew about us numbered maybe thirty at most in the whole world. But the waiter's non–reaction made me begin to wonder, had we been lied to? Did everyone know?[5]

---

5   I realize now that this young man was just covering up his total ignorance, which is something all creatures do across the galaxy, so I do not judge him.

After the waiter left, Greg and I chatted until we got our food and started eating. The food was amazing, Greg was amazing, everything was amazing, but the guilt of having this amazing evening was starting to creep up on me. I pushed it aside, hovering instead in the perfect euphoria. As our meal wound down, Greg excused himself and when he came back, he had someone with him, a nondescript man just a few inches shorter than he was, with dark hair and small dark eyes.

"Aria, this is my friend [Andrew?]," Greg said, pointing to his friend (I cannot recall the man's name, but I am sure it started with an A).[6] "He's one of the chefs here tonight, so if you liked your food, he's the one to thank. [Aaron?], this is Aria."

I smiled and bobbed my head.

Greg's friend looked back and forth between us for a bit longer than seemed polite before responding. He seemed amused. "Nice to meet you, Aria. Greg's great—you got yourself a pretty good human being there."

"Yes." I blinked a few times, flustered. "He is not technically *my* human being, but he is good." They both laughed, and I cleared my throat. "You two are friends?"

The man nodded. "Greg was in one of my cooking classes over at Virginia Tech. 'Course, Greg moved on to bigger and better things, didn't you, Greg?"

---

6   Or it might have started with one of the other twenty-five letters in your alphabet.

Greg rolled his eyes. I glanced at Greg, looking him up and down. He could cook human food, too? My heart[7] stuttered.

The two men stood by the table, chatting for a few moments, and I watched Greg's eyes crinkle in a smile even when his mouth was not smiling. I only barely stopped myself from reaching out to touch him.

Greg's friend was giving me a penetrating look. He stepped closer. "How did you two meet? What do you think of Greg? And how long are you in town?" he asked with a conspiratorial smile.

Greg chuckled and whacked him playfully on the arm. "It's a first date. Give her a break."

The friend was still looking at me. "But . . ."

Greg shooed him away. "He's a great guy," Greg said after his friend was gone, sitting back down at the table. "I'm glad we caught him—I wanted him to meet you. And sorry, he's kind of overprotective."

"Like Penny." I glanced over my shoulder, trying to spot her, but I did not know where she would be sitting, and she was too good at hiding when she wanted to.

Greg took a drink of water. "Yeah, she seems very . . . loyal. How'd she take you leaving her behind?"

I cleared my throat. She could undoubtedly hear our conversation. "I am not sure. Knowing her, she followed me

---

7   My culture does not use this organ as a symbol for love. But "my elbows stuttered" just does not have the same impact in English. So I will stick with *heart* for your benefit. Extra points if you find more instances of this throughout the rest of my story! Though, I do not know what you need points for.

here rather than be left behind and is now listening in on our whole conversation."

He laughed and then leaned forward. "I guess we need to talk a bit quieter and closer, then." He winked.

He had not said anything blush-worthy, but I could still feel myself blushing.[8] *Ahem.* "Actually, we were supposed to go home today, so Penny is already mad that I delayed us."

"Home to Booshlaboo?"

"Well . . . no. We do not live there anymore." I looked down.

"That must be hard, to be away from your home?"

I sighed. I'd been barely more than a youth when we left. Our refugee situation here was not the best, but I'd adapted to it.

Still, there were so many parts I missed from home. Before the plant uprising and Manyleaf War and before our backyard garden[9] ate my parents and kicked us out, I had many pleasant memories. I could not share any of that, however. I looked down as Greg reached across the table to hold my hand, his fingers loosely entwining mine. A zing of energy zipped up my arm and settled in my chest.

Watching our hands, it was like our hearts were entwining as well. It was a magical moment, the dim light making it hard to see, hard to breathe, iridescent bubbles blown from somewhere, gently floating, adding to the dreaminess of the

---

8   Luckily, he could not see me blush because it was blue and on my shoulder blades.

9   Our homes were very humble, even for all our royalty. We used to have very elaborate gardens, however. This royal tradition was done away with for obvious reasons.

moment. I knew I should pull back, pull back my hand and my heart. I was crossing a threshold here, one I could not back away from, one that maybe I had crossed the moment I first saw him. None of this was fair: not fair to my people, not fair to me, and not fair to Greg. And it was my fault if it went any further. I had to cut it off now or my heart was going to be irretrievable.

I watched as his thumb stroked mine in the magical candlelight, willing myself to pull back.

Willing, but failing.

Instead, he was the one that pulled away. "While we're on the subject—" his tone was light, but his expression betrayed a sudden nervousness, "what's with that whole honorary dishwasher title thing you do?" He blushed, and when I did not answer beyond a noise of confusion, he went on. "Don't get me wrong; it's charming, but it's almost the only thing I know about you, and it sounds like, well, nonsense. And where are you from, again?" I opened my mouth, but he went on. "I looked up Booshlaboo or whatever."

"Boovashoo," I corrected, clearing my throat.

"You say it differently every time you say it."

"It is conjugated differently depending on the speaker's mood."

He blinked. "Huh. But nothing close to that is a country, city, municipality, or village that I can find, anywhere on Earth." He leaned back in his chair, tapping the table with his fingers.

Booger. "Well . . ."

"At first, I thought you were teasing. Flirting. Like the poisonous forbidden fruit thing. But you're really doubling down on all of it. I have to ask myself, why would you double down on such an obvious fabrication?" He flushed pink again at this. I shook my head at him, but he was not slowing down now. "And assuming Aria is even your real name, what's your last name?"

I should have been more prepared with things like last names and a credible origin city before this. Penny was always telling me to be prepared. But I kept forgetting humans had things like last names in the first place. Also, preparation had seemed boring and unnecessary until that moment.

Greg looked up at me and smiled, but it was with a tinge of sadness. "Look, I get it. You can't tell me. But I'm in government, so I'm not a complete stranger to these things. I figured it out. I know what you are." He paused, as if waiting for confirmation. I opened my mouth again, but my mind was a blank; what could I say? When I did not answer, he just nodded. "I should have known from the start. You are just *way* too interesting to be true. So, I guess my only question is, why are you here?"

I closed my eyes. He knew I was an alien. What would he do now? Were there already UNOOSA[10] agents here about to jump out with a giant catapult? Could I run away? Was Penny overhearing this, ready to tackle Greg from behind? When I

---

10   If you have not heard of UNOOSA I would tell you to go look it up for yourself, but since you no longer have the internet, I do not suppose that would help, so you'll just have to take my word for it. UNOOSA stands for United Nations Office for Outer Space Affairs. For the last thirty years, they had that website and those fliers that read, "Access to space for all." Their unintentional delivery on this promise might seem particularly painful considering the current situation, I suppose. I understand they are secretly running the Government of Human Survivors behind the scenes now.

opened my eyes again, the bubbles behind Greg were starting to blow our direction, but the magic of the moment was gone. Scrunching my napkin, I watched my traitorous little hope pop away like the real bubbles around us did not. I tried not to let my disappointment drown me, but some of it spilled out my eyes[11] anyway.

Of course he knew. Had known the whole time. This very danger was why Penny warned me to stay away. Now he was going to tell me he could not possibly have an alien for a date, especially one who broke rules, and my people would be kicked right off the planet.

I took a deep breath, trying to steady myself. "So if you knew, why did you still ask me as your date? Why did you not report me?"

"So it's true? You admit it?" he whispered. I could feel his foot tapping on the ground below the table.

I did not answer. It was time to get out of there. If he had any intention of reporting me, I did not want to be here when he did. Maybe I could still salvage something for my people, stand up for them, finally be the buffer I was meant to be, as suffocating as that felt to think about. I looked into Greg's gray eyes for the last time. I tried to memorize his face, the flicker from the lantern reflecting in his eyes, the smells, the feelings, but a glimpse of movement behind him distracted me.

It was a face I recognized, a face that could not be there: only a flash, and it was gone.

I stood, scanning the faces around us in the lamplight,

---

11   Yes, we cry. Alien tears, though. Which are just like human ones.

searching where I had seen the anomalous person, but bubbles kept getting in my way, blocking my vision. *Bubbles.* Why were there so many bubbles?!

Everyone around us started coughing, batting at the bubbles, which were multiplying and swarming like *choig* locusts. I continued to scan the faces behind Greg, swatting the bubbles out of the way. Had I imagined it?

Then, as Greg turned to see what I was looking at, a sudden gust of wind popped the bubbles all at once. As if in slow motion, a wave of shimmering light next to the pier burst outward, creating a luminescent blooming explosion of red, orange, yellow, blue, purple, and black.

[04] I leaped forward, swept my arms around Greg, and pulled him down and away from the blast. There was a deep, enveloping boom as the wave of sound caught up to us and then all was silent but my own labored breathing in and out. I felt Greg's hair against my cheek, our arms still around each other. Then the sound whooshed back around us: crying, coughing, and screams echoing as if through a tunnel.

Greg was talking. "What happened?" he yelled with a cough. It sounded like he was speaking through water.[1]

"An explosion," I yelled back.

"What?"

"I said, there was an explosion!"

"I know, but I mean, what . . ." He shook his head and pushed away, kneeling and gasping for air.

I stopped myself from reaching out for him again and instead looked around for Penny. It was too dark and hazy to see much, the night seeming even darker after the brightness of the blast. But then Penny was at my side. I'd forgotten what the disguise I'd created for her looked like, but I recognized her by her intense expression. She examined me for injuries and, finding none, immediately ran toward the source of

---

1   I should know. I spent a month underwater once. The conversations were boring, but it was not the water's fault most of the time.

the explosion. Penny's job is as much an investigator[2] as an adviser when the need arises, but for once I was annoyed to be on my own again so soon.

I looked around at the dozens of humans surrounding me. A female was crying. I tried to take a deep breath. Surrounded by distress and chaos, I felt dizzy, disconnected, directionless. Alone. I turned to Greg the same time he turned to me, and our eyes met. Time slowed,[3] and in that moment, we understood one another entirely. It was a meeting of minds across space, languages, and species. And I knew this was no longer about us.

We both stood, running as one to a group of humans crouched nearby. All of them were coughing and shaken like Greg, but otherwise appeared mostly unharmed. The explosion had been like a giant, colorful bloom, bringing a wave of haze. But there did not seem to be much damage—chairs were overturned, lanterns tipped, and a nearby flowerpot was broken, spilling its black dirt across the asphalt.

We ran from group to group, checking for injuries, helping those who had fallen. The smoke was fading, though there was still a sparkly gas cloud and coughing all around. I seemed to be immune, but I wondered, should I be coughing too? I tried a quick test cough, and looked around to see the effect, not sure if I was doing it right. No one was looking at me. Everyone seemed too preoccupied.

---

2   Also, scientist. Before she became my personal adviser, her title was "Penny Four-eyes."

3   Yes, literally. It uses up some of the power units, but sometimes it is worth it.

One human woman in a blue flowery dress, closer to the direction of the blast, was coughing and gasping so hard, I worried she was going to pass out.

And then, she did.

Greg ran toward her, but he was coughing too, and it was slowing him down. I ran after him, unsure what to do, how to stop it. A human male in a business suit started up, his coughing increasing, and he fell to the ground as well. A dozen others in that direction started the same cough, and like a wave, they began falling all around us. Then a dozen more, everyone nearby us now on the ground. Greg was on his knees, coughing and doubled over. I tried to help him up, but he seemed to barely notice me.

Get him away from the haze was my only thought, and I grasped hold of it. I pulled Greg up and into a stumbling run. He grabbed someone we passed, an older woman all in pink including her hair, and put her arm over his shoulder. I followed his lead, pulling someone else to my other shoulder, a man who clutched a coughing child. A few others we passed joined us, holding onto our chain where they could. We ran, a huddled chain of coughing, hacking, crying people stumbling through the night. As we got farther from the blast point, the haze started to clear. I spotted a cement bench not too far away that seemed free of haze, though it was hard to tell in the dark, and made it my goal.

It happened so fast, I could not stop it; one moment I had a hold on Greg, and the next he tripped over a curb and crumpled to the ground, dragging me and the chain of coughing people down with him. We collapsed into a heap on the sidewalk. He lay sprawled, unconscious and bleeding at the temple, and the rest of the pile lay around him, coughing or out cold.

I had studied human anatomy enough in order to disguise myself and Penny, but that did not tell me how to diagnose or cure whatever was happening to Greg and the other humans.[4] I leaned down my ear to Greg's mouth. He was still breathing. Which meant he was alive. Beyond that, I was completely hopeless. The scratch on his head was dripping blood across his face, a strange shock of red.[5]

I made space, then sat down with a bump and pulled Greg's head onto my lap. I was pretty sure I still had spare power units, but what could I use them to do? Disguise those around me as bald green aliens? Talk to them in various languages? I did not know how to help, how to save human lives.

To which a voice in my mind responded, *They are just humans. It is not your job. Your responsibility is to your own people.* The voice sounded very like Penny's.[6] I shook my head. I could only hope that something about our physiology meant Penny was no more affected than I seemed to be, that she was fine somewhere: fine and getting answers.

A siren started up nearby, and I breathed a sigh of relief; human emergency personnel had the skills I lacked. They would make Greg and the others better. I gently placed Greg's head off my lap, then stood to try to find a human doctor.

---

4   We may be similar on the outside, but humans are a big crazy mess on the inside!

5   Our blood is royal blue. Which does not matter at all right now. But this is perhaps why red seemed so strange.

6   If you want to imagine what her voice sounds like in my head, it is like a cross between one of your wild bears and your garbage disposals.

I did not have to run far. Six ambulances stopped in a brightly lit parking lot for Blasters Neighborhood Market, and emergency personnel in white protective suits[7] covering their heads piled out of the vehicles. I waved down a few of the faceless emergency people, and they followed me back to my pile of humans, other emergency personnel dispersing toward the dozens of others.

I held Greg's hand while someone assessed his head injury, took all kinds of data like heartbeat and temperature, and then a group loaded him and the others onto stretchers and pushed him toward one of the ambulances.

"Are you the wife?" asked one of the faceless people pushing Greg's stretcher.

"What?"

"What's your relationship?" They held me back when we neared the ambulance.

"I am his . . . date?"

I could not see the person's face well inside the plastic front, but they did not seem impressed by this information. "What's his name?"

"Greg."

"Greg what?"

"Greg . . . Human? Greg Helper of the Alaskan Senator? Greg Keeper of my Heart and Secrets?"

"What's his *last* name?" The person said, their tone tight and clipped.

---

7   This is oddly close to what we wore when we arrived on your planet. We were trying to look the way you might think Aliens dress, but actually, they were our spa suits.

Oh, right. I kept forgetting that humans had last names, not titles. Greg had been annoyed not to know my last name, obviously not realizing we do not have them. Perhaps I should have asked him what his last name was then?[8]

"I, uh, do not know."

With no further response, the human lifted Greg into the ambulance, then closed the doors on me and drove away. I sat down on my curb again, the glow from a streetlight surrounding me like a halo. It was cold now that Greg and the other humans were whisked away and gone. Where was Penny?

As if called there, Penny appeared beside me and took a seat on the curb too. Clearly sensing my melancholy, she waited silently for me to speak first.

"Did you learn anything?" I asked her after a moment.

She made a gesture to signal the negative,[9] her face pinched. "What should we do, Your Majesty?" It spoke to the desperation of the moment that she was asking me. She *never* asked me.[10]

I glanced at her. Her human eyebrows on this new disguise I'd created for her were so thick and low I could not even

---

8   I know. I was beginning to realize how self-centered I was to not consider this sooner, but on the other hand, as queen, I was used to everyone around me being just as me-centered as I was.

9   We do not shake our heads or shrug, or at least not with the same meaning attached. In a moment when you might shake your head no, we give a swift foot kick.

10   This was not to say that I never offered suggestions, but simply that, as my adviser, she was the one that was asked for suggestions, not the other way around. This may still seem strange to your preconceived notions of what the queen should be like. But I told you it was not like you think.

see her eyes. It was distracting. I used some power units and a clap to change her back to the disguise she'd worn at the gala, counting on the fact that everyone around was too distracted to notice. Then I tried to pull my thoughts together.

What should we do? Investigate what had happened? Sit there and cry until someone made us get out of the way?

Go home to the Compound?

I may not be overly proficient at many things, but one thing I am practiced at is making and evaluating a list. If I'd had my writing tablet or one of Greg's sticky notes, I would have written it down.

I knew going back was the right answer (though sitting and crying sounded like more fun). Our people needed us back; they were not used to having me gone for more than a day or two at a time, and tended to panic easily.

There were other dangers if we stayed here longer as well, such as Greg—a man so adorable, he threatened my entire civilization. I could *not* stay and risk giving in to such a dangerous temptation.

But lastly and most importantly, the alternatives to going home were ridiculous. Stay out here and *investigate what happened*? I had witnessed something terrible and mysterious, but this was a humanny thing, and therefore not my problem. I had enough problems as it was without adding humanny ones.

Going home was our only real choice. And I knew this.

But there was one problem.

"I saw Woods," I told Penny.

She blinked. "What?! When?"

"Right before the explosion. I thought I was imagining

things, but he looked right at me, disappeared, and then everything blew up."

"That is impossible!"

"I know."

"And what, you think he is . . . responsible? For the explosion?"

Was he? I breathed out. "I do not know."

"But that is impossible!"

"I know."

"But . . . how'd he get here? You and I have the only gravitator!"

"I know."

"And also, he died seven years ago!"

"I know," I sighed.

"Did he look like . . ." She wiped her mouth with the back of her hand.

"Not dead, but yes, like himself, like us. Not human. He was wearing a hood, but—"

"How could he be here without being seen?!" she huffed.

I shook my head. ". . . Well, I am not sure that is the point, but . . ."

"Because he is dead!"

"Yes."

Her eyebrows were so low that she was in danger of blocking her eyes again. "You must have been mistaken. It could not have been him. It was too dark there with all that 'mood lighting' to see properly. And you were distracted by Greg."

She was probably right. But what if I was the one that was right this time? "If there is even the slightest chance that it truly was him, that he is somehow here and caused an explosion, this *is* our responsibility. *My* responsibility. We cannot go home until we know. Not yet."

Penny's face drained of color. "But . . . we have to go back! If we don't return in eight and a half more Earth-days, our people will . . ."

"I know. We will return before then," I responded firmly. "We have to."

She nodded, and I let out a breath. She had agreed so much easier than I expected. While I was confident the humans would not notice my absence (it had been months since anyone broached the Compound door beyond food delivery), ten days was a long time to be gone. It was unprecedented. And yet, eight and a half more days did not seem like enough time.

The question was, enough time for what?

[05] I swear I was not thinking about seeing Greg again when we decided to delay our return home to the Compound. I was thinking only of finding Woods, and if he was alive and responsible for this mess, then taking him back to be punished. Again. Hopefully before the humans discovered him. And before our eight more Earth-days were up.

Penny notified our communication adviser of our delay via her thingamabob,[1] and then we sat there in the circle of the streetlamp light on the dirty curb, watching humans be whisked away in the night by noisy ambulances like *collvop* berries being swiped by a large *balefo* tongue.

I was tired, not to mention soiled from sitting on the sidewalk, my special human-date outfit totally ruined. It was time to get up, make a plan to find Woods, and get back home to the Compound.

And never, ever see Greg again. Not even to know if he lived or died.

But that was as it should be. Truthfully, I was a little embarrassed by my behavior with Greg so far, by the way I had let some little fantasy of holding a human's hand while he whispered in my ear get in the way of my duty, risking my people's very lives and happiness. I'd only known Greg two

---

1   This is an accurate translation. The thingamabob is like one of your cell phones, if your cell phone was a flat circular disk that could change shape to become any medical, research, scientific, or cosmetics device.

Earth-days; we'd had only three interactions. We hardly knew each other.

Yes, he had a good smile. And great shoulder blades. And a nice forehead. And he spoke with intelligent sincerity. But those things did not add up to love.

A small memory squeezed into my mind, of the moment our eyes locked, and goosebumps shivered down my arms.[2] But I shoved the memory back out again. I did not even know his full name, which apparently was important for humans. I had simply gotten carried away in the moment. I know some of you have experienced something similar, right? Try not to judge me too harshly. True, my mistake ended up having much more dire consequences than yours might have,[3] but that is beside the point.

We sat watching as the last of the humans were whisked away and emergency vehicles and officers moved through the area. Several blocks around the explosion were being evacuated for the rest of the night due to the lingering gas and haze, so there were soon approximately a hundred evacuees huddled in the parking lot behind us, along with a few more being treated for mild injuries. I realized we probably should have left sooner when a police officer in a dark blue suit made a beeline for us from across the parking lot. I worked very hard not to flinch, my usual reaction to your law

---

2   I only add this for your benefit. No, we do not have this as a physical reaction. But if we did, we would not call it *goosebumps* or *goosepimples*. *Goose pimples?!!*

3   Such as explosions, the end of a world, etc. But I suppose I should not assume anything about you.

enforcement. Penny's fists started to come up next to me, her usual reaction to *my* usual reaction, but I put my hand on her shoulder.

"*No*, Penny. No killing police. Okay? That is a command: say it back to me."

She huffed. "Fine. No killing police."

"Or maiming."

"Or maiming," she reluctantly repeated.

"Or even hurting unless it is self-defense."

"Fine," she sighed as the policeman approached.

He stood in front of us, looking us up and down. "You two were near the explosion?" he asked.

"Yes." I forced out a cough as evidence.

"You think this is funny?"

"No, I was coughing . . . because of the . . . smoke." I coughed again.

He squinted at me. "I notice you didn't leave with the ambulances."

"Uh, no, we um. Yes, we are fine. Not counting the coughing obviously. Like all the humans. Like *us* because we are humans. But we decided not to go to the hospital because . . . we do not like nurses." I coughed again for good measure, and Penny groaned under her breath. The officer looked at us, one eye squinted closed, his mustache twitching.

He motioned to a pink-skinned dark-haired officer nearby, and she joined him, pulling a notebook out of her pocket.

The first officer turned to us again and coughed. "So, did you notice anything unusual?"

My body was starting to tense up. "Um well, I . . . the restaurant's menu had two typos. And the fish was way overcooked."[4]

With a *tsk* of impatience, the other officer stepped in. "Did you see someone or something suspicious or out of place in connection with the explosion?"

Something out of place? Besides us? And a supposedly–dead alien? "Um, no. Not as . . . No," I lied.

Penny shook her head awkwardly.

"Doesn't she talk?" the male officer asked, his eyes bouncing over to Penny.

"Her English is not great. We are not from here."

"Foreign." It did not seem to be a question.[5]

"Yes?"

"Where y'all staying?" he asked.

"With a friend."

"Mm–hmm. I see. We might have some more questions for you, so don't leave without giving this officer here an address." He walked away, and I stood, Penny standing with me.

"Sorry, please excuse us," I said to the female officer. "We are very fine, so I think we will go home now." I gave her my most winning, unassuming human smile.

She looked us up and down. "You should really be checked for shock."

---

4   This was a lie. The fish was perfect.

5   Nor did he make it sound like a compliment.

"Oh, no, that will not be necessary, it was only mildly surprising, no shock here."[6]

Her concerned expression froze on her face. "Then if you could just leave me with the address where you're staying, we can contact you if we have any more questions."

"Oh. I should perhaps say that while I know the way there, I do not know the address[7] offhand. Or onhand."

"Oh? Can you call the friend you're staying with to get it?"

Penny shook her head, glaring at me. I needed to stop talking to these humans and we both knew it. I was out of practice. "We do not have any telephone devices, either."

"Aha," she said, her voice getting hard as *clox* ice. She flipped a braid of her hair back. "We can escort you back to your friend's place in a squad car then."

"You know," I said, "actually, I *am* feeling a little . . . pained, in my, uh, body. Maybe it would be a good idea to get 'checked out' here after all."

The officer sniffed. "Alright, Miss—uh, what did you say your name was?"

"Aria, Keeper of—"

Penny elbowed my side.

"What was that?" The officer squinted at me.

---

6   Even with the translator installed in my brain, you may notice I still occasionally struggle with idioms, colloquial phrases, homophones, etc. This is a limitation of the device, and no fault of mine.

7   This might be the only thing I said in this conversation that was absolutely true. Your human addresses (especially in your larger cities like Washington DC) are very complicated.

". . . Aria . . . Keeperov? And Penny . . . Candy."[8]

She wrote in her little book. "Go ahead and have a wait over there with the evacuees, and tell someone you need medical attention. Don't leave until you check with me." She pointed toward the group of evacuated humans standing in a loose huddle in the middle of the parking lot. We scrambled over and hid ourselves among the tired, poor, huddled masses,[9] and tried to blend in as if we too had been evacuated from our homes. We copied the others' reflex checks and breathing patterns while medical personnel poked and prodded us.

The group of evacuees made perfect human camouflage on top of our human disguise; however, we could not seem to sneak away once we joined them. We tried to leave when the two officers were no longer watching, but before we got far, their eyes always seemed to find us. So we stayed, continuing to blend in while waiting, blend in while being examined, and then blend in some more while they filed the evacuees onto a bus.

After a short trip, the bus stopped and unloaded us at a high school. A big outline of a bloated, green head with huge eyes was displayed across the front with the words "Home of the Aliens" underneath.[10] When we got inside, someone

---

8   I've been told Penny Candy sounds like an exotic-dancer name. Please do not tell her. I do not think she would appreciate it. She cannot dance.

9   Since this is what the Statue of Liberty calls for, I think that means these humans were very patriotic to your United States.

10 Unless there was another race of Aliens hiding on the earth that I did not know about, this was a lie. See? Humans lie too.

checked our vitals again,[11] after which we tried to leave again. But it seemed like everywhere we went, those two officers were there *again*, sauntering around and glaring at everyone. We kept scrambling through doors to get away and ended up in a utility closet that smelled like bleach.

Penny turned on a light using the little chain hanging from the ceiling. I sat on a pile of white[12] toilet paper rolls.

"What now?" I whispered. "We have to get out of here. I cannot keep pretending. Last time someone checked my reflexes, I accidentally slapped him."

Penny glared around at the shelves filled with paper sanitary products. "Perhaps we can just stay in here? Eventually, the officers will leave . . ."

I put my head in my hands and growled in frustration. I did not want to stay in this tiny closet. We were always hiding in tiny spaces: I hated tiny spaces. They reminded me too much of our time in space.[13]

"Well then what do you suggest?" she asked.

"Use some power units to gravitate out of this place?"

"Your Majesty, we probably shouldn't unless we cannot find another way. We may still have plenty of power left right now, but who knows what the next few days will bring? Those power units are a precious gift from our people, not to be used lightly, and gravitation requires more units than anything

---

11   Yes, we can fake these, but it takes concentration and practice. Like flying.

12   Ours are violet colored. You know you were wondering.

13   One of the reasons I hated our time in space was because it reminded me of my first closet. Which I hated because it was too tiny.

else. Do you know how many units it will take us to gravitate from here to the Compound?"

"No, how many?"

She threw her hands up. "I don't know either because the equations are too complex! It's something like your height plus your girth minus the day of the month divided by your intelligence quotient, but I can never remember precisely and that is the point!"

". . . And *what* is the point?"

"We've never stayed out this long, we don't have Harold Royal Calculator to help us so we only have a general idea how many power units we need in order to return, we are still using units every moment for maintenance, and we have eight more Earth-days in which we may need to use more!" She was pacing now, tiny steps in the tight, tiny space.

I stood up. "I know, but—"

Right then, someone opened the door and we screamed, as did the female in green scrubs in the doorway.

She put a hand to her ample chest, taking deep breaths. "What are you two doing in here?" Without waiting for an answer, she pulled us out of the closet and pushed us ahead of her, back into the large open room with everyone else. "Don't wander off—you need to stay with the group, okay?"

"We only want to leave and go home, is that possible, uh, nurse?" I hoped the police officer had not told her we disliked nurses.

"If you aren't in need of medical attention and you have someplace to stay outside of the evacuation area, you can check out with that officer over there." We both ducked when she pointed to the policeman that hated us, but luckily, he was not looking our way.

"Are those the only two options? Can we not check out with *you*?" I whispered to her.

"When it comes to something like a possible bombing, the counter-terrorism unit is in charge, and they want all those evacuated officially accounted for. Look, by tomorrow, things may calm down. It's—" she glanced at a wristwatch, "—already two in the morning as it is. You should get some sleep, go set up your own bed roll. Just grab some from the pile." Then she dashed off, her black, curly ponytail bouncing against her back.

We hurried to the pile she'd indicated and grabbed what looked like rolled-up black and gray blankets and then moved to the group of people who were already camped on the scuffed-wood floor.

Someone had turned off the long overhead lights on one side of the large room, but Penny and I did not try to sleep.[14] We closed our eyes whenever an officer or medical person passed close by, but otherwise, we whispered ourselves around in circles.

"If I did see Woods, if he is alive, how did he get here?" I whispered. "It cannot be a coincidence that I saw him right before an explosion, not with his . . . proclivities."

---

14   Anyway, if we had tried to do our version of sleep (we call it charging) in front of you, you humans would have started stabbing us with the nearest pitchforks. I am glad that pitchforks seem to be in short supply now, with the end of your world. Such a crude weapon. But I understand they were normally for stabbing hay and other plants who deserved it, which I support.

"You say that as if he were a bomber! He was a chemist."

"With violent tendencies."

She glared at me and rolled her eyes. "You *didn't* see him, so it doesn't matter!"

"Do not be upset, Penny," I said gently, and she turned away. I lowered my voice even more. "Am I being a little insensitive about this . . . considering what he was to you?"

She was turned away, and it was too dark, so I could not see her face to gauge her reaction. "That was a long, long time ago. He's been dead for seven years."

"But you have not had a relationship with anyone since, so I assumed—"

"No. I'm fine." She turned back toward me. "I simply do not want to see you make the same mistake, putting a dalliance over the wellbeing of our people."

"Is that what you think you were doing with Woods?"

"Sometimes."

She'd never admitted as much to me before. She knew from the start I had not liked the two of them together, but we'd never spoken of it. This vulnerability was her most convincing argument against Greg so far, but at this point, it was unnecessary. Greg was out of my thoughts completely. 100 percent.

. . . 99.7 percent.

A confident 80.

[06] In the morning when the light came back on, we still had not found any solutions to the Woods situation, at least not that we could agree about. A female officer we did not recognize approached our group of evacuees, all still lying on our bed rolls spread out next to the wall of closed bleachers. Most of us stood, and Penny and I eased to the back of the group.

"We're going to lift the evacuation order today, so anyone not in need of medical attention can check out in a few hours."

"Where was the explosion? How close were we?" asked a human male with a long ponytail, rolling up his wool blanket.

The officer sighed, rubbing her eyes. I noticed her blond hair was standing on end, and I wondered if it was a style choice or because she had spent the night pulling on it instead of sleeping. "It started by The Wharf, in the yacht called the Lady Blue," she said.

The Lady Blue? The explosion started at the site of the government gala we'd sneaked into two days before? I turned to Penny, and it was clear by her expression that she already knew, had known since exploring right after the explosion.

"Why did you not tell me?" I whispered.

"Because I knew what you would think, but I still don't believe this has anything to do with us. There were important humans there too," she whispered back.

"Are we in danger?" a female asked the officer, hugging a small child.

The officer shook her head. "We believe the danger has passed. I can't tell you much else, but I can tell you the same things I just told the reporter outside. Of those we transported to Saint Bridges Hospital yesterday, we have one dead and twenty-six people in mild to critical condition. I can't give you any names yet because I don't have them."

One dead. I told myself that it was *not* Greg.

And if he was not dead, I now knew he was at Saint Bridges Hospital. I had not realized I had been waiting for this information until I heard it. What she was saying faded back into my awareness. "—so either the explosive was vaporized in the blast, or this was something more mundane like a gas leak. At this point, we suspect an accident, so no, we aren't calling this a bombing at the moment. But make sure we have your info so we can update you."

I turned to Penny. "I am going," I whispered, starting to back out of the group.

"*Don't you dare,*" she hissed.

I lowered my voice even more. "Penny, I have to check that he's alive. He is my responsibility. I will only gravitate halfway to the hospital; that way we will not waste as much power. And we can meet at our safecondo." With that, ignoring the look of outrage on Penny's face, I crouched down, activated the gravitator, and disappeared.[1]

---

1 In case you are wondering about this technology, gravitating can go anyplace I know the name of or can picture. To gravitate from one place to another feels like nothing. Well, like standing in the middle of a tornado made of electric eels. But otherwise, nothing.

I appeared behind a big smelly garbage dumpster and stood up, glancing around to make sure I had not been seen. Then I followed the signs, walking the last four blocks until I reached a large building with the words "Saint Bridges, Washington, District of Columbia" on the side, and hurried to the front desk where a few women in scrubs sat chatting.

"I am looking for a patient here," I said.

A plump, pink-skinned human woman at the desk glanced up. "Name?"

"Aria, the Seventh Daughter of Morr, Keeper of the Sacred Sponge, Heir to the Fallen Branches of Bough."

She paused. "That's the name of the patient?"

"Oh. No, it is Greg."

"Greg what?"[2]

"I do not know."

She narrowed her eyes at me.

I cleared my throat, hoping to appeal to their sympathy. "I ask because we went on a date last night during the um . . . *explosion*." I whispered that part in case they did not want the ignorant public to know about it. "And he was injured, and now I need to know if he is alive." The woman's annoyed expression had not changed. "Because he is the man of my dreams?" That last part just popped out.

Still nothing. Did this woman have feelings of stone?[3]

After a moment, the woman stopped glaring and smiled, but it felt sharp and pointy instead of warm like a human's

---

2   Why are humans from this culture so obsessed with last names?

3   *Bodoo* stones are especially unfeeling. But this woman had feelings of a *hardcop* stone.

smile should be. "You were on a date with some man, you don't really know his name, and now you want to get some personal information. How was it going before the . . . *explosion*." She mimicked my whispering.

"What?"

"How was the date going?"

It was a weird and nosy question in my opinion, but I was not sure if this was unusual.

"Fine," I responded with an uncomfortable gulp.

She smirked. "I can't tell you anything unless you're family. So unless he ended the fine date with a proposal, I can't help you."

The woman next to her glanced over and rolled her eyes.[4] "You are so mean, Bonnie." Then she turned in her chair and started sorting through some papers behind her.

I stood there for a moment, unsure how to proceed.[5] "Can you at least tell me if he is alive?" I finally asked.

"Look," said the other woman, turning back around but still busying herself with paperwork. "Bonnie didn't need to say it that way, but she *is* right. We can't tell you anything unless you're family or if he gives us permission. But I can tell you the death from the incident was a female, so unless he was identifying as a different gender, he's still alive. Sorry, sweetie, it's the best I can do." She turned around again.

---

4   We roll our eyes in my culture as well, but it is a symbol that means, "I am done eating now if you could take my plate away." I am pretty sure that is not what she meant here.

5   I have no idea why these women were so mean. Nor whether or not they were nurses. But it occurred to me that maybe I *did* hate nurses? If you are a nurse and reading this, I am very sorry, I am sure you are a very nice human.

I stepped back. He was alive. I had told Penny I only needed to know he was not dead, and now I had done that. They would not let me see him, but I did not need to. Seeing him now would only complicate things, as would picking a fight with these difficult human ladies, despite how much I wanted to, and even if leaving now meant I would never be able to find him again. Which of course I did not need/want anyway.

"Thank you," I said to the desk ladies' unfeeling backs, then turned and eased out the sliding glass doors.

I stood outside the door and put my face in my hands. Why had I left Penny on such a foolish errand? She was going to give me a very stern talking to for that. When would I stop being stupid?

"Need a ride?" said a voice behind me.

I turned and there he was. Greg. Standing in the hospital entrance. A sheepish smile on his face.

$[07]$ Some of you may have noticed something about me as I give this report. Even though I do lie a lot, you may think I am not very good at it.

This is only partially correct. It is not so much a matter of being a bad liar as it is a matter of being bad at improvising. You must understand, I usually have whole teams of people writing my lies for me,[1] so making up my own on the spot was not something I had any practice at. Therefore, I apologize. First for being a liar, and second, for being a *bad* liar, which I've heard humans say is worse. You are a very unique people.

Perhaps you can feel better in knowing I am every bit as bad at lying to myself as to others. As I saw Greg standing there, despite my very sincere justifications that I did not need to see him, it all *flew out the window*, as you say. And then all those same foolish feelings from before came flying back in through that same window, and I ran and hugged him. He responded like we were old friends, hugging me back. I could feel a deep rumble in his chest; he was laughing at me, and I loved it. After likely too long a hug, I stepped back, flushed, and apologized, watching him through my lashes. He chuckled again. We stared at each other in awkward silence for a moment, unsure how to proceed.

Greg cleared his throat and spoke first. "I'm assuming

---

1   It is nice to have lie writers; you should definitely try it if you plan to incorporate lying into your personal or professional life.

you already have an extraction plan and a team and a car and everything?"

"No, I do not have a team. It is only Penny and me."

He nodded. "I called a YouRide. Want to share? The senator said she'll cover it."

I tried to shake my head but nodded instead. I blame your complicated head motions for the confusion. "I need to go back to my condo." We were all politeness now. Like strangers. Which, I had to remind myself, we *were*.

A dusty green car came to pick us up and we settled with a space on the seat between us, me looking forward, Greg facing out the window. I gave the driver directions to the safecondo, and we were off.

It was going to be a short ride, and I knew I needed to tell Greg goodbye for good, but I was having difficulty choosing the right words. *You are beautiful but too human for me?* Or, *I have too many annoying responsibilities to spend time with you?* Maybe he would be the one to say something instead, and all I would need to choke out would be *Goodbye forever.*

"So," he said, "did you come to the hospital looking for me? Or were you already there? I may have overheard some of what you said to those nurses."

I was once again glad he could not see me flush.[2] I kept my eyes forward. "I was just looking for you," I said and then realized I should maybe not have admitted that.

---

2   Because, again, it was on my shoulder blades. Our clothing generally does not cover both shoulder blades, just the immodest one, but I was careful to choose clothing that covered both shoulders when in human disguise for this very reason.

"Can I ask why?" he asked, his tone conversational.

"I just needed to know if you were okay. Are you okay? You were injured." I pointed at the bandage on his head.

He touched his bandage gingerly. "Oh this? It was just a scratch and a bump. I'm fine. The last thing I remember is walking away with you and that chain of people, and then I guess I fell down and hit my head. But they tell me I'm fine. Did *you* get hurt?"

"No. I am fine, too. I am glad to know you are all right," I said. *And now we need to say goodbye.* I opened my mouth, but could not get the words out.

He gazed at me. "Is that the only reason you came to find me? To check on me? No other reason?"

"Yes?" *And to say goodbye, but the words are stuck.*

Greg glanced up at the driver of the car, but the man seemed to be ignoring us, engrossed in his music, so Greg turned and examined me for a moment again. "I guess what I'm asking is, was meeting me an accident, or . . ."

I glanced at him. "As opposed to . . . fate?"

His mouth quirked into a half smile. "I am sure everything about you is classified and I have no right to ask, so, don't answer if you can't, but why are you here? Is it about the explosion? I really can't believe you would have anything to do with it . . . but, did you? Or is the real question whether *it* had anything to do with *you*?"

I took a deep breath. "Yes. I do not know. I hope not. And now it is my turn to ask a question of you. Are you going to turn me in?"

He cleared his throat, scratching his neck. "I know I probably should. But for some reason, I feel like I know you, and I have to believe you are one of the good guys. You are, aren't you? One of the good guys?"

I breathed out, and turned away from him again, looking through the car window as buildings and people rushed by. I'd studied enough of your culture and its outlook on aliens to suspect what he was talking about. I do not lay eggs in people's chests or infiltrate governments,[3] or abduct people to probe and run tests on them.[4] I was and am a liar, but I hoped that would not count me in with the bad guys. Humans lie too, right?

"Yes. We are the good guys,"[5] I breathed.

He nodded. "Then, no, I won't tell on you." He leaned toward me. "So, how busy are you while you're here? Because if you haven't already, you've gotta try half-smokes—they're basically DC's signature food, and I know this really great place—"

"Greg," I moaned.

His expression fell. "Don't tell me, you aren't allowed to date—you were breaking the rules when you came out with me yesterday."

"I am breaking laws even *talking to* you." But by his expression, I knew I needed to be clearer and say what I'd been trying to say from the beginning. "Which is why this will be the last time I see you."

He nodded again, exhaling.

I pushed on. "I may have to stay for another seven days,

---

3   On purpose, anyway.

4   Except one time, but that person was asking for it.

5   In retrospect, I see how this might have been another falsehood. Good and nice Aliens do not destroy planets.

or less if we can find the person we are looking for and find out what happened. But you need to go back to Alaska, do you not? And I need to . . . make wiser choices." I avoided making direct eye contact, so I would not accidentally change my mind, and instead looked at his forehead.[6]

Greg grasped his hands together in his lap, looking out the window. "I have to stay for a week or so too, actually. My boss left yesterday, but she wants me to rest up after the explosion. And to stay in touch, let her know what happens with the aftermath. So. Looks like you and I have the same goals. Sure you couldn't use any help?"

I considered this. We had almost no experience on Earth outside of our very short yearly excursions. It would be nice to have some assistance. But then I saw Greg's face, felt how much I wanted to say yes, and sighed. "Thank you for the meal yesterday. And the ride. And I am glad I met you. But I think this needs to be goodbye for good."

He took a long breath in and out and nodded again. As if on cue, the car pulled up to our safecondo.

I got out and turned back to him. "Goodbye."

He did not respond, only smiled. I shut the door, went inside, threw myself on the soft bed, and held on,[7] because if I did not, I was afraid I would jump right back up and follow his YouRide.

---

6   Which turned out to be a mistake. I think I have mentioned he has a great forehead. I was mesmerized.

7   And also because my mattress was very soft, and I appreciated it and wanted to let it know. It is very therapeutic to hug a mattress, you should try it if you ever manage to have a real mattress again after the destruction of your planet.

Penny arrived a few hours later to find me still in the same position, face down, arms hugging the mattress.

"Is he dead?" she asked me.

"No," I sighed, my voice muffled. "Alive and well. A mild abrasion."

"And you could not have waited a bit longer to learn that? You should have stayed with me. You have no idea the trouble I had getting here. They kept talking and talking, asking questions I had to pretend I couldn't understand. I had to knock out three people in order to get away."

"I am sorry," I said into the mattress.[8]

She sat down next to me. "So does he know what we are?"

"Yes."

"Will he get us into trouble?" Her voice turned sharp.

"No." I tipped my head to face her.

"But he hurt you?"

"Yes, but not in the way you imply. He still wants me. I think. But I have decided to do my duty."

"And go home?" she asked.

"No. And avoid him."

She patted my back, a quick, soft smack. "I did learn something after you left, but not much. Most of the injured humans were damaged from smoke inhalation rather than from the blast. Truly, I am not sure there is anything more to

---

8   This was an apology to Penny, not the mattress. Perhaps I should have felt sorrier to Penny, but I knew she was actually not-so-secretly pleased to get the workout. Penny is not ever happy unless she gets to fight at least one person when we go out. And she is rarely allowed, so she always comes back grumpy.

learn. Even the two police officers who were watching us seem to have given up now. They all believe it was an accidental explosion. I am inclined to agree."

I sat up, smoothing the sheet. "Could it be that I imagined Woods? I do not know why I would."

"Perhaps he was a vision brought on by unresolved guilt?"

"No, I truly feel none. . . Do you think I should?" I'd not considered Woods worthy of her, even before he went *boonuts*—whenever she was with him, she went from the strongest person I knew to a weak and submissive pile of mush. But I'd never tried to stop their relationship from moving forward. Until I had him executed, of course. And I still believed I had made the right choice in the end. Did Penny?

She turned away. "His conviction was right. It was treason. But regardless, none of this seems like his style. Even if you did not imagine him, even if he is still alive, I think we must face the possibility the explosion was not about him or us." She started gathering up some discarded clothes on the floor beside my bed. "Do you want something to eat and then we can simply return? Go back to the Compound where our people need us and where we can investigate without a deadline? Without distractions? We have to be back in seven Earth-days as it is."

The mention of food put some feeling back into my toes. "What do you have in mind?"

"There is a taco truck a block away. I passed it on my way here. I hear tacos are delicious, especially with fresh tomatoes." She glanced at me out of the corner of her eye.

"Well, I am not agreeing to going back, but I *guess* we

can go eat," I said, yawning. We both knew she had me at *fresh*.

"How many power units do we have left, now?" asked Penny as we started walking.

I glanced at the Royal Everything Device gauge. "Two hundred thirty."

"We are burning through them so quickly. Have you put on weight?"

I shrugged, stepping around a crack in the sidewalk. We joined a long line to a red boxy truck, a line that was growing larger behind us. I let my melancholy ease away and instead embraced my enthusiasm for a good line to wait in. Penny kept rolling her eyes at me.

I cannot help but like it: all the humans so falsely polite, always first come first serve.[9] I simply love to queue.[10] Could anything be more average, middle-class, human?

We received our food and started walking back when I noticed something: a wave of bubbles, some bigger than my fist, blowing around us from behind.

"Not again," I heard Penny mutter as the inevitable giant boom sounded and an iridescent wave overtook us.

---

9   In my world, we eat by rank and then by need. Sometimes we have competitions to see who is hungriest. I always eat first, because of rank, unless my uncle Borno is there, in which case his hunger outweighs everything else. I've seen him eat an entire *bilgebeast* in one sitting including all four wings, the floating eye, and the seventh head.

10   For you confused Americans out there, this means to wait in line. Or, I suppose I should say for those confused *previously-known-as-Americans* out there. Sorry.

[08] A giant wave of colorful plasma, even bigger than the last, expanded in a blast, overtaking us in seconds, throwing us off our feet, and knocking us to the ground with a bump. I opened my eyes to see a world shrouded in sparkly smoke and haze, even thicker than the first time.

Penny and I recovered quickly and stood to help make sure everyone got away from the blast, but all the humans seemed to be running away on their own this time. I saw a few coughing and ushered them away.

"Come on." I turned to Penny. "There will be more humans closer in."

Penny protested, but I was already running the opposite direction of everyone else, into the smoke and haze. We helped a few stragglers, but then the emergency personnel got there with masks, and we avoided them, still running in the direction we'd seen the explosion. There were fewer and fewer humans the deeper we got into the sparkly haze. It was not until we were less than twenty meters away that I saw where the explosion began.

The high school, Home of the Aliens.

We'd been there, at most, four or five of your hours before. Another explosion so near us? Surely, this was not a coincidence. Especially considering I *had* seen Woods at the restaurant. And if so and he was responsible, was he still here somewhere, watching? I had to find out for sure.

I was running as fast as I could now. Haze billowed and

swirled out of most of the doorways and broken windows of the school, but the structure seemed otherwise intact. Could Woods be inside?

A side door hung on its hinges, and Penny grabbed my hand as I tried to enter. I turned back to her. "Penny, if Woods is here, we must find him before he can cause any more damage. I am going in." And then I pulled away from her and went through the dark doorway. Penny followed me inside, grumbling.

The interior of the school was in worse shape than the exterior, with more haze and glass and books and papers everywhere. We ran from one end of the smoky school to the other, but the building appeared to be empty. Which meant all the humans had gotten out, and no Woods either.

Frustrated, I stomped back to the big room we'd stayed in the night before. Several long tables that had been filled with supplies were now crammed against the walls, like they had been thrown out from the center by a giant wind, heaped and bent in piles along the perimeter of the room. This was clearly where the explosion had started. Penny circled the area.

I felt a hint of rising panic, and I tried to squash it. Woods was gone. Without any leads, we would soon have to go back to the Compound whether one of our people were involved or not, and then it would be months before we could come out to investigate again. And what if there were more explosions and human deaths in that time?

Penny crouched down, looking under the tables, her eyes

making a giant sweep of the room. She made a thoughtful noise.[1] "Strange . . ."

"What?"

"There doesn't seem to be any debris or shrapnel from the bomb."

"Maybe it disintegrated?"

"But there should be *something* left behind."

She was right: the middle of the floor was empty. There weren't so much as scorch marks.

Penny sniffed. "There is not even the expected smell. The odor is too fresh."

I inhaled too. "There is a hint of lightning smell, though. Or like burned electronics? Maybe that means it truly was something like bad wiring that caught fire, both times, and there was not a bomb, coincidences be *snoobered*."[2]

"But there aren't any electronics right here in the middle of the room. And judging by the way the tables and chairs are piled, this is where it started." Penny narrowed her eyes, stepping into the center and staring at the spot directly in front of her as if it were not just air.

I examined the spot as well, trying to see what she saw. Penny often had instincts I did not. Which was annoying when you were a youth trying to hide ten stolen *choco* desserts, but useful in moments like these.

She looked down at the floor and then back up again.

---

1   It would sound like a bodily noise to you. If we had spent more time around humans, we would have gotten out of the habit of making such a sound.

2   Do not ask.

"No scratches or scorch marks on the floor . . . I think the explosion started . . . in midair. Right here." Penny slowly waved her hand back and forth through the air in front of her shoulders, like she was pushing something away.

"In midair? Like it was floating?"

She glanced at me, her hand still held in front of her, her head tipped in contemplation. Then she reached into her utility belt, whipped out her thingamabob, and pointed it toward the same spot she'd been waving through.

"What are you doing in here?" said a woman's voice behind us. We turned around to see a group of humans in heavily padded suits, their eyes wide through their transparent face shields. They stared at us for a moment, at our likely-guilty expressions, at Penny's thingamabob which looked like a tiny copper toilet plunger.

"Hi," I called brightly with a casual wave.

One of them grabbed a radio on their shoulder and yelled into it.

Ah, booger.

So we ran. We'd have been caught immediately except for the fact that the group of bomb squad officers were forced to waddle their pursuit, but I could hear them cursing into their radios as they ran, barely twenty or thirty meters behind us. We burst out of the broken side door, the effort ripping it off its final hinge so it crashed to the ground. Soon, we were running along the street, sirens and angry voices starting up and echoing somewhere behind us. We ran until my feet, legs, and chest burned, and I knew at any second they would catch us and start asking all the wrong questions.

"We have to hide!" I gasped as we passed an alley full of cars parked along the curb.

Apparently, Penny had the same opinion because she suddenly turned back around the corner into the alley. Pulling me behind her, she jumped up onto the bed of a truck parked there, yanked open the door of a tall, skinny, blue plastic box strapped in the back, and shoved me inside, where we both collapsed onto the small seat in the center. I only hoped we were far enough ahead that our followers had not seen us enter the alley.

I realized right away what the blue box must be because of the smells,[3] and jumped up off the seat again.

"Why are we always hiding in such tiny smelly spaces?" I said in a whisper to Penny, who shushed me.

The sirens were not going away. Minutes passed.

"Change our appearance!" Penny breathed.

I shook my head. "What good would that do? Will not they be suspicious if two random humans come out together from a box in the back of a truck?" I whispered. "We have nowhere to go. Why did they even strap this box here? Presumably to transport the human poop? We are going to be found hiding in a human poop transport box!"

"Stop talking! I'm trying to think," whispered Penny. It spoke to the desperation of the situation that there was not even one apologetic "Your Majesty" mixed in with all the whisper-shouting.

And then there was the roar of an engine and the box

---

3   You humans make weird smells. We of course make smells too, but they smell like love and sunshine. You and your planet were very nice though.

started moving. I admit I squeaked in surprise as we were lurched against a wall, but the increasing sirens and engine noise were so loud, I hoped they drowned me out.

"What is happening? Did they catch us and now they are taking us away?" I did not even bother to whisper now.

"I don't know! So be quiet until we do."

Several more minutes passed with us bumping back and forth, our arms braced against the walls to keep from touching the seat. The close quarters and Penny muttering next to me were quite a bit like our ride to Earth from Brooshaloo if I discounted the smells, and I ground my teeth.

Before long, the truck stopped moving and the engine noise cut out. We shimmied around so Penny was in front, closest to the door, ready to jump out and fight whatever came, and I tried to position myself behind her to see our soon-to-be attacker over Penny's shoulder.

The door opened, and Penny flew out, jumping on the person who opened the door, and throwing them to the truck bed.

I saw who it was and gasped, leaping forward to pull her off him.

"Nice to see you again, Penny," coughed Greg.

[09] I helped Greg up, he dusted himself off, and Penny stepped back, but she looked like she was considering attacking again even knowing it was him.

"This is not your truck," was all I could think to say once we were all upright, standing in the truck bed.

He rubbed the back of his head and winced. "Ah . . . uh, no, it isn't."

"Yours is orange. And old. And round. This one is new and square and white." I did not know why I was letting the thought of Greg in this new white truck bother me. The old rusty one just seemed to fit him so much better. But it was not important just then.

"The orange one wasn't mine, either, I was just borrowing it. And I still have it; it's right there." He pointed to the truck that we had pulled up next to, and I realized we were in some kind of covered lot, parked next to the orange truck.

"But how did you happen to be driving this shiny white truck with a poop box strapped on the back, and with us in the poop box in the back?"

He chuckled, but it seemed uncomfortable. "I, uh, stole the truck, I guess, but I have every intention of taking it back before the owner notices. So maybe it was more like borrowing?"

"So, you happened to be borrowing a truck with a poop box and us hiding in the poop box in the back?" I asked, blinking rapidly.

Penny stood between us, looking back and forth, her stance tense.

"No, I took it *because* I knew you were in the poop bo . . . the uh port-a-potty[1] in the back," he said.

I swallowed. "I do not understand," I admitted.

He rubbed the back of his head again. "Do you mind if we talk about it after I return the truck? I don't know when that guy will need his truck back. He was very nice to leave his keys in the visor, but I doubt he was planning on being gone long, and I'd rather not get arrested right now."

Go back? After all the trouble we went through to get away? My legs were still wobbling from all that running. "We cannot go back there!"

"No, you guys can stay here; I'll be back shortly, I promise. We aren't that far from where it was parked before. You can wait here in the truck. The other truck. *That* one." He pointed to the orange truck again.

So, we got out, Greg drove off, and we got into his orange truck, me sitting in the middle of the brown vinyl bench seat with Penny on the side. Penny looked me up and down with a disapproving frown and clicked her thingamabob on again, turning away from me.

"How nice of Greg to save us like that," I said.

She did not answer.

"Yes, I know I said I would never see him again, but this hardly counts. I did not ask him to come. And if he had not driven us away, we might have had to gravitate out of

---

1   Port-a-potty, by the way, is not much better of a name than poop box. It means *excrement-portal mover.* I am just saying.

whatever jail[2] they threw us into, and the humans would surely notice, not to mention we would not have enough power left to gravitate home and we would be walking[3] from here to Alaska, which would definitely have taken longer than the seven Earth-days we have left," I said.

She continued to ignore me.

I sighed. "What were you looking for with the thingamabob in the school?"

She tapped the thingamabob a few more times, then finally responded. "Remember how the humans kept coughing and falling at the first explosion? I thought there must be something toxic in the air, so I was reading the chemical compounds."

"And? What did you find?"

"I took a sample, but I am still looking through the readings." She changed the shape of the thingamabob to be a flat disk and spent a few moments swiping through all the data while I looked over her shoulder. She grumbled and shook the thingamabob. "I don't see anything strange here. It is just air. Oxygen, nitrogen. Like everywhere else on Earth. Like most livable planets. Like Boovashoo."[4]

"All planetary air ratios are not the same, though, right?"

---

2   I realized later we could have gravitated out of the port-a-potty, but we were too distressed by the sirens and smells to realize it at the time. Mostly the smells.

3   You are probably thinking we could have just taken any one of your many transportation options: flying, car rentals, boat, Alaskan cruises. But you may have forgotten that most of those required things like identification and last names, which we did not possess.

4   Except ours was higher in nitrogen, traces of poisonous spores, etc.

This, at least, I knew from her long monologues on the subject. "Are the concentrations unusual?"

"I don't . . ." She trailed off, looking uncertain, then she
shook her head. "I don't have the resources to analyze what I
found to be sure. The thingamabob is limited in that respect.
For the trace elements, it just lists 'common particulates.'
This device is for collection, not evaluation. I need more
computing power."

Penny grumbled and shook the thingamabob repeatedly
over the next several minutes, and then Greg was back. He
opened the door with a creak. "So, need a ride somewhere?"
he said, hopping into the driver's seat and shutting the door.

"Were you followed?" Penny asked and I translated into
English for Greg.[5]

"No. I passed one or two cops in the area, but they asked
if I'd seen anything and I said no. And they just ignored me
when I walked away after I parked the truck again. I don't
think they're looking for you anymore, just working through
the explosion stuff."

"We need someplace to analyze the results of an air sample we collected," I burst out.

"Aria! No!" Penny protested.

"Like a lab?" asked Greg.

I nodded. "But we only need a ride there, that is all: this
one thing, and then we need to say goodbye again."

---

5   I suspect that Penny was faking it about not speaking any English. But
     I did not call her out on it because I did not want to embarrass her. She
     never had cause to practice speaking even during most of our excursions,
     but she learned to understand English from watching Hallmark Christmas
     Romances.

He smiled. "You're in luck. I happen to know a guy with a lab." He turned to Penny, as if asking for her permission.

She looked down at her thingamabob, her eyes boring into it. Then she swore and gave him a little nod. Greg sent a message on his phone and started up the old, orange truck.

"So," I said as we rode, "are you going to tell us how you managed to be there right when we needed you? Or needed *someone*? Not necessarily you."

He cleared his throat. "I wasn't following you if that's what you're worried about. I was just nearby."

"You were?" This seemed very improbable.

He sighed, his thumbs tapping the steering wheel. "When that explosion happened, it looked like it was in the same direction as your apartment. So, I went looking for you. I parked nearby and was wandering around on foot when you went running right by me."

I had passed him and not known it? That must have been when I was blacking out from exertion.

"Then I saw you go into that port-a-potty, and I saw some cops not too far behind you, and I realized taking the truck away before they figured out where you'd gone was your only hope. So I . . . borrowed it. I was just lucky the keys were in there, otherwise I would still be sitting in the cab of someone else's truck like an idiot. I've never done anything like that before." His eyes were wide.

"Oh, Greg . . ." I could not decide if I was grateful or annoyed. He had saved us from being caught, but he'd likely now put himself in serious danger doing it, and broken some of your laws, which seemed out of character for him. I did not know any of your police officers personally, but I knew in general they do not like it when you run away, or when you break laws. Had he been seen? I was obviously very bad at what you call "breaking up,"[6] because here Greg was back again, in danger, and I was allowing it.

We drove for only a few minutes—Penny staring out the window, and me trying to decide whether to scoot closer to or farther away from Greg—until we arrived at a flat, boxy building.

Greg opened the car door. "My friend is already inside, and he says I need to come in with you. Then I can drive you back to your condo after." He did not give us time to disagree before showing us to a gray metal door with a glass window. The door opened before we could knock.

"Hey Aria, nice to see you again," said the chef from the restaurant where Greg and I had our date, the one whose name began with an A. Greg introduced Penny, and his friend showed us in. The hallway was short and opened into a large white area with metal counters spread throughout.

Something was strange about it. "Is this a science lab? It seems . . ."

⌈Allen?⌋ ushered us through the middle of the room to a table at the back. "Did he tell you it was?"

Greg looked around. "I mean, it *is* a lab . . ."

The friend laughed and spread his hands wide. "Welcome to the Virginia Tech food lab."

"*Food* lab?" I asked.

"Right. This is where I used to teach night classes. Greg

---

6   Your metaphors for romantic separation are very violent. And accurate.

took a food science class from me a year ago, right here in this room."

Penny walked past him and went over to a table with some electronic equipment.

"Oh, um, help yourself to the computer," said [Adam?].

We watched for a moment as Penny started plugging and unplugging things from the thingamabob (currently in the shape of a copper rectangle sort of like a phone) until she found a connection she was satisfied with.

"Sorry," Greg said to his friend. "I guess maybe they didn't need a lab, just a computer? I blame the language barrier. But it's good to catch up with you again anyway."

"Don't worry about it. How's the boss?" the friend responded.

The two went off to the side, chatting, while I hovered over Penny's shoulder. After not too long, Penny turned and bared her teeth at me, and I gave her some space.[7]

"So you experiment on food here?" I asked Greg's friend. He smiled.

I was not even sure what that could mean. Yes, we experiment on *our* fruits and vegetables too, but they are sentient and evil. Once it becomes food, your human food is not sentient, so it was hard for me to imagine how much you could hope to gain.[8]

---

7 It is a lesson I learned early with Penny. I've seen her break someone's finger for crowding her. And it was not even one of the unimportant fingers, either.

8 Even now, a year later, I still do not quite understand this. Do you inject casseroles with dangerous chemicals? Make a hamburger go through little mazes? Make pizza push red and blue buttons to be fed more cheese?

I did not ask about this, considering it impolite. Instead I asked, "Do you enjoy it?"

"I love all things food related, but cooking is my first love, and testing out something new is the most exciting. I don't get to do it much anymore, but they still let me use the lab whenever I want." He smiled at me again, but it was the look of someone trying to figure me out.

He opened his mouth to ask me something, but I jumped in. "Because you cook at the restaurant instead?" I still was not very prepared with answers to questions, so I felt it best to avoid them.

"Yep, though I don't do that as much as I like either. Have my fingers in too many pies." He laughed like it was a joke, which I hoped it was, because putting fingers in pies is very gross and wasteful.

"And Greg took your class?"

He nodded, leaning against a tall table. "Culinary science. But Greg didn't love the science of it, I think. He's meant to be in a kitchen, not a lab."

"In a kitchen in the safety and privacy of my own home," Greg added.

"Come on. You have talent. And can you really say you prefer politics to cooking?" asked [Avery?], leaning toward him.

"What I do can't be called politics. I'm a low-level staffer. I organize and write agendas. I bring people donuts."

His friend nudged him with the back of his hand. "Donuts you made, of course."

"Of course. Why do you think a senator would keep me on staff? My agendas are a mess."

"All right, enough," said Penny in Booshy. Everyone stopped to listen like they understood even though they did not. "I'm done; time to go."

Penny tugged me out of the room, and everyone filed after us down the hall. She continued talking to me as we left. "So, I think we couldn't find fragments of an explosive device because there *was* no explosive device at all, at least not one built with any of the usual explosive substances, but that's not even the most important news." And then I knew she was serious, because she switched into Balavuro, which is like our own private pig Latin version of Booshy: unnecessary since nobody here understood even when it was not backward.[9] "I found something unexpected. There was *kishwellium* among the other particulates."

"Kishwellium?" It sounded vaguely familiar, like I'd read about it recently, but I could not place it.

"It is a very common element. *On Brooshaloo*. There is no way it could be here, and yet, it is. A Booshy element. On Earth."

A Booshy element on Earth. There were many implications of such news, but one was clear to me.

It meant we were not going home to the Compound yet. We were staying to find out about this element. We were staying to find Woods.

---

9   Your tongues and brains are the wrong shape for it, I am told. I've never seen a human brain in person, though, so it is all hearsay.

[10] Greg's friend [Alex?] waved at us from the doorway as we drove off. Sitting there in Greg's truck, I tried to prepare myself to say goodbye to Greg forever. Again. I pretended to listen to and understand Penny's chattering about what was probably a very important clue while secretly examining Greg's profile next to me instead. He still had a big bandage on his forehead.

One thing I know about your physiology: your human brains are important to you, and fragile. And I suddenly started to worry Greg might have damaged his, and that Penny might have hurt it further when she knocked him down. I touched the bandage, my fingers wandering to his hairline. Greg flinched when I touched him, but then he grinned a slow smile at me.

"Does it hurt?" I asked, pulling my hand away.

"My head?"

"Your brain?"

"*My brain?*"

How could I tell for sure without opening up his head? "Are you not supposed to be able to answer questions to show you are undamaged? Like how many arms you have? Quick! Tell me the number of appendages you have divided by the number of face orifices!"[1]

---

[1] You thought I was going to give you the answer to this question here. But how would you learn that way?

He snorted and the car swerved. I was sure this meant we had brain damaged him. *I* had brain damaged him. I noticed Penny had stopped talking and was glaring again. I glanced at her and then back at Greg's forehead.

"My head doesn't hurt," Greg said, his eyes on the road again. "But I *am* hurting right here." He took my hand, entwined our fingers, and placed our hands over his chest. A zing went from our fingers up my arm.

In my mind, I scrolled down through what I knew of human anatomy, trying to remember everything in the human chest. "Your lungs?" I asked.

He laughed, making me flush, and then I remembered about the symbolism of the human heart.[2]

I pulled away. "Greg!" How could he joke about this? I was not sure I could reject him any more than I already had, so why was he making it harder?

"I'm sorry." He put his hand back on the wheel. "And sorry for being cheesy—I just think we need to revisit this." He motioned between us.

I huffed. "No, we do not."

"Is it really a matter of international security?" he asked, his eyes still on the road.

"Intergalactic, but yes."

He snorted. "*Right.* So you're saying we are putting billions of people in danger or something just by being together?"

"9,876 people. But yes."

He sobered. "That is specific. Look. At this point, I know

------

2   I have mostly come to use this idiom comfortably now, but sometimes I still get it mixed up with the spleen or elbows.

almost nothing about you. And I haven't asked because I assume it's all classified. But you haven't killed me, and I haven't turned you in. And right now, it seems to me like you could use every asset at your disposal. Just nod if you can't tell me right out, but are you here trying to figure out the cause of the explosion? Chasing down the one you think is responsible?"

I nodded. "Yes, we are chasing someone."

"And you're trying to make sure nobody else gets hurt?"

I nodded again. "Yes, if at all possible. But—"

"So we both have the same goal, then, and I have connections that might be useful to you. What do you say to working together—" Penny snarled, and Greg held a hand up, "only professionally, and I promise not to push for more. Colleagues only."

"So what would you get out of this arrangement?" I wanted to know.

"I get to spend time with you. My *colleague*. And if or when ten thousand lives are no longer at stake, you . . . let me know."

I did not respond. Maybe we needed help, but I was not sure I was strong enough to work with him, as *colleagues* only. Or unselfish enough.[3] I had no practice at unselfishness. And would I not also be putting him in more danger every moment we were together?

Penny took my pause for evidence I was considering his offer, which I was. "No, Your Majesty, absolutely not."

---

3   Turns out, I was not, as evidenced by the earth's destruction. But he was very convincing.

I switched to Booshy. "I know, but—"

"Just say no. We don't need him."

But the longer I thought about it, the more I was convinced maybe we did. ". . . I think maybe we do need him," I said.

"Why?" she asked, glaring at Greg.

"He already saved us once in the poop transport box. We have no help here, we are using up precious power units, we are on a deadline, and we are out of leads and connections. Plus, I . . . have a feeling."

"You have a feeling? So when you say we need him, are you sure you don't mean *you* need him?"

"Of course not," I said, trying to glare at her. But she turned her glare back on me. And she was much better at it.

"What do you say, Penny?" asked Greg.

I turned to Greg. "She agrees wholeheartedly with your terms, but I have one condition. Whenever I say I cannot tell you something or cannot answer a question, you forget you even asked. When I say get out, you get out. Without hesitation or argument. I will not be the cause of you getting hurt or damaged again. Penny can be very dangerous when she wants to be." Penny would probably not hurt him again as long as he kept his distance, but even at a distance, being near me was increasingly dangerous for more than one reason. I hoped having some rules might protect him and everyone else.[4]

He nodded. "Agreed. Goes without saying. I'm nothing if not obedient."

This did seem to be true. I sighed. "Fine. Deal. One more

---

4   It did not.

request, though. Can you help Penny and me get a hotel room?"

His eyebrows shot up. "Sure, but don't you have a place already?"

"Yes, but on the off chance that it may have been compromised, I do not want to risk being recognized there now that we are working with you as well."

Greg shrugged. "As you wish."[5] He stopped the truck by a tall pink building and pointed. "Is Fantasy Inn & Suites all right? Doesn't seem like your kind of place, but maybe that's better if it isn't? They tend to be more discreet."

Greg helped us check in and then walked us up to the room on the second floor. Fantasy Inn had two suites and we'd chosen one at random, which turned out to be outer-space themed. I was afraid this was too conspicuous given the abundance of "alien" decor throughout, but since the other room with the "Queen's chambers" theme might be just as bad, we stayed put.[6]

I stopped Greg at the door as he was about to leave. "Oh, and Greg, I have a question."

"Anything."

"It is important."

"Absolutely." He stopped and stood at attention.

"What is your last name?"

"Huh?"

---

5   I have since learned that in some cultures, this means I love you. Or that may be only for princesses and farm boys?

6   Even though the little picture of a green alien in the corner of the bathroom mirror scared the *boogoolies* out of me.

"Your last name, what is it?"

"Jones?"

"Is that a question, because I am pretty sure you are supposed to know the answer, and if you do not know it, you are definitely brain damaged . . ."

"No, not a question. It's Jones."

"Greg Jones. Nice to meet you."

[11]   In my culture, we use titles, roles, and occupations as a part of each name, which means you know a lot about someone by the name alone. Simply by meeting them, you know Barley Eleventh in Line gets to be the eleventh person in line to eat at any party no matter how hungry they are. Jay Grounded cares for the gardens and teaches our version of yoga. Harry Always Hits Below the Belt . . . well, that one is self-explanatory, but you get my point.

I did not actually feel like I knew Greg any better now that I knew his last name, but I found myself repeating it under my breath anyway all that night and the next morning. *Greg Jones, Greg Jones, Greg Jones.*

Just as we finished getting ready for the day, there was a knock on the door to our room. I opened it. "Greg Jones," I said aloud.

"Aria . . . honorary dishwasher and arranger of fallen branches."

I smiled.

Greg glanced at Penny and nodded at her. "Penny."

She swore at him in Booshy again, and he grinned back. It was beginning to be their special thing, and it made me unspeakably and illogically happy.

I pulled him inside. "I think maybe we should not go out during the day, Greg." I said. "Do you mind waiting until it is dark? We have now been seen by several officers, in suspicious circumstances: two officers in particular that talked to us at length and hate us. We could be recognized. In fact, I would be surprised if our faces are not already on all your signs and screens everywhere." As much as I'd dreamed of having my picture on a most-wanted sign, this was not the best timing for it.

Greg shut the door behind himself. "Alright, no cops. But aren't we in kind of a hurry? Don't you think it would be enough just to go out in disguise so nobody recognizes you?"

It was true that we were short on time, and only working at night would be limiting. But was changing our disguise the best option? I fiddled with the Royal Everything Device power gauge around my neck, twisting the three little silver dials on the sides of the round body. One hundred and eighty units remaining. I had left our disguises up all night since it used less power than turning them off and on again—which meant there were more than enough units to change our appearance now and still have enough to gravitate back to the Compound.

The trouble was, I did not want to. For some reason, I was attached to this human disguise. I liked the dark skin and dark eyes and long silver hair, and I liked the way Greg looked at me when I was wearing it.

Greg looked back and forth between me and Penny. "Maybe you have a different word for what I'm talking about? It wouldn't have to be much. Maybe just a wig, or hair dye. The silver hair sort of stands out," he added.

"A wig? And that would be temporary?" I asked.

"Yes." He squinted in confusion.

I clapped my hands. "Yes. You are right. We should go out in disguise."

Greg offered to be the one to go get us disguise supplies

when we told him we did not already have such things. He came back a half hour later with plain brown dye for me,[1] as well as a series of wigs of varying colors to choose from, and Penny and I spent the next little while in the tiny bathroom deciding and getting ready. Of course the dye would not work on the digitally disguised[2] silver hair, but the wigs worked perfectly.

When we finished, I had the sudden wild urge to cover my head. I knew from a glance in the mirror that with my short brown hair, I looked perfectly, averagely human. Although I had appreciated Greg for being average, I was surprised to find myself sullen with the change in my appearance. I always thought I was making myself invisible with my human disguises. Now that I was truly normal-looking, I realized how much I still attempted to stand out among you on our excursions.

We came out of the bathroom, me running my hand through the brown wig, and Penny awkwardly fluffing a long curly blond one.

Greg nodded. "Nice. Most people won't even look at you twice, now."

---

1   By a strange coincidence, "DYE for Me" was also the name of the tiny shop where he picked up said dye and wigs.

2   This is how the facebender works according to the original packaging for it: "A digital template of your choice adheres to your head, hair, and skin, temporarily becoming corporeal for days on end, as long as the disguise is not turned off or switched. Wow!" It cannot be removed like a mask or wig. Even when an already placed disguise is disconnected from the power source, it remains in place for ten to twelve Earth-days on the residual power, and then can be turned off at will by the wearer. This is nice when the queen leaves on irresponsible excursions, but her people assigned to guard the door must still retain their "alien" disguise.

I gulped down the pang of disappointment this gave me. We each donned a pair of sunglasses, Penny put on a hat, and we were ready.

"So, where do we start?" Greg said, sitting on the edge of the room's small desk. "How can I help? Are you trying to find your suspect, or do you already know where he is?"

"We are still looking for him. But we are not sure where to start."

Greg nodded. "What about like an APB? Or maybe a missing persons report would be better? I have a friend that's on the police force. She could probably help us out."

"I thought we said no police?"

"Oh, right." Greg looked me up and down. "You sure? Nobody would recognize you now, and we wouldn't need to give them any personal information about you."

I swallowed an uneasy lump in my throat. "Let us save talking to the police as a final resort." I ran my hand over my wig again. "I want to learn more about the air sample we took yesterday."

"The air sample might lead us to your suspect?"

"We think so."

Greg nodded, rubbing his hands together. "But you can't give me more than that?"

"We do not *have* much more than that." I glanced at Penny who was still fluffing her hair in a side mirror. "I can only tell you Penny found an element in the aftermath of the explosion that should not have been there. We learned a bit about it yesterday, but we need to learn more, and find where it came from, and that is where we are stuck."

"So the element is unusual?" Greg asked.

"It is very common where I come from, but here, yes. Impossible."

"Hmm. Interesting," said Greg, nodding and pulling out his phone. "So, we need to know more about it. Maybe we should have stayed at the lab yesterday to learn more."

"Maybe. Could we go back there without your friend? Do you have your truck?" I asked.

"I decided to leave it home, in case it was noticed yester-day.[3] [Abe?] is waiting for us in his car out front."

I brushed a hair off my forehead. "But Greg, is that a good idea? We should instead get a taxi or a YouRide."

"Yeah, uh . . ." Greg nodded and rubbed his neck, standing up. "I can see how that might be better. But I may have exaggerated a little when I told you how much of an asset I could be to you. The truth is, [Anson?] is the one with all the connections. But don't worry, he is also completely trustworthy. I didn't tell him anything compromising, only that you were a friend in need. So . . ."

I started doing our equivalent of wringing my hands,[4] then I turned to Penny.

She looked back at me in the mirror's reflection and groaned. "It is up to you, Your Majesty. You started us on this path, and you must decide how to finish it. But *I* trust [Anthony?] more than *Greg*."

Greg stepped closer. "Come to think of it, I just

---

3   This was a good call as it was very orange. We do not have orange on my planet. Just mentioning as an interesting and unrelated sidenote.

4   Which Greg might have found strange, but it is internal so he could not see it.

remembered that [Ames?] knows someone that could help, which might be better than going back to the food lab. He has a buddy that used to work for NASA as a geologist or elementologist. Barry *something*. From Russia."

I considered for a moment. At this point, I'd already broken so many Accord rules, I supposed adding one or two more people to the group did not make much difference. I took a deep breath. "Okay. Let us talk to this Barry Something. But nobody else should be involved. Is 'Something' Barry's last name?"

"No," Greg said, typing on his phone while we left the room and headed for the stairs. "I can't remember it, but [Al?] will know how to get in touch with him."

"You do not know his last name?!" I asked, shocked. He smiled.

Greg and I walked along the sidewalk in front of the inn toward his friend's waiting car, Penny trailing behind.

"What is [Adrien?]'s last name?" I asked.

"Smith," said Greg.

"Okay. Smith. Yes. That is a good one."

[12] Greg's friend waved at us out the car window.

"Hello, Mr. Smith," I said as I opened the back car door, pleased I knew his last name.

"Hello, Aria, Penny," he responded, eyeing our new hair.

Greg and I climbed into the back, and Penny got into the front, glaring at us and swearing under her breath. There were a few big boxes of spatulas and frying pans in the back seat,[1] so we placed the box pile between us. Once we were seated, I could only see Greg's spectacular forehead over the top.

"So," I said to Greg over the boxes, "*Smith. Jones.* I do not understand about your last names. What is the purpose? What does Smith portray? What does it mean?"

"A smith is like someone who works with and shapes metal?"

"But I thought [Aidan?] is a chef," I said, confused. I looked toward him in the front seat of the car, but he was apparently in the middle of telling Penny a story about a grand cooking adventure, not listening to us.

Greg tipped his head. "Yes, he is. He must have had an ancestor that was a smith, maybe."

That made no sense at all, but I tried not to show my

---

1   Truthfully, I have no idea what was really in those boxes, I just assumed. Does not every chef have large boxes full of spatulas? Just in case there is a shortage later? Or in case there are a hundred pancakes that need flipping?

confusion, although Greg could not see my face over the pile of boxes anyway. "And Jones?"

"It's been a while since I looked it up, but I think it means son of John?[2] Or something. But my dad is Miles, not John, so . . ."

"What? So some last names mean something and some do not, but the meaning does not actually apply either way?"

"Yeah, you're right, it's confusing. How do your last names work?"

"We do not have them, only titles."

"Really? I mean, I guess that is kind of similar to the way we used to do it here."

[Ace?] took a corner and the top box pushed itself over onto Greg. We both cried out, and Greg chuckled, trying to right the pile.

"Sorry!" called [A.J.?] from the front, then went back to chatting with Penny even though she politely[3] ignored him.

"Hey, did you eat breakfast yet?" asked Greg quietly when the box was back in place. "I know we're in a rush, but wanna get some flapjacks after this? While we make our next plan of attack?"

"What are flapjacks?"

"You've never had a flapjack? A pancake? They are sort of like a fried, sweet, slab of bread. Don't you have anything like that where you come from?"

I shook my head, but then remembered he could not see

---

2 By the way, *Jones* also means an intense need or craving. Just thought you might be interested to know that. *Ahem.*

3 If you count scowling and grumbling every few minutes as polite.

it. "No, I do not think so. We do not really have bread because we do not have many viable grains."

Greg slapped his knee. "Oh, that is unacceptable, we are absolutely going for some after this," said Greg. "Assuming we don't find another clue we have to follow right away at Barry's."

I shrugged and smiled, but he could not see it so I raised my eyebrows[4] instead, which maybe he could see, but which likely made no sense in the context whatsoever.

We pulled up to a long and skinny, single-story, teal-colored home with real seashells and starfish embedded along the exterior walls. I liked it immediately.

[Alejandro?[5]] knocked and a human with almost no hair on top of his head and giant thick glasses opened the door like he'd been standing right inside, waiting for us.

"Come in," he said as if it was one word, and hurriedly motioned us inside.

We all squeezed through the gap, and the man shut the door.

"Through here," he said, leading us through a yellow painted hallway at so fast a pace, I would have struggled to keep up even if I had three extra tentacles and was following underwater. Which, to be clear, I did not and was not.

"So, what do you have for me?" the man said in a heavy

---

4   In my culture, this means "You *know* I cannot hear you when you try to talk to me from the other room." It is not a particularly useful expression since the one you are making it to also cannot see it. But this does not stop angry housemates from doing it.

5   This one is definitely not it. I have seen one or two Alejandros, and this man did not possess that Alejandro quality, if you know what I mean.

accent, his words quick and smooshed together. We entered a large room, and he turned around, rubbing his hands together. I am afraid I might have given a sudden *yip* of surprise: he was wearing nothing but a robe and boxers. I had always understood boxers to be human underwear that should not be worn in view of others. If all his hurrying around was to make everyone believe he was important, the outfit did the opposite. Luckily, I seemed to be the only one who noticed.

[Arcturus?] motioned toward us. "Hey, Barry, these are my friends, who would like to remain unnamed, if you don't mind. You remember Greg, though, right? They need a favor."

"Oh, a favor, yes? I don't care about names, but I need *something*. Who are they to want a favor from me?" The man scrunched his eyes up.

Greg cleared his throat. "This woman is an undercover reporter for a very important anti-government blog," he said.

The man, Barry, nodded vigorously. "Which blog?"

Greg frowned. "Uh, it's new. But while working on her story, which we can't tell you about, she found a substance that shouldn't be here, which I understand is your expertise." The man suddenly looked very eager. Greg continued. "But you should know, Barry, that everything we do here is top secret. In fact," he turned to [Archie?], "Can you step out, buddy? I told them I wouldn't involve you unnecessarily. For your own safety."

[Anderson?] shrugged, but he narrowed his eyes as he went back out in the hall.

Barry was still nodding. "Don't worry. I know how to keep a secret. My mind is a vault. And all the forums I use are highly encrypted. Yep, yep. Send me your discoveries."

The two men looked at us expectantly. I turned to Penny, who just blinked.

"How do we send them to you?" I asked.

"Beam it to me?" offered Barry.

I had no idea what this meant, and I had opened my mouth to make some guesses when Greg jumped in. "Didn't you say you have a sample of it?" he suggested.

"Yes. But it is a gas."

"That will work, I can do that," said Barry, scrambling to bring over some kind of gas collection device with tubes and containers of water. Penny and I huddled over her thingama-bob, blocking it from view while we changed it to something that could allow a small tube to enter it, then she activated it so that a small amount of the collected gas went out into Barry's tubes. Barry spent a few minutes looking over what we had and making notes while we viewed the room.

We were in a wide area with dark paneled walls. Every surface was filled to the brim with computer equipment, mag-azines, various sundries. I suspected it was a lab of some sort[6] by the number of beakers around and sinks set in every table.

Barry suddenly whipped around. "Is this real? You found this nearby?"

"Yes?" I responded, unsure if he should know that or not.

He bounced back and forth between looking at his notes and typing on his computer. "Your sources are right. It absolutely should not be here." He looked sideways at us. "Meet element X. I have heard all about it in the forums, but

____

6   Definitely not a food lab. Although I did see a very old tuna sandwich on
     top of one of the computers that seemed to be growing a friend.

I thought it was a hoax." He flipped his robe closed, but since we'd already seen underneath, I was not sure why. He rubbed his nose and continued. "As far as I know, there are only the smallest traces found anywhere on Earth, first hinted at in the forums about eight years ago. Its profile is unmistakable. And it is unlike anything else on Earth."

"In what way?" asked Greg.

Barry sniffed and wiped his nose again. "Because of its critical sublimation point. In regular temperature and pressure, it sublimes quickly, going directly from solid to gas within minutes, faster than dry ice, even. But as a solid, it acts like a metal. Nobody on the forums has ever shown real evidence of it in either form, however. Because it is *highly* classified. As in nobody is even supposed to know about it; they shut down any online conversations about it, make people go missing. That kind of thing." He grinned and Greg frowned, but Barry did not seem to notice. "I don't know what plans the US government has for it, but they want it for themselves. I cannot believe I have some true element X in my possession! Oh, the fellows are going to be so envious." He looked over at Greg. "Don't worry, the fellows won't tell, and my internet connection is untraceable."

"So, wait," said Greg, "you're saying the only ones with access to it are the government? The US government? *Our* government?"

Oh dear. Governments should never be involved in science. And suddenly I remembered where I'd read about kishwellium recently.

"As far as I know, yes. We elementologists, of course, can't be completely silenced when it comes to these things,"

Barry said proudly, his mouth a wide smile. "Truth can't be covered up entirely."

"So how would a trace of this element end up here?" I asked, Penny whispering in my ear about how this human already knew too much. I shushed her.

Barry leaned his side against the table. "That's the question, isn't it? Give me a minute to put some feelers out." He rushed over to a computer and started tapping away at it, his nose maybe three centimeters away from the screen.[7]

We watched, but I was impatient as he worked. Penny started circling the room. She picked up a dark metal ball that was sitting in a cradle and started examining it.

"Barry, what is your last name?" I asked while we waited.

"Hickenbottom," he answered.

". . ." I said.

"Ooh, this is interesting," said Barry.

"What?" asked Greg.

"Hickenbottom?!" I wanted to clarify.

"[Name redacted] says he has some new information about element X, but he has to move to a new location to share it with me first. Must be good," said Barry, grinning at us over his shoulder.

I shook my head. "But . . . your last name is Hickenbottom? That cannot be right."

"Barry, we don't have that kind of time," said Greg,

"Fine, I will tell him to give it to me now in code," said Barry.

"Hi–cken–Bot–tom . . ." I said.

____

7   His eye lenses did not seem to be doing their job if he had to go this close.

Barry pointed at the screen. "My friend [other name redacted] also says he has some info. He tends to know the really good secrets . . . about half the time."

"And the other half?" asked Greg.

"Nonsense," said Barry.

"Great," said Greg.

"Hickenbottom. Hick-en-bah-tuhm," I said. Penny elbowed me.

Barry continued. "So, [name redacted] says he got wind that the government is testing and building things with element X in secret locations all over the world, but—"

"Hickenbottom-Hickenbottom-Hickenbottom."

"—[Other name redacted][8] says he has proof that agents within the government have been stealing and selling the element to other countries. But I don't know, he's kind of a nut, to be honest."

I tried one more. "Hick-En-Bottom. Nope, I give up. I do not understand last names."

Greg snickered. "Where are you from, Barry? I thought you were Russian, but, no offense, Barry Hickenbottom doesn't sound very Russian."

"Ukrainian. But of course I changed my name when I got here."

"Changed . . . to Barry Hickenbottom?" I squeaked.

Greg chortled.

"We better take off," said [Ashley?], peeking his head in

---

8   Why are some names redacted, you ask? None of your business. But also because their names were something stupid that my brain purposefully blocked out. Like BondChemicalBond007.

the door. "I gotta get to work. Did you guys get what you needed?"

Barry waved us away. "That is all I have for now, anyway. I will contact you when I find something more." And with that he rushed us all back down the hall and out the door.

"So, friends," [Andres?] said as the door shut behind us, "How did it go? Where can I take you before I head to work?"

I glanced over at Penny and Greg, unsure what our next step should be.

"Time for flapjacks?" said Greg.

[13]   If I was queen over your people, I think I would standardize some of your names for things. All your languages have a problem, but English is the worst offender. I would make it so there would be no more of this arguing over what to call the pan-fried cake, or the fizzy drink, or the luminous bug, or the athletic shoe. And no more of, "Is it a flying bat or a baseball bat?" Oh, and *whom*. *Whom* would be right out. Gone altogether. Banished.

While we drove away from Barry's house (Greg in the front this time), [Austin?] and Greg argued about whether it was called a hotcake or a flapjack, finally settling on pancake but only because it was the term they both hated equally. I glanced at Penny. I suspected that although I had been distracted, she may have gotten something important out of all that in there. But she was not talking yet, just glowering at the thingamabob.

"So, what do you say?" asked Greg. "Should we settle this with a cook-off?"

"Not today," responded [Alistair?]. "I have to drop you guys off for now. But don't let Greg mislead you—his hotcakes are all right, but mine are divine. Come back to the food lab again sometime, and I'll let you compare. Especially you, Penny." He winked at her over his shoulder.

Greg turned and eyed me. "So, do you ladies want to come to my boss's apartment then? I can cook you flapjacks while we . . . regroup?"

Regroup. It was a good word without giving much away to his friend, though I supposed as long as [Augie?] did not know we were aliens, we might be safe.[1] But speaking of extra people I did not want involved, I was positive it would be a bad idea to go to Greg's boss's apartment and involve her too, of all people. The Alaskan senator almost *definitely* knew too much about us already, and we were best to stay clear of her.

As if reading my mind, Greg went on, "She isn't there at the moment—it's where she stays when she comes to DC. She went back home to Alaska already, but she's just letting me use her apartment here to rest up after the explosion. We would have the place to ourselves."

"No,"[2] said Penny in English. Maybe it was the fact it was in English, but her objections were starting to sound halfhearted.

"But Penny," I said in Booshy, "we already agreed to work with him." She grumbled at this since we both knew *she* had not agreed at all, but I pushed on. "And we do need to *regroup.* And also, I want to try flapjacks, for research. Plus, we can speak Booshy, so Greg will not get any information he is not supposed to get while we figure things out. And since the senator is not there anyway, it might be good to switch up our locations and avoid suspicion. Right?"

Penny pursed her lips and stared back out the window.

So [Asa?] dropped us off at Greg's boss's apartment.

---

1   I realize now this was a silly supposition. If he thought we were involved with the terrorists that bombed DC (which in a way, we were), that might be just as bad.

2   The other word she knows.

It was very modern and white, with a proportionally large kitchen. As we sat there at the island bar, watching Greg mix and fry and flip the little cakes in the pan, I felt so safe and warm, I could have continued watching him forever.

But I could feel the Penny storm cloud[3] brewing beside me, reminding me we had a bigger purpose here and were needed elsewhere soon, so I knew *forever* was off the table.

"This is going to take a while," Greg said, glancing at Penny's scowl over his shoulder. "You two go ahead and chat, and fill me in on what you can."

I turned from Greg (reluctantly) to Penny, speaking Booshy. "So. Does that all mean what I think it means?" I asked to start her talking.

She grunted. "If you think it means the United States government is using a Booshy element to cause explosions, either on purpose or accidentally? I don't know. Maybe. The first question is how did they get it?"

I cleared my throat. "Yes, well, actually, I may have some ideas about that."

She frowned at me. "What?"

It was so rare for me to know something Penny did not that I was tempted to savor the moment, but the situation was too dire for that. "We might have maybe definitely given it to them."

"What?!" she said again, her mouth agape.

"While Barry was talking, I remembered where I had heard of kishwellium recently. I was studying the Accord, and

---

3   If you think she's been grumpy so far, you do not want to be here for the real storm to come.

it was listed in the addendums and disclosures. Kishwellium was one of the tools and elements we handed over to UNOOSA as part of the 'share all technologies' rule. The Royal Interns assured me the humans could not use it for much anyway. I remember kishwellium specifically because we had so much of it in storage and it did not seem particularly useful, so I . . ."[4]

"Not useful?!"

"Well I certainly did not know it could be used to make explosives, did I? I would never have given them something so dangerous."

"Kishwellium is not dangerous! It is not an explosive; it doesn't burn. I can't fathom how it could be involved in any of this. But—" she pointed her finger at me, "—it *is* useful: it was just in storage because in its pure state, it sublimes too quickly in Earth's atmosphere, making it hard to manage unless combined with another element. It has to be frozen to keep it solid here."

I leaned back. "You know I have no idea what any of that means."

Greg turned and put a towering dish of flat cakes in the center of the table, then went back to whisk some white cream in a bowl.

Penny continued in a hushed tone. "The important thing is that we *do* use it. Combined with copper it becomes an important component in all our electronics. Without it, technology like the gravitator would not function. I can't believe

---

4   It may seem strange that Penny was not aware of this, but you should know that at the time, she was not a royal adviser yet, so she had almost no involvement in politics. She took over as my main personal adviser because all the others could not handle me.

you gave it all away. Did you give them our coolers to carry it in as well?"

I rubbed my neck. It was too late for guilt. "I do not remember. But I think we can safely say yes, at this point." So they'd received an element they did not understand, but had kept it frozen, studied it, and were now experimenting with it. It had been there, at the site of the explosion. Someone must have discovered a way for it to become explosive, despite what Penny said.

"Everything okay?" Greg asked, putting down a big bowl of white fluffy cream and fresh red strawberries on the bar in front of us.

"Yes," I responded a little too enthusiastically. "No. Yes. This looks so good, Greg!" The question was, were the explosions an accident, or were they using our technology for evil on purpose? "Are those fresh strawberries?"

"Of course! Best way to eat flapjacks." He smiled, and started pulling more bowls out of his boss's refrigerator. He dropped a bowl of blueberries and chocolate chips next to the strawberries.

I turned back to Penny. "But then how is Woods involved?" I asked her. She scowled. "Penny, I know you cannot quite believe it, but we *know* there was an element from Brooshaloo there, and you know I have no reason to imagine him. I *saw* him."

She was looking stormy again, but it was with sadness when she said, "Kishwellium *was* one of his specialties . . ."

I had not realized that, but if so, such a coincidence was too much, even for her.

"So, anything you can share, or need help with, or is it

all top secret?" Greg asked, sitting down on a stool across from us.

I tried to be as vague as possible. "What we learned from Barry was important, but I do not yet know how it is connected. We need to find our suspect right away, but we do not yet have many clues, the how, why, or where."

Greg piled himself a small plate with a few cakes and toppings, then handed us both empty plates and motioned to the food, "So do you think there are others involved, and is it someone in the government? My government? Like Barry implied?"

How much did Greg need to know to be helpful without being in danger? I did not know, but hiding things from him was hard. "Officially or unofficially, intentionally or unintentionally, yes, your government is probably involved. Or it is possible our suspect stole from your government, and the government has no knowledge of any of it."

"So, your suspect is someone from *your* government."

I shook my head firmly. "He is with us, but he is not *with* us. He does not have the approval of our government." I decided not to tell him yet that our government was *me*.

"And once you have him, what are you going to do with him? Will you give him up to our law enforcement?"

I looked at Penny, and she frowned but still did not say anything. It would be up to me, but I knew there was a lengthy discussion on the subject coming later. "I do not know yet."

Greg nodded and took a bite of his flapjacks. "So all we have to do is find the guilty parties. Right? And before they hurt anyone else."

"Yes. And not get arrested by your police while we are at it."

Greg swallowed a bite of food. "Okay. I think our first step is to put this cream and these fresh strawberries on some flapjacks. And then, to eat at least three flapjacks each."

"That is an excellent first step," I said, smiling. I do love a good to-do list.

Penny sighed and took my empty plate, piling it high with flapjacks, cream, and strawberries and putting it back in front of me before attending to her own. Greg paused in his eating to watch her do this, making me self-conscious about letting her serve me even though she had done it for as long as I'd known her, even before she was my royal adviser.

"I can of course get my own food," I said in my defense. "I know how. It is only that Penny likes to serve me."[5]

She would have glared at me for that, but she'd taken a bite of the food and was now eating with such enthusiasm—various sounds of enjoyment occasionally escaping her lips—that I was not sure she even knew who she was anymore.

I gave an apologetic smile to Greg, then cut into my pile and took a very small bite so as not to get too overwhelmed.

I groaned in ecstasy and Greg chuckled. "Yep," he said. "Flapjacks."

Penny was even more engrossed than I was.[6] I had never

---

5   Both of these statements are untrue. She does not *enjoy* serving me even if she is used to it, and I was only so-so at getting my own food unless it was something I can just eat whole without preparation. Like a peach. Or a taco.

6   I did love it, but I think fresh fruit does not need to be dressed up so much. It is perfect on its own.

seen her eat like this. Once she finished her first plate of flapjacks, she started loading up another, all before I had even gotten halfway through my first serving. Greg put his empty plate aside and leaned his elbows on the bar in front of Penny, smiling at her. She did not look up, but she did let him drizzle a small amount of strawberry sauce on her flapjacks.

"You're starting to warm up to me, aren't you, Penny?" said Greg, shaking a finger at her.

She glared at him, but he seemed to take that as a yes. And I was pretty sure he was right to do so.

Greg's phone made a notification sound, and he pulled it out to look at the screen. He cleared his throat and exhaled. "So, it turns out there's a public press conference in a few minutes at the courthouse." I looked up at him in surprise and he sighed. "I didn't tell my cop friend anything, but she knows I'm in town and she sent me the announcement. Bella isn't in charge, but I think she can get us in. Look, maybe if we go, we can get some more information, answer a few of the other questions: the 'how' or the 'why.'"

I rubbed my forehead. This would involve being in the presence of police officers again, the two that hated us, or the others in bomb suits. Even with our wigs, it could be a danger. Penny just looked back down at her cakes and started eating again.

I put my hand over hers. "At least it is a plan, right? And our disguises do seem to be working, since we have not been recognized or arrested yet," I said in Booshy.

Penny called Greg something that I am too polite and royal to relay. But I took it as agreement and finished shoveling fruit and flapjacks into my mouth, planning to get at least one more plateful before we left. Or two.

[14] Once we entered the courthouse, I almost backed right out again. The entire police department was there, judging by the abundance of blue uniforms. We stayed only because nobody paid any attention to us whatsoever, probably because the conference had already started. The city officials had opened the meeting up to the public, with an overflow in an adjoining building, and that is where we were sent. We were ushered into a room with a big projector screen at the front. A large light-skinned man with a bulbous nose was talking on the screen. "—But we do have a final count of the injuries and fatalities from both explosions."

Greg found us seats in the very back and stood behind me and Penny.

The man continued. "Forty-six total casualties,[1] including one fatality. The second explosion was reported to be bigger, but because there were already authorities, police officers, and medical personnel on site, they were able to evacuate everyone from the location quicker." He leaned forward to hear a question from someone in the front. "I don't know anything about that—you would have to ask

---

1   I do not understand this terminology. I have never found what they are describing to be very casual.

her,"[2] he responded. "But let's save any more questions till the end." He straightened his black tie. "Let me reiterate: we are not terming these explosions acts of terrorism at this time, and we still haven't ruled out accidental causes."

At this, there was an uproar of objections from the crowd at the courthouse and around us in the overflow, which the officer quieted by pushing on, louder.

"I realize two accidental explosions seem improbable. But our experts still insist that the evidence is inconsistent with purposeful bombings. We have found no explosive device, debris, shrapnel, nor any expected residues. In addition, the casualty numbers are extremely low for explosions of this size. Most injuries were mild, due to window glass blown out from the shock wave. And the shock waves were atypical for a bombing. In fact, the evidence is more consistent with what you see after a small meteorite hits the atmosphere. And except for the fact that the blasts were strange and so localized, an aggressive meteor shower would be our prevailing theory. That said, if anyone finds any suspicious holes in ceilings or craters in the ground, please contact the local police department right away."

A tall white-haired human in front of us began examining the ceiling, a hand over his balding head.

---

2   I still do not know what question he was answering here, but I have imagined a few possibilities. 1: "Is your sister still single and will she go out with me?" 2: "How much does Aria like Greg now that she has eaten his cooking in relation to how much she liked him when they first met?" 3: "FBI Agent Maria Marcus has said we can't attribute all of the injuries directly to the explosions, that some were injured out of surprise after seeing a chicken crossing the road. Would you care to make a comment?"

The officer on screen straightened his tie again. "The main point I want to make here is that we recommend going about your day as normal while we continue to investigate." There was more murmuring at this. "And, for those choosing to remain in the city, feel free to shop, enjoy your gatherings, participate in your local government, and report anything suspicious. For those choosing to evacuate, please do so in an orderly manner."

"Thus negating everything you just said," mumbled Greg from behind me.

"Also, in terms of protecting yourself and your loved ones, we have learned that the aftermath of both explosions left an unusual haze that can be harmful if inhaled. We believe the crisis is over, but if not, possible injuries could be reduced even further by wearing KN95 face masks. We will be giving them out for free after this meeting, here and at several other public buildings, including the police station, community center, and at the local high schools."

"That is a great idea," I whispered over my shoulder to Greg.

"Mm-hmm," said the human sitting on my right, and I realized it looked like I was leaning over to whisper in her ear, but she did not seem to mind. She smiled at me.

"So, what do you do," I asked her with a smile back.

"I'm a barrister," she whispered back with what I recognized as a British accent.

"Oh, how exciting! I have always dreamed of becoming a barrister."

"Really?" asked Greg.

"Yes. Why? Is that unusual?" I breathed.

He chuckled quietly. "Not at all, I just didn't picture you as a lawyer."

"Oh," I whispered. "I thought it was something else. What is the other one, the person who gets coffee for people?"

". . . A barista?"[3] he asked.

"Yes!" I sighed. "I have always dreamed of becoming a barista." I smiled at the human next to me again, but she scowled and leaned away. A few people shushed us, and Greg tried to stifle his chuckling.

Someone at the front was asking another question we could not hear, and the officer leaned over the pulpit to hear better. "Bubbles?" he asked to clarify, his eyebrows pulled low. I sat up straighter, but I could not hear the asker's follow-up question.

The officer shook his head in unbelief. "Yes, a few have reported, I can't believe I'm about to say this, *bubbles* at the scene, but rest assured it wasn't related to anything other than creating a romantic mood at The Wharf." Some people in the audience laughed, and the officer rubbed his head. "Let's keep this to serious questions only, please."

After a few more minutes of questions we could not hear, the press conference was over, and we all filed out.

"Wow," said Greg, "that didn't quite go where I expected it to. 'Aggressive meteor shower'? Wild."

He grabbed a face mask on our way out and I made sure Penny and I each grabbed a mask too, for appearances. The

---

3   I stand by this dream. I do think I could be both queen and barista. But I am building up to it. It is slightly more difficult now that there is no more Earth coffee or coffee shops.

scene outside was a jumble. Everyone donned their face masks immediately and hurried off. I wondered how many people would believe the danger was over and be willing to stick around. Judging by the general confusion on the street, I suspected the answer was not many.

Greg touched my elbow. "Aria, I know you said police involvement should be a last resort, but since the police department is just right there," he pointed across the street, "I could just run in, ask her if she can put out a missing persons report, and come right back, without really involving you. What do you say?"

I agreed, so Greg left toward the police department, and Penny and I turned to meander in the opposite direction.

My brain was a large blank[4] after what we had heard in the press conference. The only way the explosions could have been from a meteor shower was if the meteors were invisible. And did not burn. And sent out colorful clouds of haze. Which is impossible. And I know impossible: I once saw a *drooloo* balance a *fromorgny* on its pinky. And Penny laughed at it. So, two impossible things.

Greg was suddenly back, his expression sheepish. "So, my friend told me they can't do anything without a description and a picture. Which I can't give. Sorry. Should we just forget it, or do you want to take a chance?" It was a sincere question.

I sighed. "What if the police officers recognize us?"

"I don't think anyone will recognize you, honestly. Not only because of the disguises, but also because there are so many people in there, we shouldn't stand out. And my friend

---

4   I promise this was not the norm for me. Or it was not until then.

is trustworthy. She said you can remain anonymous, and they won't ask you any questions outside of the description. Plus, I don't think even *I* would recognize you right now. But look, if I'm wrong, we can just get out." And then he gave me his sweetest smile, and I decided this was better than no plan at all.

I put the hat I'd had in my pocket on my head. "*Fine.* And while we go, you can tell me what a missing persons report is."

We were only a few steps away from the squat brick police station when Penny stopped. "This is a waste of time. And it's dangerous. I am not going in there. I'll just . . . I'll stand guard outside." She backed away from us and strode off.

"Where's Penny going?" asked Greg, stopping next to me.

I blew out a puff of air. "She still does not think I am right about the suspect, so she does not think this will be useful. But I know I saw him. He is involved, I am certain."

"So why is Penny so sure he wasn't there?" Greg opened the glass door for me, and we entered with a slew of other people.

"Because he is dead."

"Ah. That's a pretty good reason."

"And also because," and I had to admit this one was even harder to get around in some ways, "it is the way he looks. If he had been seen by anyone but me, at the explosion or since, we would have heard about it. Even without a missing persons report."

Greg and I sat down to wait our turn inside the police station. The tense atmosphere inside the station was even worse than outside. Apparently, a lot of people had seen something 'suspicious:' I sincerely hoped none of the tips would be about disguised alien queens. I pulled my baseball cap lower, bowing my head to hide my face from the crowd of humans around us.

"So, he's distinctive and suspicious-looking," said Greg, "But couldn't he be in disguise?"

This was one thing I was sure of. "No. I did already see him disguise-less, for one; and also, he does not . . ." I paused, trying to find an explanation that would not give too much away about myself. "He does not have what he needs to disguise himself." Namely me and the power units only I could control.

I knew Greg likely had no notion of what the Booshy people looked like. Even among the .000001 percent of the population who knew about us, only a fraction of that percentage ever had actual contact with us, and they had only seen the fake alien visage we presented. Certainly, zero percent of humans were aware of our facebender technology: it was one of the technologies we had hidden so we would not have to give it away. I was hoping that somehow Greg believed I looked like the human disguise I wore.

Greg shook his head in confusion. "He doesn't have what he needs? Couldn't he just *get* what he needs? Like we did? Get a wig, contacts, and makeup from a corner store? Maybe even steal them if he has no money, though obviously he has resources if he's building bombs."

Oh. I had forgotten again that humans had their own methods of disguise, even though I was currently wearing one. "That is true, I suppose he could." I thought for a moment longer. "And this is what he must have done, because otherwise, where has he been hiding all this time without being seen? Or only being seen by me?" As I spoke, we were called up to the front of the line.

Even with how busy the station was, the process to report Woods as a missing person was very quick. Greg's police friend, Bella, got us a semi-private location to talk in. She was a harassed-looking dark-skinned woman with large eyes and a big puff of curly black hair on her head. The two friends reminisced about high school for a bit, and then Bella got down to business. She wrote down everything we told her. She wrote Woods's name, wrote that he was an unbalanced, out of work actor who liked disguises, and that we had last seen him at the site of the first explosion so he was possibly injured. And then she handed us off to a sketch artist since we did not have any photos. The red-faced male artist worked very swiftly and did quite a good job drawing, only getting annoyed after the fourteenth picture I asked him to draw.[5] And then it was over.

I breathed a sigh of relief as we shoved through the crowds on our way out of the station. Just as I turned to Greg to tell him how quick and painless the process had been, about how glad I was that Penny was wrong about the risk, I caught a glimpse of two of the nearby officers, and I froze in place, making several other people bump into me. It was

---

5   He finally walked out when I asked if he could draw a bowl of fruit. Well, after I asked him to draw a *second* bowl of fruit. I liked the first drawing of fruit so much, I wanted one for myself. Could there be any worthier subject than fruit? I would have asked him to draw Greg, but I did not want it to get mixed up with the Woods pictures. Nobody would suspect a bowl of fruit of anything nefarious. Well, not human fruit, that is.

the two officers from the first explosion, side by side: the ones who hated us. Greg followed my eyeline. He put his arm around me, pulling me close and nestling my head against his neck.

"Just stay with me," he whispered and chuckled, his eyes tight. Was it a fake laugh, or had one of us said something funny, I wondered, but then I stopped thinking all together. We pushed through the crowd and out of the building and did not part until the officers were out of sight.

Ah, he was hiding me, I realized as he let go and stepped away. "That was . . . you are very smart, thank you," I said, off balance now. I was glad when he kept hold of my hand.

Penny arrived by my side and asked if she could speak to me in private. Since Greg did not speak Booshy (and neither did any of these other humans), *all* our conversations were private, but I humored her. "Greg, leave."

"You bet," he said cheerfully and walked away into a crowd waiting outside the station.

"I saw the senator," Penny said.

"What? Which senator?" I asked.

"Our senator. Greg's master."

I felt a wave of unease. Did Senator Kilcher know we were here? No, of course not. We were in disguise. In *several layers* of disguise. And it was a big city.

Still, the unease remained. "Did not Greg say she went back to Alaska? That she left after the gala? Is the Senate in session?"

"No."

I looked around. "I wonder what she is doing back here."

"Your Majesty," Penny pulled me farther away from

the crowd, "is it possible that Greg lied? That he *knows* she is here?"

"Why would he do that?"

"He works for her. He works for the United States government. He is a human, and his loyalty is to them. If she discovers us here and shares this information, it will be very bad for us."

I squinted at her, thinking. Yes, Greg was human. Did this mean he would betray us in favor of his own kind? He had said he would not. But was that a lie?

"No," I said aloud to my own question. "No, Greg does not have some secret plan to get us in trouble."

"But—" she began anxiously.

"No, I believe him. I trust him. I choose to trust him."[6] He had chosen to believe we were the good guys, and now I was going to do the same for him.

Penny narrowed her eyes, but nodded.

"Greg," I called out. He popped his head around the corner and moseyed back over to us.

"Did you know Senator Gwyn Kilcher is still here?"

Greg's face waffled between confusion and surprise, and I felt any remaining anxiety about him ease; I had made the right decision to trust him.

"Gwyn Kilcher, my boss? Here where? Here in DC?" he asked.

I nodded. "Penny just saw her."

He looked around. "Where?" he asked again.

"She was going into a clothing store," Penny said,

---

6   Of course, this turned out to be a huge mistake.

gesturing in the direction of nearby shops, and I translated. Greg rushed off toward the building, Penny behind him.

Rather than stand there, attracting attention waiting for them, I wandered along the nearby stores, trying to come up with and write down a plan for our next steps on a piece of paper I'd taken from the inn. Sometime later, Greg and Penny caught back up to me.

"We couldn't find her," Greg said, out of breath. He scratched his head while we walked along the sidewalk. "Her flight was two days ago. I bought her the tickets myself. I suppose maybe she could have come back here again. She goes places without informing us all the time. But it's suspicious that she would just leave and come right back. And where is she staying? I'm in her apartment."

He put his hands in his pockets, looking around. "Or maybe she just never left, and tried to make it look like she had, for some reason? I tried calling her, but she didn't answer, as usual. Let me look into it. If she's still here in DC, someone will know."

I turned to Penny.

"Do you believe him?" she asked me in Booshy.

"Yes, I do."

"Then so will I. She must have lied to Greg. Or, I suppose it is possible that I was mistaken, and it was someone else."

That did seem unlikely. Penny never forgets a face from any species.

[15] You are a planet of interesting contradictions. You value truth, but not if it encroaches on politeness. You protect personal freedoms only so far as they do not infringe on general safety. You celebrate diversities but fear what is different. Some of my people find these contradictions to mean you are untrustworthy. Not me—I am only relaying this from others. I find your contradictions fascinating. And spending time among you has always made me want to trust you,[1] as I did Greg. Even if I cannot always follow his thought process.

"Anyone up for bowling?" asked Greg as we rushed along the sidewalk. We had not settled on the exact destination yet, but a brisk trot helped us feel productive.

"Bowling? But, I made a list!" I held up the sheet of paper with the plan I had made a few minutes ago. *Press conference* and *report to police without getting caught* were written and crossed off in a most pleasing way. "Also, what is bowling?"

"Bowling's a game," said Greg.

Penny glared at us both as she passed, then continued on in front of us. Since she could not really contribute to the conversation much, she had taken to circling us like a vicious *snorb* bat.

Greg grimaced. "Yeah, I realize a game doesn't sound

---

[1] I am fully aware that you might not care, since at this point in the story, you likely do not trust *me*. This also has almost nothing to do with this part or the rest of the story. I am not sure why I included it.

like the best choice right now. But they say if you want to figure out clues, you should stop thinking about them and let your unconscious mind work on it. Bowling is great for not thinking."

When he saw my disappointed expression looking at my to-do list, Greg took the paper out of my hands. "Okay, you're right. What's next on the list?"

I tried to take the paper back, but his reach was much longer than mine. He looked the sheet up and down, then squinted at it, giving it much more attention than the short list demanded. Then he smiled sideways at me and flicked the paper with his finger. "So the next one says, 'come up with some ideas.' No problem. I *do* have some ideas, but I think maybe we should get away from the streets to discuss them. And the last one on the list says, 'come up with a better plan.' That's a good one, I like it. But again, we may want to be somewhere less conspicuous. We could go back to your hotel or my boss's apartment, but I bet at a time like this there won't be a single other person bowling, and there's an alley right up here. What if we write *go bowling* on the list right now, and then when we get inside, we can cross three things off at once, and come up with some more to write down from there. What do you say? I'll even let you use my special heavy ball point pen."

Crossing off three things at once? I turned to Penny who was passing around one side.

"For the record, this is a stupid idea, but . . ." Penny said, making a gesture that meant she'd already washed her hands and feet and tentacles of my decisions.

Nobody could deny it was a convenient location for

getting our bearings; I could already see the front entrance. So we turned into the wide doorway with a big fiery ball painted on the window.

We were the only ones there except one human who owned his own ball[2] and the teenager working the counter, both of which were out of earshot with the noise of the heavy balls on wood. In case you do not know, bowling is another of your ball sports that has gone the way of the Earth, but for lazy people. I particularly liked it because you could eat at the same time you played, and was intrigued by the food that was not at all fresh, but somehow still tasty.[3]

"I keep thinking what a terrible plan this all was," Greg said as we watched Penny push the ball down the lane on her hands and knees.

"To go bowling?" I thought it a strange admission since bowling was his suggestion. And I had already written *Base of Operations, Bowling Alley* at the top of our plans paper.

"No, not *our* plan. *His. Theirs.* The person or people causing the explosions. I mean, what were they even trying to do? Hurt or kill people? They've done a pretty poor job if so. This is a big city. Yes, one person died, and some went to the hospital, but for a bombing, it's been a complete failure. There are tons of important people here. The *president* is here. But most of the injuries were simple cuts or due to smoke inhalation, and no one in government has been anywhere near the

____

2   I assume this by the way he was polishing, cradling, and kissing it. Nobody would so care for a stranger's bowling ball.

3   I suspect that none of these descriptions of the bowling alley and the food there will surprise you. But maybe they will make you feel nostalgic for the old days when you could go bowling? Is not that nice?

explosions when they happened. Also, the smoke inhalation problem is now conveniently solved with cheap masks."

"Maybe our suspect is simply trying to hurt *me*? Both explosions have been at places I recently spent time."

"Well then why hasn't he? Even if he's your arch enemy with a grudge or something, he chose a pretty poor method of hurting you, right? You're one of the only people in the vicinity of the bombs without even a scratch. Instead, he hurt a bunch of other people not at all related to you. So if hurting you was his goal, he missed. By a lot."

This was true. What was more, I was not affected by the smoke like the humans were, which was something Woods would surely know. I stood to take my turn rolling the ball toward the little white blobby things at the end of the aisle.

"You are right," I said. "And also, the man we suspect, Woods, is a genius. He would never make any plan that would fail so completely. Which means we still have no idea of his motivations." I clapped when my ball hit one of the blobby pins.

"Can you tell me more about this Woods guy, or is it top secret? Did he fake his own death or something? I thought that only happened in the movies."

"I cannot tell you more, not because it is secret but because we do not know. I was there when he died; he *should* be dead." I looked over at Penny, but she was pretending not to pay attention to me, and was instead examining the machine that threw up balls.

Greg took a deep breath, gazing at me contemplatively. "The only thing the first explosion accomplished is that it made people scared, but that was short-lived. And the second explosion really only put the police and public on even higher alert, asking everyone to keep an eye out for strange things. Which will make it harder to set any future explosions, but maybe that isn't their goal." He stood to give me a few pointers on which fingers to stick in which holes on the heavy ball. "Come to think of it," he continued, "now the police might even have a few suspects."

"They do? Who?" Now that my fingers were in the holes, I was not sure they would come out again. I suspected this bright pink ball was for a child, but it was *pink*, which everyone knows is a royal color.

"Their suspects are you and Penny. In fact I can only think of one possible goal that is having any amount of success so far."

"What is that?" I said, finally dropping the ball and watching it roll into the gutter.

"To get you outed. Maybe even caught by authorities."

I glanced at Penny, who was still standing by the ball roller. Her expression mirrored my thoughts, which were agitated.

Greg went back to drying his fingers and palms with the hand dryer. Penny started muttering, and I sat down and put my head in my hands.[4] It was a pretty complicated plan, but Woods always did have plans too intricate for me to follow. And it seemed to be working. If someone wanted me and Penny to be caught by the humans, maybe to get us out of the picture completely, this was one way to do it.

---

4   You may have noticed I do this often. This is because my head is very heavy. I think it is because I am very smart.

So was it revenge? Revenge on me for having him killed? Or was his goal to get us thrown off the planet so we could find another without so many rules? If so, there were many other barriers to this, chiefly that our ship was no longer functional, and being catapulted into outer space meant death, but maybe he had found solutions for those issues as well.

Although I would not put seeking revenge past him, this goal of getting us kicked off the planet seemed more in line with the Woods I remembered. Woods hated Earth. And while I perhaps disregarded the severity of the Accord, Woods had outright revolted against it. So he'd created havoc near us, revealed himself so we would stay, continued to create confusion until our unusual behavior inevitably made the humans suspicious, then continued to cause enough damage until he could get us evicted. We'd fallen right into the whole plan like *boroshmooshmoos* jumping off a *quaking duckuss*.

There were still a few holes in this theory. Where had Woods gotten the kishwellium? And he was a genius, but how could he have known all the rest of it would fall into place? We were supposed to go home directly after the gala, but we did not. And we did not the next day either because of my date with Greg. Surely Woods could not have known all of that would happen. He could not have known about Greg, could he? It seemed impossible, but Woods had proved he had better foresight than I in the past.

Penny dropped her ball straight into the gutter, dusting her hands together with an air of finality, and then sat in the vinyl-covered booth next to me. She watched Greg as he stood to take his turn. "What Greg suggests—this does seem Woods's style. This human is much smarter than he looks," she grunted, her eyebrows lowering. "And his flat cakes were delicious."

I sat up and responded in Booshy. "Yes, he is smart. And yes, they were." If anyone would be able to discover Woods's motivations, Penny could. But so far, all she had done was mistrust me and mistrust Greg. It was time to get her on board.[5] "Penny, listen—"

"We should go back to the Compound now," she cut in. "Take a train and the ferry and gravitate the rest."

I shook my head. "Penny, wait."

"That way we cannot be caught, if that is his goal," she continued, a kind of desperation in her voice. "We would be far out of reach. Our people would be safe. And we would never have to face him." She looked down at her hands.

I considered this. "Then you believe Woods is alive? And that he is trying to get us caught?"

She grunted again, still looking down at her hands. "More likely, he wants us to be forced to leave. He hated our situation trapped there in the Compound. Would have done anything to put an end to it."

It was as close as I was going to get to her admitting she'd been wrong. I glanced at Greg, who'd stopped playing and was now sitting on the bench seat across from us, rolling his neck.

Greg was right about Woods's motivations. I felt it. And if so, going back would thwart his plans. We should have gone right away, but I'd kept delaying.

"We cannot leave," I found myself saying to Penny

---

5   On board, off board, overboard, whatever it took.

in Booshy. And even though I'd dreaded going back to the Compound all along, I realized my reason for refusing now was not what I expected. "I am sorry we did not leave sooner, I know that is my fault. But I do not think it would solve the problem now. The humans can catch us in Alaska as well as they can here—easier even, since we would already be locked up. And if he causes another explosion, more humans would be in danger. No matter what Woods's motivations may be, he is our responsibility. We must find him before he takes this further. We are the only hope."

Penny looked down and nodded. I was relieved that even though she is always right, for once, I was even more right.

"What are you guys talking about?" Greg asked, draping his arms across the back of the bench seat.

"Penny has decided to believe me," I responded. "And it is my turn to play."

We took the next few minutes finishing up our game,[6] and with Penny's more-willing help, making a list of Woods's possible hiding locations, and then we changed our shoes and left.[7] As we filed along the sidewalk, I noticed Penny lagging behind.

When I slowed down to walk beside her, she sighed. "I'm very sorry I took so long to believe you, Your Majesty. That was un-friend-like. And un-adviser-like. I should have believed you from the start. But truthfully, I think I didn't want to."

------

6   I bowled a strong sixty-three, in case you are wondering.

7   I did want to keep the strange shoes. The shoes I was changing into were ballet flats and I do not even do ballet, which felt insincere.

"Very understandable under the circumstances."

"Thank you, Aria. You are a true friend." She took a deep breath. "I've thought of a way to find and follow Senator Gwyn Kilcher, or at least find out for certain whether she is here."

I blinked at her. "What? But, why? Greg said he will take care of that. And we have a list!" I held up the paper.

"Yes. But if she is here, that means the senator has been lying to Greg regarding her whereabouts. Why would she do that? What is she doing here? It doesn't feel right. I want to investigate."

We stopped walking and I put a hand on Penny's shoulder. "This hardly seems like the time to go off on a separate mission, Penny. We have to find and stop Woods, we only have six Earth-days to do it, and there is nobody better to track him than you. You are my adviser."

Penny nodded, her face dark and determined. "That is true. I am the best, and we don't have much time. But I don't need to be with you to advise you. And I think this is important. As Alaska's senator, the senator must know about us, so if Woods is doing as Greg suggests, the senator could be involved. We must be sure either way. Greg is smart—he can help you track Woods." She closed her eyes. "And also, when you *do* find Woods . . . . I don't think I want to be there. I think I might only be a hindrance." She sighed and started walking again. "The two of you can catch him and stop him without me, and Greg can watch after your safety. You still have plenty of power for the emergency shield if you need it. And I will find out what the senator is up to and make sure nothing she does can hurt our people."

I had not expected this amount of openness from Penny and was not quite sure how to respond. I'd always considered her my friend, but like most of my relationships, it was one-sided when it came to sharing: always from me to her. So I agreed to her terms. Penny gave Greg the one-armed-one-leg Booshlaboo salute, which Greg returned with a clumsy wave, unwittingly agreeing to the passage of my safety over to his care, and then Penny left.

I told Greg Penny wanted to investigate the senator on her own, and then I told him he was not allowed to ask more. So he did not. Instead, he called a YouRide so we could check the first place on our list.

As we rode away, I could not help noticing that Greg and I were suddenly alone. Sort of. Not counting the stranger in the front seat. But besides that, so, so alone. And I was trying very hard not to like it.

[16]   I want to tell you something you might not know. Well, something *else* you might not know. Besides all of the other things in this story you do not know.

Some of your alien movies have suggested reasons why humans are unique. Some say it is your passion, strong emotion, beauty, art, poetry: like those are things only humans have to such a degree. Mostly incorrect: I've seen these attributes in many other places around the galaxy. Do you want to know what truly makes humans unique? Awkwardness. I am pretty sure that is a human invention. You might think I am the most awkward one in this story, but it is a trick of your mind.[1] I did not even know what awkwardness was until I came among you. But walking around the empty streets of Washington DC alone with Greg, trying to be just colleagues and never being sure what that meant, I certainly knew about awkwardness now. And it was bliss.

"Where's next on the list?" Greg asked. We'd been at this for more than twenty-four hours not counting meals and sleep for Greg,[2] but we were still just getting started. I looked over the locations listed as we walked along a sidewalk, passing a series of restaurants and shops.

---

1   It could also be because you are reading the story wrong. And by the way, how dare you think that: I am a queen.

2   I do not need to recharge as often as humans do, but I am afraid I got very little done while Greg was sleeping on the couch of our Fantasy Inn Suite. He is just so cute while he is sleeping. Like a baby *flabgop*.

"That is the last of the public and private chemistry labs in the area." I tapped my mouth with the pencil Greg had loaned me, and made it click a few times, looking down at my notebook. "Even though nobody recognized Woods's picture at any of them, is it possible he could still be there somewhere, sneaking in when they are closed? Should we keep checking?" I glanced behind me for the fiftieth time. Greg was convinced that the only way Woods could have known where we were when he set the explosions would be if he was following us. If so, perhaps we could catch him in the act?

Greg put his hands in his pockets. "I don't know. Maybe? What do you think?"

"Penny said sometimes Woods used to live in his lab when he was in the middle of an engrossing project. I do not think an official lab would let him stay there overnight, or at least would notice if he did."

Greg scratched his chin. "How long did you say he might have been living here in DC?"

"Even if he came here to DC right away after he died but did not die, seven years at the very most."

Greg made a thoughtful clicking noise with his tongue. "So he *could* have a job at a lab by now. But if so, they would have recognized him from the sketch artist's picture we showed. So, what's the next category then?"

I looked at the list again. "Abandoned warehouses, vacation homes with suspiciously large garages, and tempera-ture-controlled storage units. Any of those could work as a lab, do you not think so?"

"I suppose anything could work as a lab in a pinch, but

maybe not for something of this magnitude? Hopefully? Let me look up some addresses to give us a starting point," he said, then he pulled out his phone, tapping and swiping at it. "By the way, Senator Kilcher still won't answer my calls. Which isn't that unusual for her, but I also checked in with the guys back at the office in Fairbanks. Reg says she called to check in when her flight arrived, but they didn't see her and haven't heard from her since. Which could mean she arrived there and then came back, or she never got on the flight in the first place and was lying about it. She is going to a lot of trouble to keep her presence here a secret, and I'm not sure why. I'll keep digging. Has Penny seen her again?"

"Yes. According to Penny, Gwyn is mostly just out shopping? I will ask Penny again when I see her at the inn tonight." I looked down at my Royal Everything Device gauge, which I'd also set to count down the time we had before we were to return home. Less than five Earth–days left. Time was running out.

As we walked, I looked around at the humans and shops we passed. The streets had started to fill up again. It had been only two days since the last explosion, and I noticed this was all it took for the general public's fear and wariness to dull. A few of those we passed were still wearing a face mask, but most wore it hanging around their chins like a saggy diaper.[3] Greg and I kept our masks in our pockets like most others. The added benefit of the public's waning fear was that with

---

3   The humans were very quick to go from being grateful for the safety a face mask afforded to being annoyed at the masks for fogging up their glasses and making them smell their own stinky breath. Having smelled some of said breath, this is completely understandable.

more and more people back to their usual routines, our investigating was less conspicuous.

We walked, rode, and ran all over the city for hours, searching all the abandoned factories, garages, and storage facilities that Greg could find with his phone. Each ended up empty or too filled with boxes/old cars/coffins to be suitable as a lab.

The final warehouse had a broken lock on the door, making it easy to see into. Add that to the fact there were actual beakers and other lab-type equipment inside, and at first, I got very excited. "This is it! Do you think we should just wait here for him to come back, and then grab him?"

Greg glanced around at the broken glass and paraphernalia. "It's probably just drugs, and if it is drugs, I don't think we want to be here when whoever's stuff this is comes back. Even if this is your guy, do you have a plan for what to do if we do catch him? I've been meaning to ask. Because I think we'll need help." He led me back out, shut the door again, and put the broken lock back on. "I say let's go back to the police station and see if they know anything about the building. That way we can check in with Bella about the missing persons report too, and then we can keep going through our list."

I blew out a puff of air. He was probably right, but not about needing outside help. "Okay, we can talk to your friend, but if this does turn out to be Woods's lab, we will need a plan that does not involve the police."

He frowned but nodded.

When we arrived, Greg entered the police station first to make sure the two officers that hated us were not there anywhere, and then I followed. Greg's friend groaned when she saw us.

Greg held his hands up in a show of non-aggression. "Hey, Bella! We just have some more info we wanted to give you. No pressure about the missing person, I swear." This was not exactly true as he had already called her twice about it today, which seemed like at least a bit of pressure.

She sighed forcefully and waved to the two chairs by her desk. "Fine. Whadaya got?"

We sat and Greg described what we had found at the storage facility and gave the address. "We thought our guy might be there, so we just stumbled upon it. It might be drugs, might be something more, but I figured either way, you'll want to check it out."

I cleared my throat pointedly.

Greg glanced at me. "Oh, and uh, keep me updated on that, if you can, especially if our guy turns up."

"I'll see what I can do," she said flatly.

"So," Greg continued, his legs bouncing. "*Has* he turned up? Anyone call in yet? Any leads?"

She threw her hands up in the air and groaned. "You know I love ya, Greg.[4] I wanna help you out, but you gotta give me some time!" She grabbed a small bunch of papers from her desk. "You want to see what the artist gave me to work with? You say your missing man might look like this," she held up a picture we had drawn of Woods's face, but with human eyes and dreadlocks instead of tentacles. "Or this."

---

4   I felt no jealousy at this. To know Greg is to love him.

She held up another picture with her other hand. This one looked more like your standard bald green alien, same facial features (Greg had given me a strange look on that one, but I thought it better be safe than sorry). "Or, one of these other *dozen* pictures."

I pointed at one. "Not the fruit one. Actually, can I have that picture? I like the way he drew that strawberry."

Her eyes bounced over to me, and I put my hands back in my lap.

She pointed a thumb at me. "And *your friend here* also described him as 'a male of any race, with any hair color or eye color.'"

Greg scratched his head. "I think we mentioned he's an actor who likes disguises? And you know how those people are, especially if he is in the middle of a psychotic break . . ."

I nodded vigorously. "We are just covering every base. That is a baseball reference," I added helpfully.

Bella rolled her eyes, dropped the pictures, and looked down at her notebook. "The only piece of solid information besides the picture of this person's face is that they are five foot nine."

I nodded. "That one is legitimate . . . although I suppose he could hunch down or something . . ."

"Regardless, do you want to know how many people there are that tall in this town?" She tossed the notebook over her shoulder. "Greg, I'm sorry, you're a good guy and a good friend, but even if I had anything actionable here, it would still take time—a few days *even if* I didn't also have my hands full investigating explosions. And anyway, even if we find him, legally I don't have to tell you unless he wants us to. I am working on this as a favor to you, but you should be prepared. You may have to let it go."

Greg frowned, looking at me and then back at his friend. "I get it. Thanks so much for all of this. I owe you. How does a dozen homemade donuts sound?"

"Two dozen. Bavarian cream," she said, not looking at him.

"Deal." Greg's phone rang. He answered. "Yeah? Oh, hey, Barry."

"Barry Hickenbottom," I said to myself.

Greg chuckled and pulled me away, whispering to Bella, "Sorry. Call me!"

She rolled her eyes.

"Okay," Greg was saying into the phone as we left, "we'll meet you there." He ended the call. "Guess who got a lead?"

[17] "I don't have a lead," Barry said. "It's more like a lead of a lead."

We were standing in a back hallway in one of your space museums, Barry's choice for an inconspicuous meeting place.

I crossed my arms. "I do not know what that means, Barry Hickenbottom, but we will take whatever you have. And could you explain it slowly? We do not have our scientist with us."[1]

"Where'd she go?" Barry wondered, his expression suspicious. I figured that Barry was always suspicious the same way Penny was always annoyed.

"She is following a 'lead of a lead' elsewhere," I responded.

Barry closed his trench coat a little tighter. "Fine. That's fine. Let's move back a little more."

I'd only seen two other people in the very large museum so far, and they were nowhere near us, so I was not sure what we were moving back from. We took a few more steps down the hall. A 1:100 millionth scale semi-inaccurate squished-up model of your solar system[2] dominated the

---

1 Penny is our scientist, but I do not think Penny would have explained what Barry said either way. She says I'll never learn that way.

2 Having actually seen all your solar system's planets up close, I can tell you one of your planets is fake. I am not telling which one, though. I do not want to ruin the surprise.

room, with a few dwarf planets and moons spilling into the hall around us.

Barry rubbed his hands together. "So, here's what I got. Element X sublimes very quickly at room temperature, so we know it has to be kept as cold as possible to remain solid."

"In Earth's standard pressure," I added.

Both men stared at me.

I cleared my throat. "If it were in a denser atmosphere, it would not turn to gas. Or so I have been told." Apparently, more of Penny's lecture had sunk in than I thought, because now I was repeating her words from the night before.

Barry scowled. "That is obvious. And are you telling this or am I?" He sniffed and turned purposefully to Greg. "Back to the topic. As I mentioned, element X isn't one of the recognized elements." He pulled a few papers out of his trench coat. "I got two guys' testimony here that they tried to have it added to the periodic table. Both say they were shut down and discredited, but one of them worked for the CIA before that, as one of their premiere scientists, and he says he was taken to a big compound somewhere in the Arctic, tied up, asked all sorts of unsavory questions, and then sent home with enough meth in his system to make him unable to work anywhere besides fast food for the rest of his life. He was kind of reluctant to talk about it, to be honest. That's what took me so long."

Barry walked a few more steps down the hallway, and we followed him. "So this ex-CIA friend, he's kept a few of his connections, and he says he finally found the facility where they were interrogating him. And he also has evidence that is where they are keeping all the element X, too. In Alaska."

He pulled out a printout of a large set of connected buildings in a mountain range, in the vague shape of a long triangle. *Our* buildings. The Compound. Of course, the real bulk of it was underground, but that was definitely it.[3]

I coughed uncomfortably.

"And now that I've shown you that, forget it or we could be arrested." He seemed pleased by the prospect.[4]

"Why does your CIA friend think that is the building?" I asked. I eased forward, trying not to bump my head on a moon the size of a basketball hanging by a string above me.

"He has seen official government documents about it, for one, but also there are plenty of clues. About ten years ago, a huge deployment of UN peacekeepers were stationed there. As far as we can see, they've never left, so we know they're guarding something. He also believes they are periodically transporting element X away from the facility in black government refrigeration trucks. He sent me pictures, sightings of the trucks all over the world."

This part was news to me. Barry pulled out another blurry picture of what looked like a black ice-cream truck. "The

---

3 Rest assured, we did not abduct this friend of Barry, or question him. Assuming this person's story was true, it was your own government that did so. Perhaps it was to protect us, but we did not ask them to do this. We do not abduct people anymore unless it is an emergency.

4 I do not think Barry wanted to be arrested, but perhaps he was enjoying the thought of Greg and I being arrested? Or maybe he was picturing something else entirely. It was hard to tell.

United States government thinks they are being so sneaky with their vehicles, but don't they realize black is the new blaring neon?" He laughed, a sound like a chainsaw.

"So, these trucks have shipments of element X?" asked Greg, taking the two images and examining them.

Barry nodded and swiped the pictures back out of Greg's hands. "They're moving it around, back and forth in those trucks, regularly. I think we can track a few of the trucks, see if any is being transported nearby, which of course it must be because otherwise why would you find some element X here?" Barry stowed the images in his coat.

Greg stuck his hands in his pockets. "Wow, Barry, this is kind of huge. But that means there is a lot more element X out there, enough to make a bunch more bombs. Truckloads worth . . ."

"Who said anything about bombs?" asked Barry, his face all scrunched up, looking around us like a whole crowd of people were there listening in instead of the dark hallway walls and dark paper planets. "Was element X used to make a bomb?"

"I do not think so," I said, and both men gaped at me again. "My scientist friend told me the element is not compatible with fire, so even if it *was* found at the site of a bombing, it cannot be from the bombs."

Barry was looking at me with a suspicious grimace again. "Your friend is partially right. From everything we know about this element, it's no more combustible than steel, maybe even less so, but that doesn't mean it couldn't be used as a *casing* for a bomb. Plus, if you know anything about chemistry and elements, which it doesn't sound like you do,[5] you would know that even noncombustible elements can be combined in unexpected ways. For instance, nitrogen can be used as a fire suppressant, but it is also a major component in a fertilizer bomb, and an ingredient in TNT. So I don't think we want to be making such definitive statements, do we?"

The way he was talking down to me reminded me of the way Woods always talked to me, but I supposed that was the way with brilliant people. It did not hurt my feelings as much from someone who did not know I was queen and was named Barry Hickenbottom, for some reason. Maybe because I'd seen him in his underwear.

"I have one other good tidbit too, if you're interested," said Barry. "This is more than you asked for, but I'm an overachiever."

"What is it?" Greg asked.

Barry looked over his shoulder to a dark corner of the hall. "Element X puts off a weird smell when it sublimes."

Greg inched closer. "What sort of smell? Is it toxic? Is that what's making people pass out?"

"I don't know if it's toxic. Maybe, but not right away and not in small doses."

Greg frowned. "What does it smell like?"

---

5   He was rude. And also wrong. While I did not personally know anything about chemistry, being a monarch means my people's knowledge *is* my knowledge. Which is why I am confident when I say I know everything, even if I do not know I know it. It is much more efficient this way, since I do not have to keep all of that knowledge in my own head, which is already very full and heavy, as I mentioned.

"Like ozone, if you know what that smell is. Sort of a household cleaner, burny kind of smell."

Greg shook his head, looking a little dazed. "Thanks Barry. The smell could give a warning ahead of time—so we might need to share that bit with authorities."

"Just don't let it trace back to me. And again, this element turns to gas unusually fast. So if it comes out of refrigeration, it would only give you a few seconds, maybe a minute or two, before it's gone. Depending on the thickness." He backed even further into the hall.

Greg frowned. "Well, that's something."

It *was* something, but I was not sure what, exactly.[6]

Barry sniffed and shuffled away farther. "That's all for now. Keep your heads down.[7] I'll be in touch." He found a door at the end of the hallway and left through it.

Greg and I exited the hallway the other way and wandered our way to an empty play area for children with a hollow metal rocket. He squeezed his eyes shut. "That was . . . I don't really know what that was. I'm not even sure what's important and what isn't. If we believe Barry, the government is involved, but I get the feeling he is kind of anti-establishment, don't you? I'm not sure we can trust everything he said."

I nodded. "Yes. He is anti-established for certain. But I also believe most of what he said is true. We smelled that fresh burny ozone smell at the school after the bomb went off. I did not mention it because I did not think it was important."

---

6   Is not everything something? I find this an unhelpful observation.

7   I did not put my head down. Barry Hickenbottom was not the boss of me.

Greg shook his head. "Knowing about that would only give us a few seconds' notice. Maybe that's enough to give us some lead time if we happened to be in the area, but I'm not sure what we could do with it. Warn people, maybe? How much good would a minute do?" He paused, leaning against the silver and blue rocket with his hands in his pockets, and I was reminded of the way he had leaned against the pillar before our first date. There were little spacey magnets all along the rocket for kids to play with, and Greg idly pushed some together.

I frowned. "But, maybe combined with the bubbles, that might give us more time to warn people?"

"The . . . what?" he was doing his confused half smile.

"The bubbles. There were bubbles at both of the explosions. Right before. You were there, do you not remember? I guess they were sort of behind you . . ."

He blinked. "There were?"

"Do you think Woods plans another explosion? Maybe he is done. It has been days since the last one." I picked up a magnet of a green alien that had fallen on the ground and stuck it to the side of the rocket with its little magnet alien family.[8]

"No, there will be more, if I'm right," he said.

"What makes you say that??" I asked, still looking at the little alien family.

"Because I don't think the job is done until you're blamed, arrested, or exported."

I let out a puff of air, and walked away from the

---

8   So it would not be lonely.

rocket. "Then we need to find him now, before any more explosions."

"Yeah. Maybe Barry will be able to get the exact address where those trucks were headed here in DC. That would be a better lead." He walked around and knocked on the rocket, making a hollow metal sound. "And if element X is the casing like Barry suggests, then that's why they can't find any debris from the bombs. Element X isn't the bomb, it just *holds* the bomb, releases it like a timer while it turns into vapor, leaving practically no trace. Seems a bit complicated when more destructive bombs are pretty easy to build, but it *is* brilliant."

He caught me staring at his profile and grinned at me, his eyes sparkling.

I shook myself. "Well, from what I remember, ease and speed were never motivations for Woods. He spent years letting his plans simmer."

Greg nodded. "Do you want to wander around for a while here, keep talking it through? I love this museum.[9] Plus, it's getting late, so we might have to wait until tomorrow to see the last few warehouses. And we can go eat at that Caribbean-street-food place I was telling you about."

"Okay," I said, pushing some stray brown wig hair out of my face. Next to the list of possible hiding locations for

---

9   I've always thought it was cute that humans used to have such an obsession with space (not realizing that space is a jerk). There is probably less of an obsession now that there is only space to be had. Maybe now you will have Earth museums? With little buttons of Earth smells and scale models of poop boxes? I would pay large amounts of currency to see such a thing, even with my aversion to your smells. But of course, it would be your stolen currency, so I am not sure it would be of much use to you.

Woods, we'd made a smaller list of foods Greg wanted me to try. I hid this part from Penny.

We walked around, holding hands, pushing buttons that shot out semi-accurate planetary smells, and poking old worn-down moon rocks. And even though I normally do not care much for space, having spent too much time there in my youth and knowing its heavy apathy,[10] it was still the nicest colleague date I'd ever had.

---

10   You may love space, hate space, be somewhere in between, but space feels nothing at all. It does not care about you in the slightest. Because, again, it is a jerk.

[18] With only four Earth-days before we needed to be back at the Compound, we sat going over our plans and progress in the Virginia Tech food lab: me, Greg, Penny, and [Angelo?]. He and Greg were finally having their "pancake cook-off" and let Penny and I be the judges.

Penny spent a few minutes updating me on her progress with the senator, who continued to spend all of her days shopping. Penny only had a few minutes before she needed to leave again, so she ate quickly, her plate piled high with flapjacks, fruit, and cream, while I waited for more pancakes to be cooked. Greg and his friend were in full competition mode, flipping flapjacks behind their backs high enough they could spin before catching them again, sometimes stealing a flapjack the other one flipped. It was like a human circus.[1]

[Abner?] turned and pointed toward Penny with a spatula. "All right, Penny, time to tell us whose pancakes are the best." Penny waved them both away, her mouth full and eyes focused on the deliciousness before her.

"Fine," I said. "I will judge you. I am *very* good at eating."

Both men made a show of getting the perfect ratio of peach, pancake, and cream onto a fork. I sat down on a stool at one of the tall lab tables and they leaned against the other

---

1 Which I have actually seen. I particularly liked the part where a human pretended to want to be eaten by a lion.

side, offering me their perfect bites. I took [August?]'s first, biting it right off the fork in his hand.

It was so good I closed my eyes, lost to the moment. An *mmm* popped out, but I turned it into a pensive *hmm* before they could notice.

"Pretty good," I said with a casual wave.

They both laughed.

"Hear that, Jones? 'Pretty good.' Beat that!" said [Alma?].

I turned to Greg. "Your turn, but that is going to be hard to beat."

I tried to take Greg's fork with my hand, but he would not release it. I thought maybe I could bite down and pull the fork away with my very strong teeth,[2] but I looked up into his face, my lips around the fork, his elbows on the table, and time slowed down again. The flavors melted together perfectly, criminally, but I found I was lost more in his eyes than the food. Close up, his gray eyes were green and blue: a burst of fresh water, of sweet kiwis and blueberries so delicious and deep, I could taste them. I was bewitched. I closed my eyes and let go of the fork, then I sat back down on my stool with a bump. I cleared my throat, and Greg straightened up again.

"Ah, man," said [Arturo?] laughing awkwardly. "No way I'm going to win now, you've got her under your spell."

"The winner is [Alfie?]," I said. "Sorry Greg, you are cute but—"

---

2   I probably would have just bit through the tongs with my pointy teeth, ruining a piece of perfectly good cutlery. But luckily, I did not. I was distracted.

[Ander?] cheered, laughing. "I think he's kind of goofy looking, but I guess there's no accounting for taste."

I looked down and started dusting the crumbs off my red sweater, "Have you heard from Barry, Greg?" I said, hoping to distract myself from the fuzzy feeling in my brain with clue talk.

"Oh, is Barry still helping you out?" asked [Arlan?].

Greg's phone rang. "Speak of the devil,"[3] he said and answered. "What ya got, Barry? Hello?" He pulled the phone away from his ear and looked at it. "I think he hung up on me."

[Acell?] chuckled. "Typical Barry." He stood and got his coat. "I need to go to the restaurant for a bit, so I think that is my cue to leave. My friend Neal is teaching a class in here later, so are you guys good to clean up before students start coming in? Penny, are you staying? Or can I give you a ride somewhere?"

She glared at him for a moment, then took one last bite, grabbed her jacket, and followed him out. It surprised me she would go with him so readily, though I supposed she *had* said she found him more trustworthy than Greg. What did they even talk about, I wondered, when they could not speak the same language? Did he have the buddings of romantic feelings for her as I was beginning to suspect? Was it possible she was returning them?

Greg was still looking at his phone. "Hey, Barry sent me a text: Looks like coordinates. I guess he found . . . Wait, he

---

3   Our devil never makes personal calls. He does however use something akin to your social media to "troll" people.

texted me again. He says this is where one of the trucks with element X is, here in DC, and to memorize and then delete the texts." Greg laughed, looking excited.

For some reason, I was very aware we were alone again, even though we had been alone for days. The fork episode seemed to have upset the colleague equilibrium: my senses were buzzing.

I picked up the plates and put everything away in the sink, trying to remember what I had been about to say. "The text. He gave us an address?"

Greg was watching me, his eyes dark pools now, a tilt to his head. He took a few steps closer. "Coordinates. My phone can figure it out and take us there. Wanna go right now?"

I suddenly realized we were standing way too close. "Yes, now."

I tried to turn my back on him, but Greg and his stupid blueberry-kiwi eyes and stupid pillow lips were a tether that I could not pull away from. I finally turned my back with a jerk, and tried to rush out of the lab and down the hallway toward the front door, but could feel myself slowing. The air felt thicker, like I had to push through it, push through the memory of his eyes watching my mouth when I took a bite of flapjack.

Even though I was not looking at him, I could feel Greg still standing behind me, not yet moving to leave.

"Aria," he said, his voice soft and low, and I turned, suddenly angry: angry at the sultry tone, angry that I had no more time, that we were facing destruction and eviction when all I wanted was to go bowling, walk around museums, dance, and stare into Greg's eyes while he stared back into mine, my real eyes, without danger.

He stood there, his head tipped, watching me.

I stomped. "Greg!"

"What?!"

"Do you know what is wrong with you, Greg?"

"No, what?"

"Nothing!"[4]

And I ran, jumped into his arms, and kissed him right on the mouth. He responded in kind, and for several moments I lost all sense of everything but the intoxicating feel of his lips on mine, the feel of his hands around my waist, the spark of energy traveling between us. When we pushed away, he was breathing heavily.

He held me at arm's length. "Um, was that a . . . like a colleague kiss?"

I backed up a few more paces to keep myself from doing it again. "Oh. I do not know. Is that a thing you do here?"[5]

He huffed out a laugh. "Not really. At least, I don't." He backed up a few more steps. "What . . . what about those ten thousand people that you're protecting, the ones that you say will be in danger if we do . . . that."

"Yes," I said. "Yes."

"Look, it's not like I planned that, but I'm fine with . . . this. To stay away from you was not my idea."

---

4   *Charade*, directed by Stanley Donen (Universal Pictures, 1963). I stole this line. And if Greg knew, he never mentioned it. I am very sorry. Sort of.

5   We do not have this on Booshlaboo. We do have kissing, but it is strictly between family and mates. And pets.

Despite his words, he took another step backward away from me.

"Well technically, working together only professionally *was* your idea. My idea was to stay away from you completely."

"Aria," he huffed.

"Greg," I mimicked his tone.

He groaned and closed his eyes, putting a hand to his forehead.

I was tempted to run and kiss him again, so I turned my back. "Let us go find the address where the truck is." I stomped out the door, unsure why I was acting like a bratty youth about it.

He caught up to me a few moments later outside the lab, and I did not look at him while he examined the coordinates on his phone. We took a YouRide part of the way, facing away from each other, then let the phone direct us as we got within walking distance, a little bubble arrow pointing the way.

Greg started to slow down. I was afraid he had changed his mind and was about to let me kiss him again. "Wait. Look where we are," he said instead.

I glanced around. It seemed a place very like any other street in DC to me. "Where are we?"

"That's the senator's apartment right there." He pointed down the road.

We were a block away and facing the back of it, but I could recognize the rooftop. I got closer to him, peering at his phone. "The apartment where you are staying? Is that where the coordinates are taking us?"

"No." He examined the phone some more. "But it's close."

The coordinates led to the entrance of a parking garage behind the senator's building. We spent an hour walking through the lot, hoping maybe someone left some clues, but we did not even know what to look for. I discovered Greg was holding my hand again. He was acting like it was normal, so I decided to pretend I did not notice.

There were not many cars in the garage, and none were black trucks. We almost gave up again, but Greg decided to risk chatting with the parking attendant. I hid behind a big van with fake wood on the side and a bumper sticker that said "Honk If You Eat Your Vegetables" on the back.

"Hi," I heard Greg say. "Um, is there any chance you might've seen my, um, dad come in here recently? He drives a big black truck, but he's getting old, and he isn't really supposed to drive, and my mom is worried about him because he has dementia, you see."

"Are you a resident at one of the buildings here?"

I peeked around the corner to see Greg rocking back and forth on his heels. "Yes?"

The guy nodded. "Look, I'd like to help you, but I don't remember anything like that. There's no camera or anything, just this mirror, and it's big, but not big enough to see the other floors or side entrances. Sorry, man. Maybe he's parked in one of the private lots? But, if so, I still couldn't help you."

"Private lots?"

"Yeah, you know, for your building? All the buildings around have private, more-secure lots that enter through here, for a monthly fee. Didn't you know about that?" I eased around, looked around the far end of the lot, and saw the four drop-down metal doors with remote locks next to them.

Greg made some excuse, thanked the guy, and came back, whistling until he got behind the van. He stood there for a moment, then crouched down next to me.

"Did you hear?" he asked in a whisper.

I nodded. "I thought those were maybe just for one car, but they are passageways to other lots."

"Do you think one of these private lots connects to Gwyn's building? There *is* parking below it, but you need a special key card for the elevator to get there, so I've never seen it. But maybe this is how you enter it from the outside? Or do you think this parking lot being so close to Gwyn's building is just a coincidence?"

"There have been a lot of those lately. Coincidences. Too many."

He scrunched his face up. "Yeah. But how do we get in to find out for sure? I think that guy might see us through his big mirror and get suspicious if he catches us trying to open the doors, now. They're probably opened with remotes, which we don't have."

"I can handle the locks with my thingamabob." I patted my side pocket where it lay, glad it had been my turn with the device today. "Will this guard man be there all night? Or will someone else come to take his place?"

"Ooh, right! Yes, we can wait until the guard changes."

"Okay. Um, changes what? Changes his clothes? Changes his mind? Changes into something else? "[6]

---

6   I did not think humans had either of these latter two abilities.

Greg smiled. I found that when he did not answer me, it usually meant he thought I was joking. So I pretended I was.

When Greg was sure the attendant stopped looking, we went up some stairs that entered the second floor of the garage and hid in the stairwell. For a while, we stood there and waited. Humans drove in, drove out, got in and out of their cars. Every so often, I peeked down the stairs. Occasionally people walked in front of the garage, and once I thought one of the people was Barry Hickenbottom—but since I was in hiding, I could not wave or call out, and he was gone around a corner before I could know for certain.

After a few Earth-hours, a new man came to the booth, and we tiptoed down the stairs and toward the back doors. Just as we reached the locks, we heard a voice behind us.

"Hey, what are you two doing there?" It was the first attendant again.

"Oh," said Greg, out of breath suddenly, moving a little in front of me, "Um, we got the code from my mom, and turns out she did have a space down here, in the private lots. So, just about to try it out and find my dad. Get him safe again, safe and sound. Can I help you?"

Even *I* could tell it was too much. The attendant was starting to pull out his phone.

Booger.

The man shook his head, angry. "You two shouldn't be back here, and I'm calling the police."

He pushed a button on his phone, and in a split second, Greg stepped up to him and swung a punch at the man's head, so wide and hard that the guy hit the ground, out cold. We ran before the other attendant could come looking, back out one of the side entrances.

"I can't believe I just did that," Greg said breathlessly while we ran. "What is happening to me?!"

"It will be okay," I said, pulling Greg into a little stairwell that went down along the side of a building. "Let us just get inside the senator's apartment and catch our breaths."

Greg nodded, still breathing hard. "The cops are bound to be on their way soon regardless. I'm sorry—that was reckless."

At the mention of cops, we saw two officers approaching someone at the entrance to the senator's building across the street, and we ducked down further, our eyes just above the walkway.

The person they approached responded with unusual aggression and that was how I recognized her: Penny. She was wearing a long brown wig and sunglasses and a hood, and she crouched as they neared her, her arms out to the sides.

I started to raise my hand to her, but Greg held me back. We watched as the two officers tried to put Penny's arms behind her back and found themselves unable, Penny swinging deftly out of the way.

Despite it being two to one and her being so much smaller, she avoided capture easily right up until one pulled out some kind of electricity gun. While I watched in horror, the officer fired at her. She shook and then dropped. I gasped and jumped out of our hiding spot, but before we could stop it, Penny was cuffed, thrown in the back of a white police vehicle, and she was gone.

[19]   "They took Penny!" I said as we scurried the other way. I was furious at myself. This was all my fault.

"Did they find out who you are?" Greg said, his voice low and quiet. "Or is this because of what happened at the garage? Except how did they get here so fast?"

I shook my head. "Did they take her to jail? Am I going to have to break her out?"

"And what was that move she did with her elbows?"[1] Greg pulled me along the sidewalk.

"We have to get her back," I gulped.

"I know."

"Where did they take her? How do we get her back?!"

"I don't know, I don't know! Let's just blend in. Come on." He yanked me through a doorway we passed, which turned out to be some sort of gaming facility for children. The sounds of metal money clinking and electronic beeping rang all around us.

"Perfect," Greg mumbled, still holding my hand as we stumbled between black flashing boxes. When we got to the back, we settled into a big booth with the words "Mega Super

---

1   In case you are wondering, this is her other signature move besides giving debilitating stern looks. You humans would not be able to do this evading move unless your elbows rotated both ways and had a mind of their own.

Alien Assault"[2] on the side, and he pulled the little half-cur-
tain closed.

"Greg, if they take her to prison, I *have* to break her out.
I cannot do this without her. She is not only my friend, she is
my adviser, my conscience. Will they hurt her?"

"They won't, trust me—our police won't lay a finger on
her." He pulled a few coins out of his pocket and stuck one
into a slot.

He was trying to comfort me, but my anxiety grew. "I
cannot say the same for her. She does not do very well in
crowded spaces. It makes her violent. *More* violent."

"They can't keep her for long, unless they charge her, I'm
pretty sure. Maybe a day, a few days?"

"That is too long. I have to get her out tonight."

"But Aria, how would you even do that? Breaking someone out of police custody . . . ?"

It would be easy. "I have a tool that can get her out right
now, if I know exactly where she is and have enough power
units left . . ."

Greg shook his head, blinking fast, and started pushing
buttons on the mounted machine gun. "But, there are other
avenues, other methods to getting her out that wouldn't
require you to break the law. We can post bail, hire a lawyer.
If we break her out of police custody, you'll have to get out of

---

2   Some of you may have noticed that there is an increasingly prevalent motif
    of alien images throughout this story. Good for you. I did not artificially
    create this pattern, I just noticed them. As an alien, I was more aware that
    alien paraphernalia was everywhere in your culture. I do suspect these
    motifs increased since our arrival, though I do not believe we were the
    cause. Maybe you always had an alien obsession.

DC immediately, be on the run. That should be a last resort. Maybe they'll only hold her for a few hours."

"Poor Penny!" I started picturing her in there, sitting in a tiny room while humans got into her personal space with leers on their faces, and I revised my statement. "Poor other prisoners!"

A kid poked his head into the booth, and Greg smiled and went back to playing the game. As soon as the kid ducked out, I gently pushed Greg's hands off the joystick. It made me very uncomfortable to watch Greg's little avatar kill all those poor tentacled aliens, even the one that was shooting baby spiders out of its fingers. The alien on the left looked like my uncle Borno.

Greg ran a hand through his hair. "Listen, just give it a little more time. I promise we will get Penny out, but at least let me talk to Bella at the police department, see what I can find out about What happened? Maybe I can get Penny released. Give me a few hours. Please."

I looked into his pleading eyes and agreed, hoping Penny would behave until we got to her. Maybe they would put her in a cell all alone? It was the only hope she would not get crowded and start punching.

We agreed that I should not go back to the Fantasy Inn for the moment, so Greg checked me into another smaller motel nearby, then left.

For hours, I paced. I turned on the tiny television mounted to the wall, my eyes watching the door instead of the screen. At around eleven, there was a knock on the door.

"Who is it?" I said through the door.

"Greg."

"Greg who?"[3]

A pause. "Jones?"

I opened the door. "You need to stop saying that like it is a question."

Greg rushed in, holding a bundle of full sacks. "Hey, shouldn't we have like a code, or something? Isn't that what you usually do, for safety? Like a code word. Maybe something like . . . 'basket of dragon fruit,' to say there is trouble."

"Basket of dragon fruit?" I asked, confused. Sounded less like trouble and more like deliciousness.

He went on. "Yeah. And when we want to verify each other's identity, we could say, 'Do you want any flapjacks,' and the answer could be, like—"

"Yes?" I suggested.

He finished arranging the sacks on one of the beds. "I was thinking something more like, 'I'll have seven to start.' Am I being really cliché right now?"

"Seven is a great number of flapjacks." I pointed at the bags. "What is all this?" I asked.

"Oh, I got some snacks. That's um, that's the good news."

"Oh good. I was afraid there was bad news." I sat on the edge of the bed.

He sat next to me, his hands on his knees. "Unfortunately, there is. The bad news is that none of my contacts could help with Penny."

---

3   I asked him this because with all the dangerous Gregs out there running around, you can never be too careful. This is the one good use for your last names, I suppose.

I nodded. It was what I'd expected.

"I tried Bella at the police station. I don't think she'll tell anyone I called: she's been my friend since junior high, but she's also pretty by the book, if you know what I mean."

I did not.

He continued. "The most she would say is that Penny has been charged, and that she's awaiting arraignment, which is in seventy-two hours. Nobody else was available to talk to me. [Averil?] won't answer my calls, and he's the one with the connections. I tried to find him—that's what took me so long—but he's nowhere to be found. We can still try to post bail. Usually you can post bail right away, but that depends on what she is being charged with. It seems to all sort of depend."

"I have to get her out, Greg. And what if they are coming to arrest me and you next? We cannot just sit around waiting. Besides, we have less than four more days anyway before we have to leave or my people suffer."

He rubbed his eyes. "I'm so sorry. I was sure I could be more helpful to you." He leaned his shoulder against mine, and I leaned my head down on to his shoulder. "So, you'll just break her out? Do you need help planning? I mean, it's almost midnight, but we could do some planning now."

"No, I need no help. But I should go right away." I closed my eyes.

"And once you get her out, will I see you again? What about that Woods guy?"

"Maybe we will find a way to come back and look for him later." But if we did, it would be at least a few weeks from now. Weeks or months.

I opened my eyes, staring at the TV that was still on; a woman in front of a wall-sized map was talking about rain and warm fronts.[4]

I closed my eyes again, nestling into the warmth of Greg's neck. His arm found its way around my shoulder, and then his lips found their way to mine, and he tasted better than a whole armful of strawberries and smelled like clean snow. His hands pulled me closer, my fingers in his hair, and I wanted nothing more than to just abandon myself to that moment.

As I was about to lose track of everything, something the television reporter was saying started to intrude back into my thoughts: "Earlier this week, a woman was arrested for stalking US senator of Alaska, Gwyn Kilcher."

I pushed Greg away to see a picture of Penny from a distance, wig half off and her arms in handcuffs, being pushed into a police car. "Greg, look!"

The reporter continued, "Gwyn Kilcher says she is no celebrity, but this is also not her first stalker."

The voice of the senator came on as if over the phone. "This is one of those security risks you get used to in government, so it isn't my first rodeo.[5] I noticed her following me and notified the police right away."

Greg leaned up. "Wait, did they say she was arrested earlier this week? That's not right."

The reporter came back on screen while the picture of

---

4   By the way, weather reports are never quite as exciting as when the weather is actively trying to kill you. I miss that.

5   I was never very sure how a rodeo applies. Or why. What happens at your first rodeo, anyway? Some kind of cow wrangling initiation ceremony?

Penny went to a corner. "When police approached the woman, she became violent and is now being held for questioning. She will likely be charged with stalking, if not more."

The reporter turned and started talking about toilet paper shortages because of the bombings.

"Stalking?" I asked. "What are they talking about?!"

Greg smoothed down his shirt. "Well, I guess they're not connecting Penny to us, or the explosion, or to me punching that parking guy. Maybe that's good news."

"Good news?" I stood up, pacing again.

"At least it means we could go post bail and not get arrested. Or better yet, get Gwyn to drop the charges altogether, if we could get ahold of her. We wouldn't have to break Penny out."

I pinched my lips between my teeth, my hands on my hips.

Greg scratched his head. "You think Gwyn told them it happened earlier this week because she doesn't want anyone to know she's still here? Something is obviously going on with her, but I don't know what."

I turned to him, taking a deep breath. I was tired of pacing, ready to act. "I do not know either. But maybe we should find out."

He jumped up. "Sounds good. How?"

"Let us ask her. If she drops the charges, as you suggest, we could get Penny out right away, correct? And then we might still find Woods before it is too late."

"That all sounds great, but I've been trying to call her for days and she never answers. Did Penny know where the senator's staying?"

"All Penny said was that the senator was staying with a friend, and spends all day shopping. I did not think to get any more information since this was not our focus. You know the senator better than I do, so what would she do? Where would she go?"

"*Staying with a friend.*" He sat on one of the beds with a bump and then stood up again. "Senator Kalani! Kilcher and the senator of Hawaii have been friends for years. I haven't even met the other Alaskan senator, but I see Senator Kalani and her staff every time we're in DC. I'm betting if we find Hawaii, we find Alaska. We can get there in five minutes if we take a taxi."

"Now, then, right? It has to be now. Penny is going to tear that police station down."

True to his word, we arrived at the Hawaiian senator's apartment building within a few minutes. Outside the door, Greg stopped.

"We might need to bribe this door guy. I've never bribed anyone, have you?"

"Yes, but not recently."[6]

He nodded. "Do you have any money on you? I spent most of my cash on the snacks."

"I do have some, but not much."

"Okay—I'll give you what I have, too. We might need every penny we've got."

"But I only have two pennies. Not counting Penny, who I do not have at the moment so never mind. Maybe we can

---

6   It was another incident with stolen choco deserts that I am too ashamed to relay.

find more pennies on the street? That is where I found these two. Why do we need pennies? Would not this hundred dollar bill be better?"

He paused. ". . . Yes, I meant . . . Never mind. Here's another twenty." He handed me his cash, and we walked through the rotating glass doors.

The aging doorman glanced up and squinted. "Mr. Jones, isn't it?"

"Hey, uh—" Greg glanced at the nameplate, "Mr. Donall! Can't believe you remember my name. Only been here once before."

"Ah, I make it a point to remember everyone's names. And I'm sorry to disappoint you, Mr. Jones, but she isn't back yet. She could be gone all night."

Greg nodded like this was what he expected to hear. "I'm actually looking for Senator Kilcher. Is she here?"

The doorman squinted harder. "That's who I meant, too."

Greg kept nodding. "Of course. Uh, the thing is, she didn't tell anyone where she was going, and as you probably know, she's in a little bit of danger, what with the stalker and everything. The guys told me to come keep an eye on her, but obviously I can't if she goes off on her own all over the place. Any chance you know where she went?"

The doorman yawned. "Sure do. She didn't exactly tell me, but I seen the invitation clear as day. It was one of them fancy mask things with dancing. Over at the Clinton Manor place. It'll be going on for hours yet."

Dancing. My interest perked up and I promptly knocked it down again. The whole city was in danger and Penny was in jail. I could *not* fantasize about dancing with Greg while Penny was in jail.

"Hey, thanks. I think we'll go over right now. You're the best," said Greg. He pulled me away and we went back out the door. Greg huffed. "No way are they letting us in a masquerade. Those things are crazy private."

"Do we just wait for her here, then?" I said, my stomach souring at the thought.

He looked at me. "Can you wait that long? What if it's another few hours? What if it's all night?"

"I do not know. I can just get Penny out *my way* right now."

"Hang on." He pursed his lips, thinking. "Okay, I think I might know somebody that could help us get into that party. As staff."

Staff. That sounded fun. I could feel my hopes rising of their own accord.

"You wanna try it? I can make some calls."

I exhaled and then nodded.

"Alright, I'll call my friend. And who knows? We didn't get to dance at the gala—maybe we could still catch a dance?" He kissed my hand with a wink and led me along the sidewalk as he pulled out his phone.

Great. I was going dancing with Greg. My head and feet were both tingling. And I was the worst friend and queen in the universe.[7]

---

7   Not actually. I know four super terrible friends and two queens that are much worse than me. But I just remembered they are all dead now. Do they still count?

[20·] Greg's friend turned out to be named Charlie and even though he was not technically working that night (and was also technically sleeping when Greg called him), he said he knew some people working the masquerade that could get us in. Within twenty-five minutes, we were being ushered through a side door into a kitchen, where someone handed us clothes to change into and trays full of food on tiny spears.[1]

"Make sure you come back and refill anytime there are less than four or five things on your tray," the extremely short male manager called out, and I was reminded oddly of being yelled at by one of those little annoying wheelie protocol robots.

As soon as we were out of the kitchens, Greg put down his tray and took off the red server's vest, and since I'd already swiped and eaten most of what was on my tray anyway, I followed his lead. He pulled out two silver masks that were clearly supposed to look like squid or cuttlefish but somehow artistically and accurately looked like my real face, with tentacle-like feathers cascading down the sides. He handed me one and I stared at it.

"What, you don't like it?" Greg glanced down at the mask before putting it on. "I swiped them from some guy in the

---

1   It is always so violent when it comes to food with you people, perhaps as a nod to the longing you feel for the times when you had to murder your food to be able to eat it.

bathroom while I changed, so we don't have a lot of other options."

I put on the mask that resembled my real face over top my fake human one over the fake green alien one over my real face. Then we entered the ballroom floor.

After a few moments searching the grand ballroom, we saw the senator as she was walking into what Greg called "a powder room." She was easy to spot since she was as tall as Greg, her distinctive long, black hair cascading down her back. We followed, trying to avoid bumping into too many other dancing humans, and entered the powder room.[2] Greg whipped his mask off.

Gwyn Kilcher was reapplying lipstick in the big gold-gilded mirror, and she did not pause when she saw us. "Mr. Jones. What are you doing here?" She removed a black sparkly mask that matched her black sparkly dress and laid it on the sink.

"I could ask you the same question," Greg said walking further into the room, his expression good natured.

"You could." She spoke like someone who was used to being intimidating. It was a common trait for your leaders, though she made it look uniquely graceful and natural. I'd been trained how to deal with such humans. It involved a lot of groveling and bowing. Here at last was a chance for me to use that training to communicate with an Earth leader, for the first time since the initial Arrival. But, somehow, I did not think those methods would work on Gwyn Kilcher; maybe

---

2   I did not see any powder in there, but I did not investigate very much.

it had never been the right tactic for any of your leaders. I decided to keep my mouth shut and let Greg do the talking.

The senator finished applying lipstick, then sighed and removed her beautiful stilettos, sitting down on a big fancy puff situated on the floor between the stalls and the gold sinks. "So who's this, Greg?"

"Oh, she's my girlfriend,"[3] Greg answered.

"Congrats. How come I've never met her?"

"It's um, it's long distance."[4] He shrugged.

"Nice to meet you—"

"Aria," I supplied. I had to quite literally bite my tongue not to add the rest of my title.

The senator looked back at Greg. "Greg, how did you get into this party? I had to schmooze some very annoying people for months to get an invitation."

Greg smiled. "You know me. I always have connections."

"True. A bit strange for a staffer, but I suppose you're from around here, makes sense you know people. So, what can I do for you both? Should I have one of the waiters bring some food in? We can sit on this pouf and have a nice chat."

"Do you have any fruit?" I asked.

Greg glared at me. "No, no, that won't be necessary, we won't be here that long. Gwyn, I just heard you on the news and we were worried about you."

---

3   I may or may not have giggled embarrassingly when he said this. You will never know.

4   We did not have long distance relationships on Booshlaboo. Our planet is much smaller than this one. There are relationships that are cross-planetary, but they never last. So, wait, I guess it *is* the same as yours.

She smiled, seemingly not buying it. "Oh, no need. I'm just fine. It happens."

"But, I mean, a stalker . . ."

"She was a tiny little thing," Gwyn said, "so I wasn't ever in much danger. She'd been following me for almost a week." She smiled at me, looking me up and down. I removed my mask. Little did this senator know how much damage that "tiny little thing" could do when she put her mind to it.

Greg nodded, folding his arms. "Speaking of that, where are your bodyguards? I thought after the other stalker-scare last year,[5] you were going to have a security detail at all times?"

"Yes, but I felt like having a few days off from all that. You have no idea how exhausting it is having bodyguards follow you around all the time. Sometimes you need some breathing room."

"Tell me about it," I mumbled. If anyone could understand wanting to get out from under the stifling thumb of protective detail, I did.

"Is that so?" Greg said.

Kilcher shook her mane of hair from side to side, pulling at some big, black-gemmed earrings. "Look, I'm a grown woman, and I don't need your permission to stay a few extra days or weeks with or without my bodyguards."

I felt a pang of jealousy. I was a grown woman, too.

Greg unfolded his arms and put his hands in his pockets. "No, no, that's true. The thing is, Gwyn, I happen to know

---

5   Just in case you were starting to think this is a story I might tell later, it
     is not.

something about you, and I've kept my mouth shut because that's what they told me to do, but I'm tired of all the subterfuge right now, plus we don't have time, so I'm just going to come out and tell you. You're under investigation. And that girl who was stalking you was undercover."

Gwyn stood. "I'm under *investigation*?! Why? Who's investigating me?"

"The FBI, Gwyn; that's who investigates dirty politicians."[6]

"Oh, so I'm dirty now, am I?" She started pacing. "Oh, those stupid [redacted] double-crossing [redacted] [redacted]!"[7]

I watched Greg with wonder. How had he come up with this so quickly?

Gwyn stopped pacing. "What is it I'm supposed to have done?"

"Embezzle government funds," Greg answered.

"Oh, ho! Embezzlement? Those [redacted] [redacted]! They're pretty confident I won't talk if they burn me, aren't they? Ho ho!"

"What are you talking about?"

"Look, Greg," she sat down again, "I don't know what you think you know. Or how you know it. But let me say that I am not dirty."

---

6   I know I've used it in the past, but I am just going to say this "dirty" metaphor is very strange. They all seem clean to me. Or if they get dirty, they shower soon after.

7   I will be honest. I am only redacting these because I cannot keep track of your swears and I cannot remember what words she used. Whatever it was, I am sure it was filthy. Oh! Maybe *that* is what they mean by dirty politicians?

"But what about the money?" Greg asked.

I shook my head. What money? What was Greg even talking about? How did he know all this? I kept my questions to myself since it seemed to be working.

Gwyn shook her head. "The money isn't illegal, and it isn't even lobbying, it was . . . a perk."

"A perk?" Greg asked flatly.

"Yes, a perk. Being one of the senators of Alaska comes with certain perks. They're completely legal payments from the government."

Greg squinted at her. "Payments for what?"

"For keeping my mouth shut."

"About what?" asked Greg, his eyebrows so high they disappeared into a curl of hair on his forehead.

But I was starting to suspect I knew. And it was not element X.

Gwyn Kilcher looked at him for a moment and glanced at me. "I can't tell you that. You wouldn't believe me even if I could."

If she was talking about what I thought she was talking about—the alien squatters secretly living in her fine state—I wondered why Greg was acting like he did not know? Did not he get the information about us, about me, from the senator in the first place? I distinctly remembered him saying he knew because he was in government.

"Oh, those stupid [redacted] [redacted] [redacted] . . ."[8]

---

8   Yes, Gwyn Kilcher had what you might term "a potty mouth." So sorry for those of you that revere her posthumously. Only Penny could swear more creatively.

Gwyn stood up again to pace. Someone tried to push open the bathroom door which I was currently leaning against, and Greg jumped back to help me hold the door closed.

"Gwyn . . . I'm sorry but are you really saying that the government is paying you hush money for a top secret . . . *secret?* And what? The FBI doesn't know about it because it's off the books? That doesn't sound all that legal to me."

"But it is. It isn't anything nefarious, I promise you. It's from the UN." She squinted, muttering, "Are they trying to burn me, or is this just a lack of transparency, a miscommunication?" She turned her back on us, still murmuring.

I could tell Greg was losing patience (and I am sure that continuing to hold the door closed while someone tried to shove their way into the bathroom did not help). "But what does your top secret *secret* have to do with the explosions?" he asked.

Gwyn turned around, looking at Greg in shock. "What? Nothing at all! What kind of question is that?"

The person on the other side of the door chose that moment to take a run at the door, and Greg and I bonked heads with a hollow cracking sound.

"Go away. The bathroom is broken!" I yelled through the door.

Greg rubbed his head with one hand. "But, what about the trucks?"

"Trucks? I drive an EV."

Greg growled, making an unexpected chill run down my spine. "Something is being transported from a secret location in Alaska to the private garage for your apartment building."

She blinked. "What do they have to do with the bombings?"

"Something inside them, something rare, was found at the second explosion."

Gwyn started shoveling her makeup tubes back into a small, fantastic beaded purse that I longed to ask where it was purchased. "I can't believe this. You're accusing me of embezzling and now of bombing American citizens?" She paused, gazing at us. "Those trucks? I guarantee you they have nothing to do with the bombings. And neither do I."

Since the person outside the bathroom was no longer pushing their way in, Greg stepped away from the door. He ran his hand through his wavy hair. "Then why are you really still here in DC and didn't answer any calls? And why did the news lie about the timeline for your stalker?"

She shrugged, her mouth a tight line. "I'm doing a little shopping. Jimmy Choo came out with some new heels,[9] and as I said, I needed a break. I have an admirer at the news station, so he helps me out sometimes. How did you even get mixed up in all this, Greg? What role do you play? You know what, I don't care. Do you have any pull? If I get that undercover stalker girl off the hook, do you think the FBI will back off?"

"Yes, but it would have to be tonight," he said. He put his mask back on.

"Done. I'll call and drop the charges right now."

I let out a sigh of relief. Penny would be out soon.

Gwyn replaced her shoes and mask, her long black hair swinging around her waist as she stood. "And now, I hope

---

9   Smart human woman indeed.

you don't mind, but I'm leaving. It's been a creepy party anyway."

I stepped away from the door, and a husky woman with a large rubber horse-head mask walked in, glaring at me with her oversized horsey eyes.

"Oh, and Greg?" the senator said, her hand on the door handle.

"What?"

"You're [redacted] fired."

Greg smiled his half smile. "Yeah, I kind of figured."

Gwyn bowed, went out the door, and shut it in our faces.

[21]   We left the bathroom a moment later: me first, and Greg trailing behind. As we hurried across the dark wood dance floor, Greg whispered my name, and when I turned, he pulled me into a dance so smoothly I could not stop it, even if I had wanted to.[1] His expression was still tight and frustrated, but within a few steps, our eyes locked and he smiled. It was a human waltz, slightly less dangerous than a Boovashoo waltz, but still similar enough that I could follow.[2] Only a few moments passed as we crossed the room, and then we were back to dashing down the hall again, but for that moment, floating in his arms, I almost forgot I had some questions for Greg.

Almost. "Greg, what was all that? How did you already know about the money perks if she didn't tell you?"

"Oh." He glanced over his shoulder at me as we moved around the other human servers. He looked uncharacteristically uneasy.

"And how did you come up with all that about the FBI?" I did not think Greg was quite so good a liar, and it felt . . . itchy.

"I didn't come up with it. It's true. Not about Penny

---

1   Which I did not.

2   And I was very glad that in the human version there were no wild *globsteri* involved.

obviously, I just threw that in, but the FBI *are* investigating Senator Kilcher. I'm going to see a bit of trouble now for telling her all that. For telling you."

"But, how did you know?" And then the pieces fell into place in my mind with a *whoosh*, like the ending leap of a wild *globsteri* waltz. "*You* are FBI?!"

He sighed, "No, not exactly." We pushed out the back door and into the chill of the night.

"*Not exactly*, Greg? What does that mean?" I stopped and made him turn around to talk to me.

He rubbed his hands together in the cool night air. "I guess it's basically over now since I just lost my job and Gwyn came clean. I'm not in the FBI, not an agent or anything, I'm only an asset."

"An asset?"

He pulled me to start walking again.

"A few months ago," Greg continued, "I was approached and asked to help the FBI in their investigation of Gwyn. My handler showed me some numbers that said she had an undisclosed source of funds, basically that she was dirty, and I was supposed to try to find out where she was getting her money from. They picked me because I was already on her staff, but I honestly haven't found anything until right now, because I was only observing. And also because I apparently wasn't any good at it. In fact, I've never really done anything interesting as an asset, and nothing like the craziness I've done since I met you."

"Oh." So, that explained some of it, at least. Gwyn had not been the one to tell him about me, the *FBI* had. I knew I could never tell Penny about this—Greg being in the FBI, even marginally? If he was not the enemy *before* in her eyes, he certainly would be now.

"I wonder what the top secret *secret* was, don't you?" asked Greg as we nearly jogged back toward my hotel.

"What do you mean?"

"I mean, what kind of a secret would the UN pay a senator for? It must be about the trucks or element X, but she seemed pretty convincingly confused about the explosions. I wonder . . ." He shook his head.

"But Greg, her secret was clearly *me*."

He slowed to look at me. "What?"

"Her secret, my secret? They are the same."

He slowed even more. "What?!"

"Do you not remember the Compound, the place where the trucks came from? That is my Compound. In Alaska! I thought you knew. They could not keep such a thing from the senators, and the information would likely be worth some of your dollars to keep quiet."[3]

"Hmm." Greg looked confused. "So, this Compound is like a black site[4] or something?"

"More sort of gray, actually."

He squinted one eye closed. "So you live in Alaska now? Is this going to be one of those things I'm not allowed to ask about?" Then his phone rang. "It's my handler," he said,

---

3   I did not know about this specific money exchange before this, but I did know the government was handing out money to anyone involved with us. Where do you think we stole the money we had *from*?

4   Back when there were still clandestine services like the CIA (I believe the CIA survivors are now strictly a knitting circle: Cozy Inspirational Arts) they had secret locations, bases, and prisons called black sites. It occurred to me only later that this is what Greg was referring to.

glancing at the screen. "I think I better go try to explain some of this since I'm now fired. I should also call Charlie and apologize because we ducked out on that job."

I shook my head. "What about Penny?"

Greg sent a quick text, and we started moving again. "Now that Gwyn is dropping the charges, I think we can get her out the traditional way. No breakouts required."

"Right now?"

He looked down at his watch. "It's one in the morning, but I don't see why not. I'll get some more money together in case they still need bail or something, and we'll do whatever else we need to do, okay? I'll meet you there in an hour after I get money and make some calls."

We went our separate ways, and I decided to walk straight to the police station. It would be quite a walk, but such exercise might help me to clear my head.

Greg's friend Bella put her head down when we entered the station.[5] "Greg, it's almost two a.m.!" she muttered against the table.

Greg smiled. "I know. We're done bugging you, I swear. Just point us to the officer that usually does bail."

She sat up and narrowed her eyes at us, but pointed toward an officer behind a glass partition on the other side of the station.

---

5   I do not think she did this because her head was heavy, though. Our heads are much heavier than yours because of brain size and density.

This is going to work, I thought. And maybe Penny and I would still have enough time left to find Woods and enough units to gravitate at least some of the way home, and we could get back to the Compound before all *glabstopper* broke loose.

But then we waited in a very long line and my optimism started to wane. It was the first time I had truly understood humans' distaste for lines. Despite it being the middle of the night, the crowds seemed to have doubled since the last time we were there. After almost two of your hours,[6] the bail officer finally met with us, but was completely unhelpful.

"She's been denied bail."

It took a few moments for my mind to catch on to what he was saying.

"But her charges were dropped!" stuttered Greg. "Or were about to be. Give Senator Kilcher a call."

The officer yawned. "Nice name-drop there, but that isn't how it works. The *stalking* charges were dropped. But your prisoner also resisted arrest, and that charge is still in force. Also, since she arrived, she sent another prisoner to the hospital. And she also came in with a very large amount of money, more than twenty thousand dollars, making her a flight risk: thus, no bail."

"But if you put her in with other prisoners, then any injury is your own fault!" I whined.

The officer coughed, a long wheezy sound. "I gotta be honest, your girl has been nothing but trouble in the holding

---

6   Even if the thing at the end of the line is a ride where you get on a flying boat and visit tiny magical places, an hour might seem too long to wait to you. Silly. But in order to pay money to get a friend out of jail? Yes, I see the annoyance.

cell back there, and I can't wait to move her over to the county jail. Next!"

A holding cell was one thing, but I would never hear the end of it if I let her go to actual jail.

My heart sank. Time for the backup plan. Which was truly my *frontup* plan. I knew exactly where she was now, and at this point, I did not care how many power units it took to move her. I surreptitiously activated the gravitator, had it select the tiny angry person currently residing in the holding cell, and sent her to our old safecondo. Penny always told me it was not possible that I could actually feel the person I gravitated, that it was just my imagination, but I swore I could almost hear her annoyance and resistance as I activated it.

Sorry!

Knowing she was out of there immediately let me breathe easier. But now I needed to leave before they discovered her missing.

"Can we talk to a lawyer?" Greg asked the officer. "There has to be someone else that can help us."

The officer sighed, and motioned us back into another unbelievable line. I tried to convince Greg we should just leave, but I could not figure out how to tell him about Penny's jailbreak in front of all the other humans. I tried to signal with my eyes, but he seemed too distraught to catch on.

"There has to be something we can do," Greg said. "I'm going to talk to Bella."

"No, wait, Greg!" But it was too late; he was gone into the crowd.

By the time my eyes found him, he was already talking to

Bella. He motioned me to join him as they went into a back room.

"Oh, um, I'll just be outside!" I called to him, and then hightailed[7] it out of there, increasingly uneasy as the time ticked by and nobody raised the alarm. Police stations were not my favorite place anyway, but staying inside one where I'd just successfully performed a jailbreak? I could not do it.

Once I was outside, I was not sure what to do next. Should I leave Greg? *Could* I leave Greg? I walked a few blocks away, but then found myself turning around again. I finally settled on hiding in the bushes just outside of the police station, crouched uncomfortably.

It was at least another forty-five minutes, nearly five in the morning, before Greg came out looking for me. "What did Bella say?" I asked, coming behind him and pulling a twig out of my hair.

"She just kept telling me to 'trust the system.' *Real helpful, Bella.* I also talked to a public defender, but then he made me set another appointment two days from now, which is way too late."

I glanced around as we walked down the bush-lined cement path in front of the police station. Remarkably, so far there had not been sounds of alarm from the building behind us, but I grabbed Greg's hand, ready to pull him into a run if they suddenly discovered they had an escaped prisoner. "I am sorry."

"So you have to break her out? And, once you break her out, you're gone."

---

7   No, I do not have a tail, high or low.

I sighed, suddenly tired. There was nothing I wanted more in that moment than to say I could stay with Greg, keep running around, solving mysteries, stealing time,[8] but it was too late. I had been away from my people too long.

"We were always on a deadline, Greg. We knew we only had ten days from the gala before we had to go back. I only have a day or two more as it is."

Greg stopped as we got to the end of the building's long walkway. A few people rushed by us, and I pulled Greg closer to some bushes lining the walk.

"But can't we . . ." Greg paused midsentence, glancing over my shoulder and up toward the police station. "Are those . . . bubbles?"

Then I smelled it.

Ozone.

I turned. Past the curtain of bubbles and through the open glass doors of the station, I saw something. A gray metal ball about the size of one of your fresh plums floated by the reception table. Along its sides, glowing cracks expanded, iridescent bubbles flowing out like it was an overactive bubble machine.

Greg started running for the door, but I pulled him back the other way. We were at least fifteen meters away, and there was no chance to stop what was coming.

With the next breath, we were blown off our feet through the air, at least another ten or fifteen meters, right into a giant rectangle bush by the parking lot.

For a second I could not see or feel anything, and then the

---

8   Except not really because this is dangerous and against the law in the known universe, punishable by extensive slicing and dicing.

pain caught up. I coughed and reached for Greg. I was lying on my back in the bush, Greg somewhere beside me. I lifted my head and looked back toward the station. It was blown wide open.

"Booger," I mumbled.

[22] Greg crawled out of the bush,[1] pausing to brush broken branches and leaves off his legs and chest, and then he fell to the ground again. I climbed over to get the face mask from his pocket, making sure it was on him properly, when a movement made me look up.

There was Woods, standing a meter or two farther away from the station, looking through the heavy haze at the aftermath of the much larger, much more destructive explosion behind us.

In the dark and with the hood Woods was wearing, he looked very like the pictures we had drawn—tolerably human but with gray skin, his large black eyes shadowed. Woods noticed me looking at him and our eyes met. He knew who I was, too, somehow. He smiled and then turned and ran.

I jumped up, rubbing my backside where the evil bush had scratched me, and followed in Woods's wake. A little voice in the back of my head protested that this explosion was even bigger than the last one. *Greg is still back there. And more people might die. Innocent people. Greg's friend. Masks or no masks.*

But I did not stop. I could not stop. I had to chase down this dead man. I'd already killed him once, and now it was time to get the job done properly. But I needed answers first.

---

1   Landing in a pile of broken glass would have been softer. Just goes to show, you cannot trust a bush, even one on Earth. I think it hurt us out of spite. It did save our lives, but I think this was by accident.

We ran for blocks, maybe miles. I cursed my adorable boots, wishing for bare feet against the cement. After several twists and turns, I slowed down, my head heavy and my legs cramping. He was nowhere in sight, even as morning approached and the sky lightened. The cloud of sparkly smog was still hovering distantly behind me, but I was not at all sure where I was.

"*Booger bubble.*"[2] I had lost him, and I was back to square one. Or square zero. As if we'd made no progress at all.

I stumbled around a corner into a thin alley and came face to face with Woods. He was not running or tired or out of breath,[3] but stood with his arms folded, watching me with what looked like curiosity, his head tilted to the side.

I lunged at him, but he stepped back out of the way effortlessly. I put my hands on my hips and glared at him, but the effect was probably marred by my hunching and heaving.

"Well met, Aria, Seventh Daughter of Morr, Keeper of the Sacred Sponge. How can I help you?" he said, his way of speaking Booshy as smooth and smug as always.

"You died!" I said, pointing my finger at him.

He shrugged. "It didn't take."

"What I meant to say is why are you trying to kill me?" This was not quite right either, but it was a start.

---

2   *Booger bubble,* like *booger,* are not the English words, but a transliteration of Booshy, And I am very sorry you had to hear such extremely foul language.

3   Why was he not out of breath? He was a scientist, and our scientists are always in top shape, of course; certainly he was in better shape than I was. In my defense, I was a queen that lived almost entirely underground in a relatively small Compound where people brought me everything I wanted. So there was very little occasion for working out.

He looked genuinely startled by this. "Kill you? No, I'm not trying to kill you, Your Majesty, Keeper, honestly." He paused, considering, "Not that I don't have cause . . ."

Something about him always, as you call it, *rubbed me the wrong way*, and I could feel my hackles rising.[4] "Alright, so *yes*, I did have you killed, but are you truly so petty about it? As you said, the execution I ordered 'did not take,' so no revenge required."

"Perhaps you're right. Regardless, I am not trying to kill you. I forgave you long ago. You did what you had to do. Our people still need you." He gave a little bow. He sounded annoyingly sincere.

"Well then, why cause these explosions? Are you trying to frame me, get us in trouble? Or is it the humans? Are you trying to hurt them? Or get us catapulted off the planet?"

"You jump to conclusions so quickly, Keeper. I'm not surprised: it is evidence of an unscientific mind. I always told Penny it was your one failing."

"What does Penny have to do with this?" I asked, alarmed. "Is she in danger?"

"No, no, I harbor Penny no ill will. I would never do anything to hurt her. And I have no intention of ever hurting *anyone*. I never did. All I want is to be left alone. And seeing you with that human earlier, I suspect you want the same."

I would not be pulled into talking about Greg. "That is ridiculous. How would causing explosions allow you to be left alone?"

---

4   This is not a metaphor, as I do actually have hackles, by the way.

He smiled. "You have no idea what is actually going on, do you? When you realize the truth . . ."

"What truth?" I demanded.

He walked past me, back toward the main road. It occurred to me that maybe I should reach out and grab him as he passed, but then what would I do? I could not hold him with my bare hands, make him return to the Compound. He was twice my size, and three times more fit. I did a quick glance down at my Everything Device power gauge, but I did not even have enough power left now to gravitate him to where Penny was so *she* could grab him. I needed backup.

"What truth?!" I asked again. "What is going on!?"

He paused, glancing back at me. "That *I* am not the one causing those explosions. *You* are." And he walked around the alley corner and out of sight.

[23]   It was all a lie of course. It had to be. If I was causing explosions, would I not notice? And also, I was queen, and he was just a dead traitor and a liar. My whole body suddenly felt hot and uncomfortable.

I could not let him get away or all would be lost. But I also could not arrest him on my own. My only chance was to follow him at a distance. I ran out of the ally and looked both ways, frantically trying to see where he'd gone in the dim early morning light.

I caught a glimpse of him turning a corner far off to the right, and I followed after him, trying to blend in[1] with the few humans on the street and still keep up. I kept dodging and zigzagging, worried he'd run again if he saw me following him. But he pushed on steadily, almost leisurely, unaware of me and never looking back. He turned another corner into a small space between two homes, and by the time I got around the corner, he was gone. I blew out a gust of air in frustration.

But I realized I knew where we were. The house I could see through the gap in front of me was blue with sea creatures glued to the walls.

This was Barry Hickenbottom's house.

What was Woods doing here? Was he hiding out here, using Barry's lab without Barry's knowledge, somehow?

---

1   Blending in is not one of my talents, as I have mentioned. Neither is keeping up. I only just managed it.

Or was Woods about to create another explosion? Was Hickenbottom in danger? I needed help *now*—maybe from both Greg and Penny, because I still was not sure how to catch Woods.

I ran back toward the haze that was hovering above the city line, a faint colorful twinkle in the air as the sun came up in full. It felt like eons before I finally arrived, exhausted, at the perimeter set up a block away from the police station.

The building was in complete ruin. Where the first two explosions had only blown out windows, the sheer size of this one had destroyed walls. Bomb squad officers picked through the rubble. Authorities in full gas masks helped the injured under canopies. Everyone was wearing a face mask, which seemed to be working since nobody was coughing uncontrollably that I could see.

Greg sat on one of the tables under a canopy with his face mask still on. Although he was facing my direction, he did not react when he saw me, but continued to watch silently as I rushed toward him, his eyes almost seeing through me.

"I am sorry I left you," I said, stopping in front of him, trying to slow my breathing.

"And Penny," he added.

"What?"

"You left Penny too." He wiped at a bit of dust on his arm, making a streak.

"Penny is fine. I sent her to our condo an hour ago. Greg, I need your help."

Greg looked away. "You sent her? I don't know what you mean. I never know what you mean."

I gulped. Something was wrong with Greg. "I would never leave you or her if I had a choice. I had to find Woods; I had to catch him. Did you see him? He was here."

Greg stared off over my shoulder.

"Catching him is the whole reason I am still here," I insisted.

"Is it?" He was gazing in my direction, staring through me again.

"Well, I . . . Yes." Of course it was. Was it not?

I'd left Greg lying on the ground after crawling out of the evil bush. He could have been dead, and my thought for him was only momentary? I was not sure why this truth was sitting so uncomfortably with me. But there was no time now to explore it.

"I'm not upset you left me, Aria. It's just that after you left, I—" he looked down. "Did you find him?"

"Yes," I said, my voice small.

"Where is he?"

I cleared my voice, hopeful that would give me more volume. "At Barry Hickenbottom's house. Barry is in danger, maybe everyone is in danger, and I need help; I cannot get Woods on my own." I could recognize with a bit of shame that I was begging now.

Greg nodded and wiped his eyes. "I don't know what I thought this would be like. You, your life, seemed so exciting, and I got caught up in it. I thought, 'I'm a government asset with the FBI, I'm meant for this.' But what was I even doing? I knocked out a minimum-wage parking attendant. We lied to the police, broke into buildings, talked about breaking someone out of jail. My friend, Bella, your friend Penny, both could be dead, could be buried under that rubble, and I have no idea which it is or if it's both. Nobody will tell me anything. And at first all I could think was, 'I hope Aria's okay. I hope she found what she was looking for.' And now Barry's in danger too? They say you guys have to compartmentalize, put your emotions aside, but I don't know. Maybe you'll have to teach me, because I definitely don't have the ability."

"Bella will be fine, Greg, I am sure of it. But right now, I need help."

"Ask the police," he said, motioning to the abundance of officers swarming around us.

"You know I cannot do that."

"Do I?" he asked. He picked up his phone and started typing.

"What are you doing?" I asked.

He would not look at me, and I noticed his hair was full of dust. "Messaging [Armani?]."

"Why?" I came closer and tried to touch his shoulder, but he leaned away.

"Because, you said you need help to save Barry, right? Well [Armament?] is . . . help." His voice was starting to have an edge to it.

"I meant *your* help," I whined.

He still would not look at me. "Go do whatever it is you have to do to save your ten thousand people, Aria. Save Barry. [Altar?] will pick you up. I need to be here for Bella, in case . . ." He closed his mouth.

I considered protesting, but there just was not time. Also, he'd always been so obedient, maybe it was time I followed his example. I brushed the back of his hand with my own, then backed away, watching him. After a moment I turned and closed my eyes tight, willing the image of him to burn into my mind as I sped away. How did everything get so complicated?[2]

I was not sure how much to fill in [Aang?], so I did not try. Instead I just told him to stop by the condo, and then to get to Barry's as soon as possible. I could feel time slipping away, everything taking too long, but I was not sure how to avoid it. I could not do this without Penny.

When we got to the safecondo, I ran from one end of the very small room to the other for at least two of your minutes before I had to admit to myself that Penny was not there.

"Where is Penny?" I demanded of [Arlo?] as I opened the door to the car again.

He gawked at me. "I don't know. Greg said she was arrested. Did you think she was here?"

I groaned in frustration. "Yes, she was in jail, but I . . . she got out this morning. She should be here; I *sent* her *here*."

"Maybe she went for a walk or something. Do you want to wait?"

"No, no this is urgent." If Woods was going to set a bomb at Barry's, who knew how long it would take? I'd wasted enough time as it was. "I will leave her a note." I ran back inside, left the thingamabob with a message recorded on it,

---

2   If I had to say one thing against the late Earth, it would be that everything around regular humans was too complicated, too complex, too tangled, too many synonyms. And antonyms. And words in general.

hoping she could also use it to track me,[3] and ran back to the car. As we drove off, I looked back at the condo building, wishing Penny would suddenly appear and join us. Or that Greg would appear, forgive me for my selfishness, and the four of us would be a team again.

But I knew they would not. It was time to work things out on my own. I was a queen. I could handle some things, without Penny, without Greg. Right?

"So, to Barry's?" asked [Anvil?] as he drove.

"Yes."

He paused. "Can I ask why? You're sure Barry's even home?"

"Actually, I am hoping he is not. But it is more about who else might be there."

[Alabaster?] smiled, his mouth closed and thin. "I see."

I sighed. "I know I have kept you out of the loop and we have not connected so far, but it was for your own protection. And now, there is not time. Someone is in there, someone dangerous, and I cannot catch him by myself, so I need your help."

He glanced over at me. "Why are we catching him?"

I exhaled. "We think he is the bomber."

"*The* bomber?"

"Yes."

"How do you know? And why not call the police?"

"I cannot tell you that."

---

3   I was never clear on the abilities of the thingamabob (because Penny would hardly ever share and let me use it), but I did know how to record a message.

He pulled over, narrowing his eyes, and I realized we were only about half a block from Barry's house now. [Ansett?] whipped out his phone. "Well then, I can help you, but I think this calls for more backup." He typed on his phone and put it to his ear.

"Not the police, though. No police," I demanded. Who were his backup? Friends of his? Maybe a gang of chefs?

He eyed me and nodded, then got out of the car before I could hear much of the phone conversation. I exited the car too, walking toward Barry's, wondering if Woods was still inside. The phone conversation was a surprisingly long one, and after a minute I was pacing.

Just as I was about to run into Barry's house without him, [Alibaba?][4] put his phone into his pocket.

"Did you find someone to help? We cannot wait any longer."

He looked at me for a long time. "Yes, I do have someone on the way. Would have been sooner if you'd filled me in sooner, but there it is. Should only be a few minutes."

I stomped in frustration.

"Trust me, Aria. When it comes to a bomber, we don't take any chances."

"Who is *we*?" As I asked this, a black van arrived, and out popped a group of ten humans of indeterminate gender in all black,[5] wearing full helmets and face masks.

---

4   I've lost track of my guesses now.

5   I think I mentioned this was the middle of the morning? Apparently, these humans subscribed to Penny's idea that black blended in, but in the day-light, it did not. They would have blended in better dressed as clowns. Who were dressed as dogs. Who were dressed as aliens.

[Aspen?] pointed to Barry's house, and they spread out, crouching low and fast, and disappeared around the back. After a minute, one of the team came to the front again and nodded.

The group did not look like police, but who were they? And how could [Abacus?] summon them to come help so swiftly?

"I thought you were a chef," I said as we crept toward the house.

"Sometimes."

"And a teacher?"

"Sometimes."

The pieces fell into place in my mind with a snap and a twist, like an old Freddor lightning player being switched on. "You are FBI. Greg is your asset. What did he call you? Handler—you handle Greg?"

He shrugged, his expression serious.

"But I told you no police!"

"I'm sorry, Aria, but you aren't in a position to dictate the terms here. I'm letting you come with us into Barry's so you can tell us what we're looking for. We don't have time for a full debrief, but you and I need to talk in detail when this is over. And Greg too."

"Are you going to take me in? Turn me in? Is that what the phone call was about?"

He narrowed his eyes, but it was not at me, it was at Barry's house. "Let's just talk when this is through."

"And what about Penny?"

Before he could answer, the team surrounded us, and we all waddled like a many-legged *bilgebeast* to the front door of

Barry's blue house. Without knocking (very rude), the team burst in, running ahead of us, and spread out through the house willy-nilly, shouting out to each other. When we got to Barry's lab, they ran around that too. Barry was there shredding documents in a fury, waving everyone away with a cry of outrage. One of the team members pushed Barry up against the wall with his forearm. The rest of the house was clearly empty of suspicious people or floating silver explosives. Then the team yelled *clear*, and [Anton?] pulled me back a little.

"You sure you saw your bomber here?"

I was angry at him for calling the FBI and annoyed that there was nothing to find, but I supposed it was better than if we had found bubbles or a floating ball explosive or dead aliens ready to kill us. "Yes, about twenty-five minutes ago, so maybe he left. But I do not know why he would come here in the first place. I thought Barry might be in danger." I turned to Barry, still pushed against the wall. "Barry, did you see—"

And then I got a glimpse of Barry's face. It was a look of pure loathing. At me.

Looking at Barry, at his expression of rage and hate, there was something else I realized, something that felt off. Barry had been outraged, but like he'd expected us to come, like he had been waiting for this day for a long time. Which did not make any sense. And there was something else. Something about his face, now that I really looked at it. If I ignored the glasses and the large nose and the lack of hair and pretended the eyes were larger and completely black, he looked vaguely familiar. I added that to the heaving-breaths-of-fiery hate in his expression toward me.

Maybe Barry was not in danger from Woods, maybe Barry *was* Woods.

Had he found a way to duplicate and power our technology, change how he looked at will, like I could? I was supposed to be the only one with a power source, but maybe he'd found another.[6]

"[Atticus?] . . ." I said in alarm, nodding my head toward Barry, and [Algernon?] turned and looked at Barry too. It was in that second that Woods/Barry Hickenbottom broke free and made a run for it.

Apparently, that was the wrong thing to do. The team made quick work of him. He was caught and tied up and thrown into a big van with a thump. They did not even know what he'd done yet, but I guessed running away was enough for these humans.

[Adolfo?] and I walked around Barry's house while his people gathered up the lab equipment. "Aria, what are we really doing here? Please tell me I didn't just break into an innocent civilian's home and arrest him and steal his things."

"No, I think . . . I think Barry *is* the bomber." I still could not quite believe it.

[Alpo?] looked around at the lab. "Look, Barry's crazy, but I've known him for years. I don't think he would simply start exploding things."

"How many years?"

____

6 I know some of you are wondering why it took so long for this to occur to me, but you should understand that the amount of power required to change one's face is small by our standards but is so huge by your standards that it would take at least two nuclear power plants to power it. Or thirty-seven billion potatoes.

"Ever since he moved here, maybe six years."

I nodded. "He has been dead for seven, so that sounds about right."

He blinked at me. "What makes you think he's the bomber?"

"I think I recognize him. I think Barry is one of my—" I wrapped my arms around myself. "[Anakin?], you know about me, do you not? I know you know. Greg knows, and he must have gotten it from you, so you *must* know. You know what I am."

He grabbed my arm and pulled me to the side, away from any of his team members on the other end of the room. "Know *what*, Aria?"

Why must he insist I say it? There was no elegant way to do so. "That I am an alien? To you. Or that you are an alien to me? That we are aliens to each other?"

We stared at each other for a moment.

[Amp?] nodded. "I think it's time we had our chat. Just let me take care of a few things first. And I need to talk to Barry. I'll have a car drop you somewhere and I'll meet you there in a bit."

He motioned to one of his people and I was whisked into another big black car, two gun toting guards on each side of me, and one driving in the front.

How had everything gotten so out of control? Barry was Woods? I could not wrap my head around it. And his capture had been too easy. Had he allowed himself to be caught? And after all our hard work, he was in the hands of your FBI. *I* was in the hands of your FBI. I'd used all my remaining power units to transport Penny out of jail, meaning we had no way to escape, and no way home. Penny was missing. Greg was probably gone to me forever. And I was apparently totally and completely incapable of handling anything on my own after all.

[24]   From the way I was being treated on the drive,[1] I fully expected to be directly catapulted off the planet, or to be sent to a lab for experimentation, or at the very least, locked in an interrogation room, and was surprised when instead the car dropped me and the two guards off at [Arbie?]'s food lab. Were they going to experiment on me here?

I made a list in my head: Woods was found and stopped, but we only had two days left on our countdown, and we would need every second of that to get back to the Compound without the gravitator. Ferries, trains, even taxis took time.[2] I needed to find Penny immediately, extract Woods somehow, and get out of there. Was I being held for questioning? I thought about refusing to enter the school building, but then I saw Greg right inside the windowed door, pacing around.

"What's this all about?" he said when I entered. He was cleaned up from the explosion, but he still seemed pale and jittery.

I decided to let [Applebee?] answer that for himself. "Is Penny here?" I asked.

----

1   I suspect the silent guards sitting by me in the car were clones or robots. They looked exactly the same and would not answer any of my questions about their births or their last names.

2   Flying in one of your airplanes was never really an option for us because of the security, plus we lacked IDs and last names, which they frowned on.

Greg resumed pacing.

"Greg?"

"She's not here . . . she's . . ." He took a deep breath.

"What?"

He paused in his pacing to look at me, but then lowered his gaze again and started walking again. I noticed he had a slight limp. "Penny . . . Penny is gone," Greg said hoarsely.

"What?"

"She's gone, Aria. I just got the call. They found her body at the police station after you left."

I looked at him, my mouth open. Why was he saying that? "No. No, I already got her out."

"Aria, they found her there! She was at almost the very center of the explosion."

"No! She was in the holding cell, nowhere near that floating bubble explosive we saw, and I moved her out of there anyway."

"Actually she wasn't in the holding cell anymore. After she put the other prisoner in the hospital, she assaulted a couple police officers, putting one in critical condition, way before the explosion even happened. So the police were in the process of getting her transferred, escorting her to the front, and . . ." He grimaced.

No. No, I was hearing him wrong. Or he'd heard wrong. Penny was *not* dead. She could not die. She would not *dare*. I looked at the door, half-expecting her to come walking through it to berate me for using up our power units and put Greg's misunderstanding to rights.

I shook my head. "She is not dead, Greg. I am sorry, but whatever you heard, you heard wrong."

Greg leaned against the wall and slid down, putting his head in his hands. I took up his spot pacing, neither of us speaking to the other. I was increasingly impatient to get this whole thing over, whatever this was, find Penny and Woods, and get out of there.

Ten or twenty of your minutes later, [Atherton?] walked in the front door. He motioned to a little classroom on the side, and we all went in, except the two guards who stayed right outside the doorway, guarding it as it shut.

[Armonde?] wiped his forehead. "All right. Barry is being very cooperative. He's already more or less confessed to the bombings." He sat down.

"Wait, what?!" asked Greg.

"Didn't you tell him, Aria? Barry is in custody. Aria led us to him, identified him as the bomber, and from some of the weird things we found in his lab, we have enough evidence to put him away even if he hadn't confessed. I still can't quite believe it. I've known the guy for a long time."

Greg stood up, his hand on his head. "*Barry* is the bomber? The one we've been looking for? I don't even . . . !"

I wondered what exactly Barry had confessed to. Did he also confess to being one of *us* in disguise? How had he disguised himself in the first place? Why had he done any of it? Why hide as Barry, but let me see his real face? Why had he blamed me for the explosions only to confess now? Even as all these questions ran through my mind, I found I almost did not care anymore. I just wanted to take Woods back to the Compound and let my thinkers deal with it. But how would I get them to release me *and* Woods?

I stood up, put my hands on my hips, and tried to channel

my queenly authority. "When can I take him?" I asked as if there could be no objection.

They both looked at me with eyebrows raised in surprise. [Alexei?] cleared his throat. "You can't. Thanks for the positive ID, but we've got it from here."

I swallowed, some of my authoritative facade slipping. "But Barry is—well if he confessed then he is not Barry at all. He is Woods and he is one of *mine*."

[Anders?] looked away, tapping his fingers on the table. "I'm sorry Aria, but you should know that once he started exploding American citizens, he became the jurisdiction of the FBI."

I sat down. "But if he is questioned, everyone will know . . ."

[Ale?] held up his hand. "Don't worry; he is in a very secure facility and only those with top clearance can speak to him."

A secure facility. That sounded ominous. Is that where I was headed as well? I looked down at my Everything Device shimmering around my neck, longing to transport Woods and I away, but the units were so low now, I would not even have been able to change a disguise. Every minute that passed meant I would be later and later returning to the Compound. Every minute that passed meant things were getting worse.

At least there wouldn't be any more explosions. But how could I get to Woods? "You must at least let me talk to him. There is so much I do not understand."

[Algy?] laughed darkly. "You don't know how true that statement is," he said under his breath.

Greg was still standing, wandering around the room. "I still don't get it. Was he in disguise as Barry but he was Woods all the time? And why did he do it? We thought he was going after Aria, but then why would he help us look for clues if the clues eventually lead us back to him?"

These were good points, I thought. "Yes. Barry told us about almost every clue we had. Why would he do that?" I asked.

[Amsterdam?] raised his eyebrows. "And did any of that actually lead you anywhere? Or help you in the end?"

Greg tipped his head. "No, it was sort of a wild goose chase, to be honest."

I shook my head. "We chased no geese. And some of his clues were useful. It was how we figured out about the bomb casing. And that there are trucks transporting element X, and where to find them. Gwyn said the trucks were not what we thought. But they *were* something. I just do not understand."

There was a long pause while [Ackerley?] tapped his fingers on the table again. "Look, I know you have a lot of questions. But so do we. He confessed he played a part in the explosions, and maybe that's all any of us need to know. By the way, Barry wanted it on the record that Aria is just as much to blame for the explosions as he is, but he wouldn't clarify how. And as far as the trucks are concerned, that was real intel. We believe he stole . . . what did you call it? . . . *element X* from the trucks in the first place. Maybe he was trying to get your help to steal more." He shrugged.

"So he was stealing element X from the government? What were *they* doing with it?" asked Greg.

[Alastair?] splayed his hand out flat on the table.

"Apparently, they were using it for some kind of experimentation, on loan from UNOOSA,"

Greg gulped. "What? UNOOSA like the United Nations Space thing? That UNOOSA?"

"The United Nations Office for Outer Space Affairs. And UNOOSA weren't the real owners, either. They got the element from *her*." He pointed at me. There was a hint of disgust in his eye.

I always feared humans would be disgusted when they knew what I was. It appeared I was right, though he'd hidden it well before now.

I smoothed my wig and cleared my throat. "Well, I told you the element was very common where I come from. I might not have mentioned that we gave large quantities of it to UNOOSA eight years ago."

Greg looked away from me, back to his friend/handler again. "So what were they doing with it? Making bombs, too?"

"That's above my pay grade. They won't tell me, but I think they were just inspecting it." [Arnie?] waved his hand. "Maybe since the element came from you, Aria, that's why Barry is giving you partial credit for the explosions. Who knows. But suffice it to say, he won't be hurting anyone else, so I would suggest letting it go and moving on."

I was starting to get angry. "So, am I also detained? Why did you bring us here to your food lab?"

"No, you are not being detained. In fact, we are sending you home. Just wanted to give you the Barry update first, since you led us right to him. And also, since we're sending you away, I wanted to give you and Greg the opportunity to talk, to make sure there was nothing left unsaid between you. For Greg's sake."

What did he mean? We sat in silence, Greg and I looking at each other in confusion.

[Aggregate?] narrowed his eyes at me. "Wouldn't you like to introduce yourself for real, Aria? Tell Greg what you really are?"

I narrowed my eyes back at him. "Greg knows everything about me: everything important, anyway. I never lied."

[Arnet?] put his face into his hands, laughing but without mirth. He raised his head. "Then here's a little truth for you, Greg. *I'll* introduce you, shall I?" He stood and lifted his hands toward me in an exaggerated sweep. "Greg, meet Aria, the alien queen."

Greg looked at [Argonon?], his face twisted in confusion. "Is that like her code name? Call sign?"

Call sign? "But you already know," I insisted quietly. "Maybe not about the queen part, but I promise I was getting to that."

[Abbott?] laughed again. "Not a code name or call sign, Greg. Aria here is a real-life alien."

Greg stared at him, his face blank now. "Like Sting?"[3]

"No, like the extraterrestrial, tentacled, bug-eyed, from-a-different-planet alien."[4]

Greg's eyes moved over to me now in slow motion, his

---

3   The musician Sting does have a very good song about being an alien that speaks to me, as you say. Or sings to me. Except the part about being English. And a man. In New York. But otherwise, it is just so very true, you know?

4   Despite the fact that this hurt my feelings, it was fairly accurate.

expression hovering between incredulity and confusion. "But . . ."

"He knows!" I insisted, "Greg, you already *know* what I am. You said you knew on our first date."

"But," he stuttered. "You're an . . . an . . . *alien?!* I thought you were a spy! A human spy! Not an *alien!*"

I opened my mouth to respond, but no words would come out.

[Avi?] scoffed. "Not a very good spy, though, right?"

"I *did* wonder," Greg admitted, "I thought it was maybe witness protection or something instead . . . But wait, when I asked if you were a spy, you said yes!"

"No! No, you asked if I was an *alien.*"

"Ah, the misunderstandings between a man and his alien lover," [Arik?] said and stood up, turning his back on us as he walked to the other side of the room.

Greg looked away from me. "[Archer?], you knew the whole time? Why didn't you tell me when I first told you about her? When I brought you to meet her. How could you let me . . ."

[Ardell?] turned back to us. "No, I didn't know either. I was as ignorant as you were to the presence of aliens on Earth. I found out only twenty minutes ago myself when I called to get back up. They've been here for more than nine years, apparently. Nine years, and the idiots at the UN didn't think the rest of humanity needed to know." He turned around again. "Gwyn Kilcher has known ever since she became Alaska's senator. Can you believe it? They've been paying her off to stay quiet. So when I called, I mentioned what Gwyn told you and demanded some answers. They sent me up the ladder, gave me some answers I wasn't prepared for. You still don't have clearance to know any of this, even now, Greg, but I don't care. You're *my* asset, so I'm making the call. Welcome to a very elite club. Both of us might have figured out about Queen Aria here sooner if we'd known 'alien' was even a possibility."

He noticed the effect this was having on Greg, and sighed. "Sorry, buddy. I know I'm being a little harsh, but it's been a rough day for both of us. I never would have told you to stay on her tail if I'd known she was an alien rather than a spy. Of course, I also didn't know you would get so attached." He put a hand on his friend's shoulder. Greg sat slack-jawed, his expression dazed.

"What do you mean stay on my tail? I do not have a tail." I looked at Greg and he flushed, but he still would not look at me.

[Ajax?] sighed and leaned back in his chair. "I know Greg told you he wouldn't tell anyone who you were, but he's an asset with the FBI. He told me everything. His information turned out mostly wrong, but that wasn't his fault."

I looked at Greg. He was still facing straight forward, but his eyes were closed now. "You lied?" I asked. Greg had lied to me? Not telling about his association with the FBI was an omission, but Greg had said he would not tell anyone about me. I am usually the one that lies, and I did not like being on the receiving end.

Greg was shaking his head now, and [Albus?] patted his back. "To be clear, some of it I had to guilt out of him, but in the end, his patriotism won out. He told me about every conversation and every suspicion. And I assured him I wouldn't turn you in for espionage, for a while at least."

Greg looked up at his friend, his eyes pained, but still kept his mouth shut. Denying nothing.

[Alric?] was back to tapping on the table. "But I'm not really sure you can be one to make accusations here anyway, Aria. Greg lied, I lied, you lied, everybody lied."

I was still looking at Greg. He would not meet my eyes.

I growled and stood up, tired of all of it. "I am ready to leave now. If you are not detaining me, I will go. Where is Penny? Did you take her?"

"What? No, I would never do anything to hurt Penny." His eyes softened.

Over the past few days, I had started to suspect that, given enough time, [Axel?] and Penny might have developed real feelings for one another, despite the language barrier. The way he said this, it seemed I was right, at least on his part.

"I thought Greg told you?" he went on. "Penny was . . ." He trailed off and turned away again.

Greg spoke up, his voice strong, but he still was not look-ing at me. "I did tell you. Penny was killed in the explosion. She's gone."

"No she is not! Stop saying that!" I yelled at him.

Greg flinched. "I put Penny and Bella's names and descriptions on the missing list. It was only a few minutes ago when someone found her. Found her body. She was already dead. [Artax?] got the news himself."

[Axxes?] still stood with his back to us, his head hanging with emotion.

I could feel my eyes filling with tears, my throat

constricting, as if my body knew something my mind had not caught up to yet.

No. She was still alive.

But . . . why had she not been at the condo? She would never leave someplace once I sent her there, not before seeing me or notifying me somehow. It was against her code. And she should have contacted me by now, or found me. She always found me.

"No. It is not true," I whispered. I put my head in my hands. *It is not true!*

[Azreal?] sniffed. "I'm so sorry," he said, his voice thick, and I discovered I was sobbing.

After what could have been minutes or hours later, I raised my head. My vision swam like I was drowning in *grop-tha* spores, everything warping around me. Greg had laid his head on the table, facing away from me, and [Age?] sat across the table, his expression tight.

"You said I can go. Can I still go, or was that a lie?" I asked, wiping my face free of tears.

[Archibald?] sniffed. "No, you can go, we are sending you back to Alaska. We'll even give you a nice private jet to fly there." His tone was bland and beaten down. "My superiors don't want anything to happen to you: they say it is in some alien Accord that you can't be harmed.[5] They don't even want

---

5   This was the only stipulation in the Accord directed toward you humans. It might seem unjust that I was not punished for breaking the Accord, unjust that your leaders kept any part of it when I clearly did not keep mine. But perhaps this came down to the fact that you'd written a whole set of almost a hundred thousand Accord rules, which had taken a lot of manpower and spellchecking, and were unlikely to jeopardize all that work now. Spellcheckers are hard to come by.

you questioned, but I say this doesn't count." He put his hand out. "You need to hand over all your technology, including that transporting technology and power source. They don't want you leaving your Compound anymore. I'll make sure it gets into the right hands."

"And my people? I broke several rules. What will happen to my people now?" I slowly unlatched and removed the Royal Everything Device necklace.

[Apollo?] took the device and put it into a small black box and locked it. "My guess is UNOOSA, the FBI, everyone will just pretend none of this ever happened." He glanced at Greg who looked shattered, and then back at me. "Go home. Take care of your people. Forget about us. Forget about humanity."

Sure. I just had to forget, forget about Greg, about Penny, about the humans, about everything good and important, everything I loved.

No problem at all.

[25] The airport was dirty and tiny,[1] and I did not even get to go through any lines with tickets or luggage checks, which was just as well since I'd lost my enthusiasm for lines and I did not have any luggage. They shoved me onto a small plane alone and locked the door to the cockpit. It was a prison on wings and I knew it, but I was already in jail in my mind as it was.

Penny was gone.

My mind and soul rejected the idea outright even as I thought it. She'd been my only real friend my whole life, even before she was an adviser, and now she was gone. She was not the first person I had loved and lost, but I was certain that once it sunk in, it would cut the deepest. At the moment, I was only numb.

And now I'd lost Greg too. I'd made many mistakes over the past eight days, but it was hard to separate them, to see where I might have stopped them before they began. And even after all those risks I took, all those dates and non-dates, in the end, Greg was disgusted by me for being alien anyway, just as I'd always feared.

I considered that maybe I should be upset with him, too. I had never lied to Greg, not outright, and he *had* lied to me.

---

1   I am not even sure you would call it an airport. There was only one air-plane, and there was nobody else there except my two guards. Perhaps they cleared it out.

But . . . I couldn't muster any anger at him for it. Who was I kidding? I think I had forgiven him instantly. My heart was his, my everything was his from the moment I'd seen him walk toward me at the gala, seen him smile, heard him laugh, got a glimpse of his magnificent forehead. And telling his handler about me was probably the right thing for him to do. Lying to me was wrong,[2] but I could not be mad at him for something I did so regularly.

Now I was on my way back to where I should have gone so many Earth-days ago. To the place I hated but where I was needed, with no Penny-buffer to protect me. If I had done like I was supposed to days ago, I would not be returning home now without my friend and with a broken heart. I was fully and completely alone, and I would never see the two people I loved most again.

When we arrived at the Compound, it was already dark outside the tiny porthole windows of the airplane. I let my human disguise fall with a clap. [Alfonso?] had taken my facebender technology, so once my disguise dropped, there was no putting it back up, but I kept up my other alien disguise underneath.

I wrapped a blanket I found under my seat around me like a *foldeplant* cocoon, and then followed the two guards back through the gates to the Compound that sat like a giant, gray, clump of fanged *chigger* grasses, waiting to take root on my shoulders and suck the life right out of me.

---

2   Yes. I do know this. Our culture may have different feelings about truth, but we also have morality. I am writing a very long report apology to prove it, am I not?

At the doors to the Compound itself, a new set of guards took over, these more familiar to me with their white and gray camo uniforms, faces and heads shielded, several weapons and guns strapped to their backs.

I nodded to them. "Jerry, Carl."[3]

They led me through a series of metal doors and corridors, all going down, down, down further into the Earth. At the end of a long and low corridor, the guards stopped, deactivated the laser grid, pushed me through the metal door, reactivated the grid, and closed the door behind me with a devastating metallic *bang* and *clink*.

I sighed, dropping my final disguise. The metallic smell of the unwashed people from Booshlaboo flooded over me. I realized I had my eyes squeezed shut and I forced them open.

Home.

I took a deep breath, trying to relieve the heavy weight on my chest.

"Your Majesty!" echoed thousands of voices. A hundred of the closest white-toga clad[4] people dropped what they were doing and converged, echoing and murmuring words of praise and comfort, a wave of polite, positive white noise.

They gently lifted me, a hundred hands and arms making

---

3   These were not their names. I never saw their faces, but I liked to pretend I knew them, and they never corrected me. So maybe those truly were their names. Jerry, Carl, if you are still alive, I am very sorry for not learning your true names, or if these were your names and you are still alive, you are welcome.

4   The togas were made of human bedsheets. White sheets were one of the only things besides "food" that we are allowed access to in the Accord, so we used them for everything: clothes, walls, tablecloths, bedding . . .

light work,[5] and carried me above their heads into the depths of the Compound, around and through some of the hanging-sheet walls and canopies, until we reached the hidden power chamber ten square meters in size at the center. It stood like a big wood burning stove, sides open to allow our entrance. They carried me inside and set me down on the cold metal bench at the center. A couple helpers brought me nourishing liquid to drink, a sheet toga to wear, and the spare power gauge device was put around my neck.

Someone touched a big bright circle on the side of the chamber to turn it on. And then all one hundred of them gathered around, swooping me up into a hundred-person doggy pile/group hug.

I activated the Sacred Sponge within me, soaked up my people's energy, and sobbed.

---

5   I am not heavy, except for my head, in case you were wondering. At least, no more than any other queen I know. And much lighter than one or two. The queen from Hallswell lives in a very dense gravity, so she can create craters when she walks. It makes her very popular at parties.

[26] I probably need to be clearer regarding the Sacred Sponge: it was so much more than just a part of my title. It was a real, physical thing inside me. True to its name, the Sacred Sponge was designed to absorb, but instead of liquids, it absorbed energy, then disseminated it at my will. This sacred device was our source of power for almost all the technology we possessed.

I could soak up several different kinds of energy with the Sacred Sponge, but the most powerful was the energy that came directly from my poeple. Before you shout about the unjustness of this, keep in mind that it was not as if I was sucking their lives away. It was more like I was sucking up wakefulness. And love.[1] Both of which were given freely and which I was also contributing, by the way.[2]

The Sacred Sponge was—as its name suggests—deeply sacred and, as such, even most of my own people did not know what it was or how it truly worked.[3] Most assumed our power was absorbed into the Royal Everything Device, or

---

1   Love gives the greatest amount of power. Obviously.

2   Not that it came without a cost: it did make the people sleepy. And grumpy. Like after one of your unplanned too-long daytime naps. Therefore, only a hundred or so people contributed power at a time, rotating to a new group every few hours to avoid exhaustion.

3   It was transferred to me from my Aunt Sonata during a sacred ceremony, only Stone Royal Trainer, myself, and my aunt present.

the spare gauge (one-thing device[4]) I now wore, but it was actually *me*, the Sacred Sponge which resided within me. Not even Penny knew about this.

Now, as a hundred of my people and I sat piled together there in the power chamber, arms draped over one another, a few of those closest to me patted me on the back, and the murmur of the comforting words swelled. I had fifteen faces so close to mine I could hear every breath and sniff between my weeping.

"Great to see you too," said someone sleepily, misinterpreting my bawling as happy tears.

When my wailing died down, someone spoke loud enough to be heard over the murmur and asked, "Where is Penny, Backseat Driver to the Crown?" and I started crying all over again.

Eventually I fell acharge[5] in my people-pile hug, my tears mingling with that of the others.

I awoke a day or two later when the charging was winding down. I sighed, and Sapphire Royal Swiper, who was still acharge next to me, peeked an eye open at me, smiled, and turned her head.

"Fair morning, Your Majesty," said someone who I had to recognize by voice alone. "Can I give you my report? Or do you need more time to recover?" All I could see of him through the people-pile was his big silver forehead: Stone, Major Thinker and Royal Trainer to the Crown.

---

4   This backup device only included a power gauge. Not very helpful, unless you enjoy looking at power gauges.

5   This is a word I made up. It means asleep, obviously. But less human.

Stone never wasted any time. I sighed again. "Yes, you may."

He lifted his head so I could see his eyes. "You were gone eight Earth-days, and during that time three unions were performed and two youngthings born. Both youngthings were put into stasis and are stable. Our monthly nourishment allotment from the humans was deposited through the delivery portal, and all seems in order."

"Report well given."

"And well received. We are glad to have you safely back with us again. You were returned through the delivery portal; does this mean the humans know now that you have been leaving? Will we have trouble for this, do you think?"

"They said nothing to me on the way in. I suspect they will continue the pattern of silence. However, I may not allow me to leave in the future." I barely resisted sighing again. Despite my emotional and physical fatigue, I was surprised at how easily I fell back into report-receiving monarch mode.

He blinked in confirmation. "This is bad news, but not as bad as it could be. I suppose we can obtain zest another way; I will put that to your team of scientists."

"Yes. Thank you." Being in the Compound underground constantly diminished the strength of our people's energy. We'd built the power chamber to enhance the process, but before long, even that was not enough. My scientists finally found a temporary solution to this diminishing power problem: although the human energy was incompatible with our own and therefore un-absorbable, we could extract from them a sort of extra zing that would enrich our power. We called it zest, and we had been extracting and absorbing your zest once a year to keep our energy fresh.[6]

Stone continued. "The life generator is down to one and one-half units, but as soon as the people-pile is finished, you can charge the generator. We were prepared to dim both the light and air filter in case you were delayed, but I am glad you were not. Last time we dimmed the air filter, thirteen people were taken ill."

"I remember. Well given."

"Well received." Stone bowed his head, his forehead bumping into the person next to him.

Penny would have been proud of me for making it on time, in the end. I swallowed. If I did not use the Sponge to charge up the life generator every ten days, the generator would not be able to power the light producer and air producer, and the people would eventually suffocate and die or contract terrible diseases[7] and then also die. It gave me a hard deadline to all trips: a curfew, which I had never pushed this closely before.

Thinking of Penny again made my throat constrict, and I forced myself to breathe normally. I was not ready to say Penny was gone aloud, but I would work up the energy to tell Stone later.

"If you don't mind my asking, Keeper, how did you manage to let your Royal Power Units get so low so quickly?"

---

6   Thanks for this, by the way. Do not worry, if you were ever to be zested, the most you would notice might be a tingly, lemony taste in your mouth for the next twenty-four hours or so. And eating anything salty would give you a mostly-harmless shock. *Mostly harmless*—like humans.

7   And then it would have been your fault for having such incompatible air.

He pointed to the one-thing device I was wearing around my neck. He was the only other one who knew this device was not the source of power, but he was a master at wording things just vaguely enough to avoid sharing his sacred knowledge of the Sponge with anyone else.

I tipped my head so I could see Stone's whole face, moving somebody's arm (Harry Long-legs) and a tentacle from someone I could not see to get a better view. Stone's face was long and droopy, and he was old enough that his silver skin and tentacles had dulled to almost white.

"I am sorry," I said. "I know the units are precious and hard to come by: we used the gravitator several times. Also, it was quite a long excursion: almost ten Earth-days. So that might account for the low number." It had felt like a lifetime in those few days.

"You must have used the gravitator many times over. I hope you enjoyed the time. I apologize we are such a heavy burden on your perfectness."

"We only used it four times, in truth."

"Ah. To go a very far distance, I presume. It must have been a grand adventure indeed."

River Care-a-Lot who lay beneath Stone gave him a maternal pat on his cheek, and Stone shooed them away.

I strained my neck to see Stone better. "It was not a very far distance. One trip did cross from here to Washington DC. But the other three trips only took us a few *gellyplant* throws away."

"Ah," he said. And clamped his mouth shut in polite incredulity.

"Stone, truly," I insisted. A few other people were starting to wake up and eye us.

"Your Majesty is always truthful, even in lies, and you are entitled to your truths and royal truth-lies when and where you desire."[8]

"No royal truth-lies here—we went no further." I'd known we were going through power units very quickly, but I'd attributed it to the fact that we had never been away so long before.

Stone turned away and looked at me from the side to avoid challenging my authority so directly. "I may be wrong—for the first time—but after your last charging of the generator, I believe you departed here with more than three hundred units of power left. To use them all, you would have to use the gravitator to circle the planet twice. You came home with only two units."

"But," I tried to think through my grief haze, "well, we did have human disguises, which we replaced once or twice. We used the air purifiers, and my royal translator was being powered constantly."

"The facebender only takes six units each time you replace a disguise, and requires none to maintain. The other devices use perhaps only one-half unit a week. I'm sorry to bring this up if it is uncomfortable."

I pushed a few more people out of the way so I could sit up. "I am not uncomfortable—I mean to say this *topic* is

---

8   I like this thought. I think it is true. Remember he said this when we get to the end, will you?

not uncomfortable. But are you implying that some power units—what? Went missing?"

Stone sniffed and his white nose wobbled. "I would estimate around two hundred units are unaccounted for, based on what you said. But 'went missing' implies they could leak out or be misplaced, which is impossible. Power must be activated purposely by Your Majesty, and the units directed."

I raised my head to look at him closer. "Maybe the gravitator was malfunctioning? Using up more energy than it should?"

"It doesn't work like that, Your Majesty. Even if the gravitator or facebender were malfunctioning, your royal power device will only send units when you activate and direct them. It would have to be you yourself that is malfunctioning, but that would be as if to say a planet can malfunction, which is nonsensical."

I knew I should have read more of the Sacred Sponge manual when I became its Keeper, but it seemed terribly boring to a twelve year old.

"So, the units cannot wander away on their own. But . . . could they be stolen?" Woods had insisted I was the one causing the explosions. Beyond the fact that I had given kishwellium to the humans in the first place, did he also mean I was the one *powering* them?

Stone shook his head. "I don't see how, Your Majesty."

I breathed out in relief.

Stone narrowed his eyes in thought. "However, if someone possessed and was able to modify some old technology out of storage—a snatcher, perhaps—then power units from your royal device could, I think, be *siphoned away* and stored. But only if the snatcher were close by and turned on at the same time you intentionally activated your power."

I jumped up, stepping out of the people-pile. A few exclaimed in protest but then they re-situated the pile without me and went back to recharging. Stone extricated himself with much more grace than I had, the people-pile closing effortlessly behind him. Standing and with the white-sheet turban around his tentacles, he looked as tall and white as always,[9] a somber contrast to my sudden manic energy.

I took a deep breath, trying to remain focused. "And do we still have any of these *snatchers* here at the Compound?"

"Yes, in the sacred archive. We have multiples of everything but the Royal Everything Device and the gravitator within it. We used snatcher technology before we developed the life generator, so we keep the devices as a backup."

"Who has access to the archive?" It was not much of an archive, more of a closet, with metal boxes on shelves surrounded by sheet walls, so I already suspected I knew the answer.

"Any one of us, but most wouldn't know how to use anything inside, or have any purpose for a snatcher specifically, since it requires your royal awareness to power it."

"So the snatcher could not possibly siphon power unless I was already activating my *Royal Power Source?*"

His mouth twisted in thought. "Perhaps it could, but it would require an alteration to the snatcher, and higher

---

9   Like a ghost, but I supposed he was very old. Are ghosts just people that got so old and gray that all color left them?

knowledge of your Royal Power Source than most have. Also, it would be extremely painful for you. You would notice."

I was starting to pace. "Woods must have a snatcher." I had not felt any pain, so he must have used it when I was otherwise activating the Sacred Sponge.

"Woods Breaker of Worlds? What does he have to do with this?" Stone asked sharply.

"It is a long story, and I am tired." Even through the exhaustion of the past several days, and of having just recharged the Sponge, however, I felt the pieces falling into place in my mind with a *squelch*, like falling face first into a pile of *crabelbrains*.

The gala on the Lady Blue, the school where they'd evacuated us, the police station: at all three sites, I had activated the Sacred Sponge to use the *gravitator*. Then Woods, following us around just as Greg suspected, had waited for that moment of activation, siphoned off power units using the snatcher, obviously counting on the ambiguity of the *gravitator*'s power needs to mask the theft. And then he had used the stolen power to make things explode at each location.

Woods had been telling the truth. He'd told me I was the one causing the explosions. I *had* powered them, inadvertently. My own technology and my own willful ignorance had spelled disaster for everyone.

It *was* my fault.

I forced myself to stand still. Woods had still done the actual exploding things. He was not without blame, but he was right. Everything that had happened was on me. Just as it always was. I was the queen.

This epiphany did not answer any of the *why* questions,

but it did not really matter now. I had to hope that Woods could not hurt anyone else while in FBI custody, especially as I—the Keeper of the Sacred Sponge and the source of his power—was so far away from him. Just one more reason I needed to stay here, away from Washington DC, away from him. Alone but surrounded, in this dark, metallic, many-person coffin.

I followed Stone to the life generator, stuck my hand in the portal, and activated the Sacred Sponge to charge, so that the generator could provide power to our other life support technology. After a few long hours (during which Hunter Trip and Fall brought me a chair and more nourishing drink), the generator reached a full charge, 111 percent.[10] I withdrew, leaving four hundred power units still in the Sponge.

There was nowhere with privacy in the Compound, but especially not for me. We do not value privacy in our culture, as a general rule. My appreciation of privacy was always one of the many ways in which I am unusual among my people.

Over the next few days, I received reports, was fawned over, and generally did not get a moment's peace. I tried many times to get some space to myself by hiding in one of the smaller domicile partitions, or by walking faster from place to place. But that only seemed to encourage my people to search me out or follow me with more gusto. Always before, Penny could convince clingers-on to back off with a look or a snarl, but without her there, I was suffocating.

At the moment, four people stood around me, discussing

------

10   This is the top charge for all our devices because we like the symmetry and are very powerful.

proper soup consistency. I tried to channel my inner Penny, puffing up my chest. "Go away, so I can have a moment. Please."

That was far too polite to be Penny, but even the weak outburst still seemed to do the trick. The people following me bowed, blinking rapidly, and left. I assumed it would not last, but several minutes later, I was still being given a three-meter berth. Not quite enough, but it was better than nothing.

I breathed in and out, trying to revel in this new bubble of freedom, but not quite managing it. I decided to walk the walls of the Compound.

To avoid extra burden on you humans when we arrived, we'd agreed to build the Compound ourselves out of our own ship. To be more precise, we essentially dug a big hole in the ground and dropped the ship inside, and then UNOOSA built a few structures over top of it to mask what was underneath.

This meant that living on Earth was much like our years in space, as though nothing had changed. I found myself walking along the borders of the old ship, my hand running along the cold metal walls. I thought about the long nights[11] sitting in a small chamber with Penny while she sang Booshlaboo war songs simply to annoy me.

Even with the speed granted us by the power of the Sponge,[12] it was a long two years in space.

My face crumpled. "Penny! Oh why, why did you have to attack those officers!"

---

11 And by the way, it is *all* night. Because, like I said, space is a jerk.

12 Unfortunately, the ship was no longer functional after its crash to earth and after remodeling it into the Compound.

"What was that, Your Majesty?" asked Bell Smiles Brighter than the LifeStar, who I had not noticed was still close behind me fixing a UV light fixture.

I waved him away. "I am talking to myself."

"Yes, of course."

Even if my people do not understand privacy the same way as you, *openly* eavesdropping on conversations, even if they are with oneself, is still rude. Bell turned away and started humming.

I banged my fist on the dark metal wall, making a family[13] inside a nearby tent yelp. If Penny had only kept her temper, she would never have gotten herself in trouble before I could get her out. I needed her. Why could she not behave? After the first explosion, I had asked her specifically not to maim the police, had I not? Yet she'd still put an officer in critical condition.

No. Wait. I had not asked. I had *commanded*. My brain started tingling. I had *commanded*.

"Stone Major Thinker!" I called out. A few of the stragglers around me scrambled away, fetching him.

"Yes, Keeper?" He was suddenly there beside me.

I glared at the other people nearby, and they skittered away. "I have realized something," I said, "and I need to leave. Again."

Stone bowed. "So soon? You have only been back

---

13   There were sadly no children in this family, since most of our children were in stasis. Due to the lack of space, we had to wait for the death of an older citizen to bring a child among us, which had not happened for a few Earth-years.

seventeen turns.[14] I am so sorry to exert any opposition, but how will you leave the Compound? We no longer have a gravitator. And will you require more power units? If we are forced to have another charging session so soon, I don't know that your people will recover. At least, not quickly. We are still recuperating."

I flinched. "Do we not have something else besides a gravitator, something older that carries a battery of its own, that would not require any Royal Power Units? Something that would allow me to remove myself from the Compound without passing by the human peacekeeper guards?"

Stone lowered his thin eyebrows in thoughtful concern. "You could take the walkabout device. It can't go far, perhaps fifteen kilometers before it needs to cool down."

"How long does cooldown take?"

"2.9 light beats."[15]

I felt a sinking in my stomach. "Ah. That is long. Maybe I could use it to get out of the Compound, and afterward take human transportation. Do we have any American money left?"

"Of course. I will send a messenger to retrieve you some American dollars. Perhaps one of your protectors should leave with you?"

I shook my head. "No, no one else has left the Compound besides me and Penny. I am afraid it would only put them in danger."

"That is up to you, but please, Your Majesty, do not put

14　About five Earth-days.

15　Much like your hours, but slightly longer. So this is just over three of your hours.

yourself in danger either. Remember that the generator runs out in five more Earth-days whether you are here or not. And your people need and miss you."

"I will be careful." It was a lie. But I hoped that this was one of those royal lies he was talking about that might also be the truth.

[27] I'd commanded her. I'd *commanded* Penny not to kill or maim any police officers with a *Royal Command*.

Disobedience to a Royal Command was not a choice. Not because she did not want to disobey me, but because when I make a command, my subjects physically cannot disobey. It is a biological imperative as a subject of the Keeper of the Sacred Sponge.

I did not like to use the Royal Command for obvious reasons. It can have unintended consequences, but it also just seemed rude. And uncomfortable. And it only worked once or twice a year with any potency anyway. Since I used it (at least on purpose) so rarely, I sometimes forgot about it altogether.

The fact that I had commanded her not to do it meant Penny could not have maimed those officers. And if Penny had not hurt the police officers, maybe her death was also an exaggeration?[1]

Since my one-thing device did not have a facebender (and I was trying to avoid using power units anyway), Stone presented me with some sunglasses, a hoodie, a pair of jeans, and some boots, then gave me a wad of cash and taught me to use the walkabout ankle device.

As I was popping out of existence, Stone called out, "Oh, and I hear that using it feels—" but he was gone (or I was)

---

1   Like Mark Twain—only less literary and more angry.

before I could hear what it felt like, which did not matter because I knew what it felt like. I was feeling it.

It felt like landing in a *broganfly* prickly bush. That was on fire. After my body had been turned inside out.

I gasped, falling to my hands and knees, sure that I was dead. After a few minutes, the sensation finally started to fade. I found myself in the middle of nowhere, the Compound a dark clump visible on one of the nearby mountain peaks, nothing else around but snow.[2] Everything was dark and desolate, and I realized that while I had money, no civilization meant no human transportation, making my money temporarily useless.

I sighed. "Booger. This is going to take a while."

Luckily, our bodies are well suited to the cold, or standing in the Arctic autumn snow might have been uncomfortable. I started walking.

It took more than ten Earth-hours, several painful walk-about device trips, and the same number of only-slightly-less painful trudges through the snow before I got even close to civilization. By then, it was late afternoon. I decided to wait until night again to avoid the conspicuousness of my silver skin in public.

After another five hours waiting inside a children's slide in a park, then one bus ride and one taxi later, I got to Greg's

---

2   The location you gave us out of the generosity of your hearts was in the highest peaks of the Brooks mountains in Alaska, where it was frigid and treacherous all year round. I like it. Though it loses some of its charm below ground.

house[3] in Fairbanks at four in the morning. I could only hope Greg was there. Five or six days was enough time for him to have returned from Washington DC, right?

As I stood on the stoop in front of Greg's house, I felt a wave of panic. I was tempted to turn around back the way I'd come—despite all the trouble I'd gone to in order to get there—rather than face him.

But I had to know: had Greg lied about Penny's death? Even with his other lies, it still seemed out of character for him to lie about something like that. Or was he simply mistaken? It felt like I had transported *someone* from the holding cell in the police station to our safecondo. And that someone had felt like Penny. If not her, who?

I was fully and painfully aware by now that I was not competent at much. My only real purpose was to keep my people alive, and I could literally do that in my sleep. I'd been sheltered and trained and instructed, but most of that instruction had either been about a planet we no longer called home or about how to deal with humans in a way I was beginning to believe was completely wrong.

But I reminded myself that besides making lists, there was one more royal task I was good at: knowing who was the best, right, most competent person to advise me in any given situation. And right now, that was Greg.

I knocked and did not stop knocking until Greg opened up.

------

3   According to his information I found posted on your dark web with our computer-like research device in the compound. For some reason, the dark web was the only web we had access to. The dark web is now the only web to survive the end of your world. Is not that funny?

I could not tell if he was happy or surprised or angry to see me. His face was a perfect blank. My skin looked dark gray now instead of brown, but otherwise, my face was about the same as before. Did he recognize me beneath the glasses and in the shade of the hoodie? I swallowed. "Greg Jones. Hello."

"Aria . . . Seventh Daughter of Morr, Keeper of the Sacred Sponge, Heir to the Fallen Branches of Bough . . ."[4]

". . . Final Monarch of the Thirteenth Planet of LifeStar," I finished for him in a whisper.

"Ah, yes. I think you left the last part out, Queen Aria." His face was still blank, but his tone was as cold as the Brooks Mountains I'd just come from.

"We both left some things out. And this is not about us. I need to ask you something. Can I come in?"

"I'm not sure yet." He shifted from one foot to the other, and narrowed his eyes at me. It was an expression that did not suit him at all. "Are you responsible for the explosions? You said you weren't, but I just need to hear it again."

I stared at him. "Yes, I am," I whispered.

He closed his eyes, face pained. "People died. *Penny* died."

"I know. And I am sorry." I inched closer. "Please let me in. I swear to you, my part in the explosions was without my intention or knowledge."

He shifted his feet again, and I thought he might either

____

4   He learned the full title at last! Or maybe he always knew it and had just been joking? Humor is impossible for my translator. And as I have mentioned, Greg is not particularly funny.

let me in or shut the door in my face, but instead he asked, "Is this what you really look like?"

"What?" That was not what I had expected at all.

"You want my help? I want to know what you look like. Are you really a tentacled, bug-eyed alien?"

"Yes," I mumbled.

"So, this is a disguise."

"Sort of."

"Show me."

"Here?" I glanced down the walkway, looking at the surrounding homes. Nobody else was out at this hour, but I still felt indescribably exposed. "Can you not let me in first?"

"No." His expression was firm.

I closed my eyes so I would not have to see his reaction, then eased off my sunglasses, removed the hoodie, and shook out my silver tentacles. Silence. I chanced seeing his fear or revulsion and opened my eyes.

He cursed.

I hastily put my hood back up and my glasses back on, covering my large black eyes again. "Am I that disgusting to you?"

He shook his head. "Still beautiful," he grunted.

I flushed. "Greg, I am sorry for my lies, even the inadvertent ones. And maybe even more for my truths. I am sorry for my lies and my truths."

He sighed. "So am I, about mine, and yours. But that still doesn't change—"

"I know, and I would not be here, but I do need your help. Please let me in."

He gazed at me, weighing me with his eyes. "Okay, then.

But I have just one more question." The intensity in his expression lightened. "Do you want any flapjacks?"[5]

I smiled.[6] "I will have seven to start."

Even though he did not return my smile, he did swing the door wide to let me in. I removed my glasses and hood again once I got inside. There was no time for or point in hiding anymore. I glanced around his home, which was small, but cozy, with some exposed red brick and natural wood furniture. Exactly what I would have pictured for him.

"What's your question?" Greg asked as he whisked some ingredients together at the kitchen island, apparently deciding the flapjacks were more than a code for verifying identity.

"Is Bella all right?"

Greg frowned. "She's better. She's still in the hospital, but they tell me she'll be out soon. Was that the question you came to ask me?"

"No. But I am glad to know it." I sat down on a barstool across from him. "You said you learned about Penny's . . . body, but did you see her? I need the truth."

He was watching me carefully as he stirred. "No, I didn't see her, but it's the truth. Would I make that up? You think I would enjoy telling you your friend died? What kind of monster do you think I am?"

I nodded. "I do not think you are a monster. And . . . by the way, neither am I one. An alien yes—monster, no."

---

5   In case you do not remember, this was the code he suggested when he thought I was a spy.

6   Smiling is one of the only gestures we have in common. Though, I think it might have surprised him to see my sharp teeth.

He swallowed and looked back down at his pancake mix again. "I didn't say you were a monster, Aria. And I could never purposely hurt you, or anyone, in such a cruel way, to lie about a friend's death."

I gulped. "But if you did not see her with your own eyes, perhaps the body they found was someone else."

He frowned. "Maybe, but I don't think so. She was one of only five people who died. [Amnesty?] went over and ID'd the body himself. He was heartsick about it when he called me. I think he was starting to have real feelings for her. I'm so sorry, Aria."

That all sounded uncomfortably airtight. Just because she had not hurt any police officers, that did not mean she had not been moved from the holding cell for another reason. Which could mean she was truly gone, and I had come out here for nothing.

No. I had to know for sure. I was not going back until I was positive.

I pushed on. "Let us say, for the sake of argument, that she is *not* gone, that it was all a mistake. Let us say that I know it was a mistake because I moved her away from the jail before the explosion, using gravitator transportation technology."

He paused in his whisking, not looking at me, but then whisked faster. "Okay."

"But if so, I do not know where to find her. I do not have time for things like missing person reports and searching warehouses. You say that [Ampersand?][7] was the one who saw

------

7   I admit I am just scrambling now.

her and told you? I need to speak to him, perhaps he can give me specifics."

"I don't think he'll talk to you. He'll just send you right back again, maybe have you arrested. This, um, fancy alien transporter technology thing—if it worked, it took her from one place and plopped her down somewhere else? With what, the power of your mind?" I opened my mouth to respond, but he kept going. "What if she wasn't where you thought she was in the first place because they moved her? Would your transporter pick up someone else? Or nobody at all?" He put down his bowl.

"It could move someone else, or possibly just a clump of air. But I know I transported someone: I felt it. And I do not think she was moved from the holding cell. She could not have seriously hurt any police officers, at least not enough to put them in the hospital. So why would they move her?"

"How can you be sure she didn't hurt any police officers? We saw her resisting arrest, and I know she's stronger than she looks. You don't think she could hurt anyone?"

"Hurt, yes. But only in self-defense. And critical condition? I would consider that maiming. No, I do not think she could." I found myself flushing as I continued. "I have a royal gift. When I make a command, my people are physically bound to obey. And I ordered her not to hurt any police, so she *could not* have."

He sat down on a stool, his flapjacks forgotten. "We'll come back to that. Regardless, let's just assume you're right and focus on what you need. You need to find her. When she got out—when you mind-meld transported her out—where did you move her and where would she have gone after that?"

"I moved her to the condo, and she would not leave until I got there. She would have waited for me. Unless . . ." I gasped.

"Unless what?" He was looking at me intently now.

"Unless there was immediate danger nearby and she thought she might need to protect me. Like, say, an explosion at a police station." Of course she had not stayed at the hotel when she'd learned of the third explosion. She had gone to find me back at the police station. I closed my eyes. "But I was not at the police station explosion anymore. I went searching for Woods."

Greg frowned. "But *I* was still there—why wouldn't she have said something to me?"

"I do not think she would have left any info with you; you may be Greg, but you are also a human."

He smiled at this, a small, sad smile. "So would she have some way to contact you if she couldn't find you, then? Could she leave a note?"

"She could have left a message on the thingamabob,[8] but I had it. And—wait no! I left it there." I had left a note for Penny. If she ever went back to the condo, she would have found it. It had been days: certainly, she would either be there at the safecondo now, waiting for me as I instructed, or at least have left the thingamabob there with a response.

So all I needed was to go to the condo, find Penny, or find the thingamabob with a message from her on it. Even if I found the thingamabob empty of any messages, that was not

---

8   Actually, come to think of it, thingamajig might be a better translation. But maybe not. I will think on it some more.

necessarily bad news. And it would still be more information than I had now.

The only problem was the condo was in Washington DC. Washington DC was where Woods/Barry was being detained, and even if he did not have access to a lab or any devices, being near him still felt dangerous. Why had he allowed himself to be caught in the first place? I was sure he was too smart for that. Our very proximity was a risk, one I'd hoped to avoid.

I sighed and stood. "Okay, thank you, Greg. That was very helpful. I still have one more favor I need to ask of you, however."

"Wait, that's it? How are you going to find her?" He stood too.

"I left her a note in our condo. In DC. I need to retrieve it."

"Are you kidding? Is it even going to still be there? And how are you going to get there? We're in Alaska!"

I waved this objection away and walked to the door. "It will still be there. I need to get a flight." We had never flown when we went out on excursions because there was too much security, but this was an emergency.

Greg stepped in front of me, blocking my way to the door. "What favor do you need, then?"

I looked up at him and took a deep breath. "I know you said [Average?] will just arrest me or send me back, but we may need to contact him anyway."

He balked. "What for?"

I gently pushed Greg aside and opened the door. "Me being in the same city as Barry/Woods is dangerous." I went

down the steps, and Greg followed me. "I know he is in cus-
tody, but something about it does not feel right. And now that
I am going back, I am afraid I will be playing right into his
hands." Greg was walking beside me now, looking troubled.
I pushed on. "We have very limited time, I am sure, and if
Penny is not at the condo, I will need help to find her quickly.
I will need backup; [Auger?] is probably our best option. All
I ask is that you delay telling him I am headed to the condo
until I check for myself. You may also want to tell him that
Barry could still be a danger. I do not know how they would
stop him, but [Applejack?] might figure something out."

Greg followed me out the door. "If that's what you want.
But can I offer a suggestion?"

"What?"

"We should take the senator's private jet. It would be
more direct and also you wouldn't cause a worldwide panic,
looking like . . . that." He glanced over at me as we walked
down the sidewalk.

Oh, right. I put my hood back up. "But were you not fired?
How do you have access to the senator's transportation?"

"I still have a few days before that's official. They'll let
me take it if we ask right. Gwyn's still in DC."

I stopped walking, putting my hands on my hips while I
considered. Then I thought back to what he'd said. "Did you
say *we* should take the jet?"

Greg pulled out his phone, and pointed the other way.
"Yes, and the hangar is this direction. I'll try not to get in
your way, but if you think you're going without me, you're
kidding yourself."

[28]   Greg stayed on the phone with one person or another the whole way to the hangar and by the time we arrived, the plane was waiting for us. He'd wisely tried calling the condo managers in DC to ask them to check our room, but gave up when he could not ever get a real person on the phone. He also had not been able to get in touch with [Ammon?], but left a vague message telling him he was coming back to DC.

We boarded the jet, similar to the one I'd flown in from DC to Alaska, all white and sleek.

"I guess I'll just go look for [Armband?] when we arrive, check his lab," said Greg once we boarded and were seated in the small cabin. Greg was sitting across from me, looking pleasantly windblown, and I longed to move a stray strand of hair out of his eyes. He glanced down at his watch. "It'll be around noon when we get there, if we don't have to stop and refuel."

"Hopefully you find him quickly; we will have very little time once we arrive." I looked out the tiny window, watching the ground fall away as we took off.

"Because Woods could start exploding things again?" asked Greg.

I clasped my hands in front of me. "Maybe. How are you at math?"

He shook his head, confused. "Is this another test to see if I'm brain damaged? Because I swear, I'm fine."

"No, it is simply that I am very bad at math, and I need

some minor calculations so we can be efficient. Woods/Barry was stealing power units from me to power the explosions, and could potentially do so again if he learns I am nearby, since he must be in close proximity. Normally, he needs me to purposefully activate the power source before he can steal any power, but there is a chance that he has learned to siphon the units by force." I thought back to Stone's explanation. "If he does begin to steal power, I think I will know it, I will feel it, and I might be able to get away to stop it. But this will depend on how many power units he might need for another explosion. And how long it might take to siphon them off. Can you help me calculate this? I normally have Harold Royal Calculator to reason out such things for me."

Greg almost smiled but hid it. "So you want to calculate how much power he might need for another explosion, and the time it would take to get it, based on how many power units he stole for each of the past explosions?"

"Yes. If we can determine this, we would know how much time we have once we arrive in Washington DC before we are putting everyone in danger. My royal thinker said that around two hundred units of power were stolen while we were gone, presumably in three separate chunks to power the three previous explosions. The explosions were increasing in size, but I do not know by how much."

Greg rubbed his chin. "So it's like one of those 'two trains leaving a station' problems?"

"What would be the problem with two trains leaving a station? Is it a competition that one must win or be destroyed?"

"No—it's a math problem."

"Oh! So like the '*groober* plant and *chapper* plant are fighting for three units of blood,' that sort of thing?"[1]

Greg shook his head, a smile peeking out again. "Sure. Uh, so, let me think this through. If each explosion increased in size, I think we can assume Woods took more power for each one. How much time did it take him to siphon off the power for the other explosions? Did it take more time the bigger the explosion got?"

I sat up, considering the amount of time between when I had used the gravitator and when the explosions happened. "No, the time between when he started stealing power and the explosion itself got significantly shorter each time. The first took a full Earth-day, and the last only took one Earth-hour."

Greg leaned forward against his safety restraint and frowned. "So they were getting bigger, but taking *less* time. Which means his system was getting more efficient, maybe? How long did the second one take?"

"Maybe five hours."

He nodded and exhaled. "I think all we can do is find the pattern and assume that pattern will continue. We could probably figure out how many power units he used for each one, and how much more efficient each one is getting, but it might take more skill than I have, and I don't think we need

---

1   The groober plant and the chapper plant of one length unit each are fighting for three volume units of blood. The chapper has spores to fight the groober, but they only last for two minutes before the groober plant adapts. The groober plant grows by two units every three minutes. Which plant will win, and how many units will each plant win before the fight is over?

to anyway." He squinted down at his phone. "If the first took twenty-four hours to charge, the second took five hours, and the last took an hour, then—" he typed the numbers in, "we can assume another explosion would only take maybe twelve minutes." He gulped and looked up at me.

It was too short a time and we both knew it.

He put his phone away. "Will you know right away if he starts taking power?"

"I was told I would be in immediate pain if power is stolen. I only hope twelve minutes is enough time to stop it. Or that he never discovers I am nearby in the first place."

Greg pinched his lips between his teeth. "Are you sure we should be doing this? Maybe I should tell the pilot to turn back."

"It is a risk, but if Penny is alive, I cannot leave her out among you on her own, without any way home, soon to be without even her human disguise.[2] She needs me. And I need her." I cleared my throat. "Thank you—your reasoning skills are more than adequate. Do you need a new job? My Royal Calculator is getting very old."[3]

"I do need a job, actually. I just got fired. But what are the hours? And what's the pay? I don't come cheap, you know."

I thought he was probably being ironic by the ghost of a smile on his lips. So I played along, mirroring his light tone. "Well, you would only be needed when it came time to do a

---

2   Because, like I think I mentioned, it only lasts ten days unless it is turned off or renewed by the power source.

3   He just passed his 2510th birthday. In your years that would be about 145 years old.

census or check the power usage, replace missing toes and tentacles, that sort of thing. And also you might get people coffee and bring homemade donuts once in a while. But you would also be on call all minutes of the Earth-day to wait on Her Majesty's whims. Do you have any experience with that? Sometimes she needs someone to do calculations quickly as a matter of intergalactic security."

Greg leaned back in his gray leather seat, looking outside the little window. "And is the queen a pretty good boss?"

"Not at all. The life and welfare of her people are completely on her shoulders, so she is always shirking responsibilities, running off to experience Earth life, pretending to be a regular girl, and hoodwinking poor, nice, unsuspecting humans. You know the type."

Greg tipped his head. "Sounds like she has a lot of burdens on her back."

"Not really, though I am told she claims so. Actually, she runs because of her selfish nature."

"I can't say I blame her for wanting a night off, personally."

I sighed dramatically. "That is kind—misplaced, but kind. If you only understood what she has done . . ."

"And what has she done?" Greg was looking right at me now.

"Lied. A lot. To people who did not deserve it, people she cared about. She also put those people and more in serious danger, and allowed terrible things to happen because of her ignorance."

There was a long pause, then Greg sighed as dramatically as I had. "As far as jobs go, it doesn't sound too bad to me—nothing compared to what my last job was like, mind you. That was paradise."

"Yes, I understand there were quite a lot of sticky notes involved?"

"Ah yes. I will miss you, sticky notes!"

"Perhaps I will see if we could get at least one sticky note for you. If you decide to take the job, that is." I tried to keep my tone light and exaggerated, but a traitorous part of me wondered what it might be like. If I could hire him for real. If I could keep him.

"So I'm hired? Do you really think a queen would take on a big doofus like me?"

"Oh, yes. She loves big doofuses."[4]

"Listen, Aria," said Greg, leaning forward in his seat across from me and taking my hand.

I tensed. "Oh, Greg, I think you should rest now. Let us talk when we arrive in seven hours." I did not know what he'd been about to say, but he looked far too earnest. Which meant it was either an explanation of why we would never work, even as colleagues, or it was a plea to start something up, neither of which my heart could take right now. Realizing we only had a quarter of an hour to find Penny once we arrived, a quarter of an hour before I might cause more pain and destruction to so many people, left my nerves raw and ringing.

Greg frowned but did not drop my hand. "Okay, but can I ask one question?"

"Yes." I braced myself.

"Do you . . . do you miss it? Your home?"

---

4   I did not know what this was. But my statement was true. Accidentally.

This was not the question I expected, but as always, something about Greg made me want to tell the truth. "Sometimes," I said.

He nodded. "What was it like there?"

"It was . . . freer."

He tipped his head, still holding my hand. "So your, um, Compound here—I'm guessing the security is pretty tight."

"Yes. We are locked in a metal box, guarded outside by dozens of peacekeepers."

"Like a prison? That's awful. I'm so sorry."

I shrugged. "Not really a prison. As long as we follow the rules, they leave us alone. It has been eight years. We have made it our home, now."

"Still, a prison isn't a home, even if you surround yourself with things from Booshlaboo, a plant or two—"

"Are you crazy?! We did not bring any plants from Booshlaboo! Killer plants are why we had to leave our planet in the first place!" I said this in my exaggerated, playful, flirtatious voice, keeping things light, but it was one hundred percent true.

Greg smiled his half smile and turned to look out the window. After a while, he fell asleep, still holding my hand. I turned away from him, trying to admire the view outside, and not the one in the plane. Sometimes I succeeded.

We landed just outside of Washington DC. As we left the plane, I replaced my hood and sunglasses again, shielding my face and head as much as possible in the daylight.

Greg pulled out his phone. "I'll keep calling [Amadeus?], but if I can't get ahold of him, I'll go to his lab or maybe see if I can find someone else at the FBI to help me. Should we meet at the condo? I can tell the pilot to wait here for a while so we can take off right away if we need to. Are you okay? Do you think Woods has started charging up the thing?"

I shook my head. There was no pain, yet, so either he did not know I was nearby, or he did not know he could steal units without my activation. Hopefully both. We still had time. Greg called us two YouRides, and we only had to wait a minute before they arrived. I ducked down in the backseat, but the driver barely acknowledged me during the ride to the condo. Hopefully that meant the hood and sunglasses were working.

Penny and I had hidden an extra room key under a bush at the corner of the condo building, and I was relieved when I found it still there. I unlocked and ducked into the door, shut it behind me, and turned on the light.

"Hello, Aria," said a familiar voice.

And there was Penny, alive. She was no longer disguised as a human. She stared at me, her expression pinched. But she was not the one who had spoken.

Beside her stood [Aslan?].

[29]   I gasped. "Penny! You are alive!"

I took a step toward her. I wanted to run to her, but found my legs reluctant for some reason. *What is wrong with you?!* I berated my legs. *Penny is here, and she is alive.* Instead I just smiled at Penny—a smile she did not return.

"So, you found my note," I said.

"Yes, thank you," she said and then looked away. I turned to [Arsenal?], who smiled. The smile was sincere, but felt wrong, upside down somehow, so I frowned back.

I took another step forward. "Thank you for finding Penny. Thank you for your help. Are you going to arrest us now?" Was this why Penny was acting strangely, why everything felt off? But how did he get here so fast? Did Greg tell [Ackbar?] to come here even though I'd asked him to wait?

"No, you aren't under arrest," said [Armpit?], his voice smooth and low. "Good to see you. Why don't you have a seat?"

I looked at the desk chair beside me and felt a wild urge to turn around and run right back out the door. But no. Penny was here, Penny was alive, and I could not leave without her. I sat, my movements slow. If this was an ambush, all I had to do was reach out and grab Penny, and both of us could use the walkabout to escape here. He could not hurt us. He did not look like he wanted to, but everything felt off, dangerous.

Penny hovered behind him now, her eyes wide as moons as she glanced at me again.

Something was wrong with her. But she was alive.

[Abscess?] sat down across from me in another desk chair, leaning forward completely at ease, his forearms on his knees. As he sat, Penny walked around behind me, swiftly removed the walkabout device from my ankle and the one-thing device from around my neck, then returned to stand close behind [Aglet?]. I was too surprised to try and stop her.

"What did you do to Penny?" I asked.

[Aardvark?] tipped his head to the side—watching me like I was a *tellurodent* in a maze. "I would never do anything to hurt Penny," he said slowly. Deliberately.

He took Penny's hand over his shoulder. The expression on his face when he glanced back at her and her responding deference was enough that everything else fell into place in my mind with a giant *whoosh* and *thump*, like a drop off the highest Hento nose spine to the deadly canyon floor.

I groaned. "Oh, I am such a complete, stupid, stupid booger head!"

"Figured that out, have you?"

Of course. There were so many clues, it was almost like he was trying to get me to guess all along but had overestimated my intelligence.

Barry was not Woods. *[Axiom?]* was Woods.

I would never do anything to hurt Penny. He'd said it as Woods and then echoed it exactly as [AWOL?].

Also, [Agog?] was a scientist too; he'd somehow known I

was queen;[1] and he had made up a story about finding Penny dead when she clearly was not.

Woods had always known what to say and how to act to manipulate a situation to his advantage, to control those around him. It was one reason I hated him for Penny: someone so straightforward that she never hid a single feeling on her stormy face.

I also hated him for Penny because of what it did to her, the evidence of which was right in front of me. How could someone so strong and aggressive become so weak and submissive? What did this man do to her?

"You are Woods."[2] I tried to snarl it, but I was too much in shock, so it sounded like a whimper.

He smiled and shrugged.

I did not fully understand it. "But, Barry?"

Woods grinned. "I'm sorry to say he simply made a good scapegoat. He was in the right place at the right time—or wrong place, wrong time, perhaps. Something around the cheekbones looked a little bit like my old face, and his personality made him easy to suspect. He was so paranoid, always expecting to be arrested at any second, so he wasn't surprised when he thought you'd turned on him. He sincerely hated you for that. And now he's out of the way in a nice little cell,

---

1   As I think I mentioned, we'd always told you humans I was only a temporarily chosen representative, and as far as I knew, they continued to believe this.

2   And now you understand why I can never remember what his chosen name was. But I am ninety percent sure it was Ash, now. That is a type of wood, right?

forgotten. I believe he's quite happy there. My being in the human's FBI does have some perks."

I closed my eyes. Why was I so terrible at this? So terrible at everything? "I do not understand. So, are you truly [Ash?] too? The one that works at the FBI? That has known Greg for a year? Teaches cooking classes and is a chef? Or did you take the real man's identity somehow?"

Woods smiled at me good-naturedly. "Oh, it's just a human alias. I didn't steal another's identity, it's all me." He leaned forward, tapping me on the knee. I flinched. "We're actually very glad to see you, Keeper. After I went to all that trouble to convince you first to stay and then to leave and never come back—I still need you here after all. To think, all those years hearing our people talk in hushed tones about the 'Royal Power Units' no one but you could control, and no one but you able to use the Royal Everything Device. I thought it was all silly superstition and taboos. Even Penny believed she could activate the Everything Device to power my items without you. But you were holding out on us. Nothing works. How fascinating."

So he did not know he could steal the power without my activation. *Good.* I looked at Penny, wishing she would turn to me and deny her part in it.

Woods continued. "My whole plan nearly fell apart after I sent you away, you know. So you can imagine my relief when Greg messaged to say he was back and needed my help. Which meant you had returned too." He shook his head, smiling to himself. "I had foolishly assumed that if you didn't have any mysteries to solve, if Penny was gone, if you and Greg had a falling out, that you would have no reason to return. But you couldn't stay away, could you? I've never been more glad to be wrong."

I tried to stand up, but Woods put a hand on my shoulder, keeping me down in the chair.

I did not struggle: I was too devastated. "Oh Penny, how could you join Woods? How could you turn against our people?"

Penny shook her head desperately, opening her mouth to respond, but Woods spoke for her. "Penny would never turn against our people, never make a single move against Booshlaboo. It is *you* who have betrayed us, Keeper." His eyes were suddenly hard, and it was so reminiscent of the old Woods that I was surprised I had not realized his identity earlier.

I scoffed, tired of it all. "Is everything you say designed to confuse me, Woods Breaker of Worlds, or are you simply incapable of truth? I know I have been powering the explosions, and I take responsibility for that. But *you* are the one setting bombs. You hurt many people."

"Your definition of 'people' is much different than mine, I think. But let's not quarrel over semantics. And I'm not trying to confuse you. In fact, let me make you a deal." He leaned farther forward in his chair, too close for comfort now, and I leaned back away from him. He grinned. "You turn on the royal power, or show us how to activate it, and I will answer any question you like, as many questions as you want." He spread his arms wide, leaning away again. "I promise to tell you anything you want to know, and not one lie will fall from my lips. We're just sitting here—might as well get all those answers you crave."

My chest tightened. "What makes you think I want your answers? I do not care. Keep your answers to yourself."

"My mistake. I don't mind if we don't say a word. We can keep sitting here in silence for as long as you want—for weeks, if that is your wish. And not a single human would know. I've already talked to Greg. I told him you confirmed Penny's death, and that I sent you on your way back to Alaska again. So he won't be coming for you." He tipped his head and tapped his chin, squinting his eyes in mock contemplation. "Of course, *our* people would miss your absence. Especially when, without you there to recharge the life generator, they could no longer breathe. But that is your choice."

I pushed to stand up again, and Penny moved to block the door, not making eye contact with me.

Woods sighed. "Ah now, I don't want to have to tie you up, but believe me when I say, I can and will."

I looked back and forth between Penny and Woods. His human face and expression looked so unassuming, forgettable almost. But underneath, I glimpsed something bigger, the same dark powerful bioluminescence I remembered. Our scientists are all natural fighters, but he had always been a step above most of the rest besides Penny. I would not stand a chance.

I turned to Penny, pleading, "You could never do that to the innocents, to the youngthings back home that would suffer if I never returned. You are bluffing."

Woods's voice turned sharp. "Do you realize that some of those innocent youngthings don't even remember Boovashoo? They don't know Earth either. They have never, maybe *will* never, see the sky? Breathe fresh air? Taste. . . fruit,[3] from any planet?"

"And is that reason enough to let them suffocate now?"

His eyes and thin mouth hardened even more. "They're suffocating already. But what happens to them now—that is in your royal hands alone. This is my way out for them. My way to stop you from hurting them."

I was still watching Penny. She was looking away from me, but her breath was quick and tight now. He *was* bluffing. At the very least, that was what Penny believed, or she would not still be standing there.

"No," I said. "No."

Woods exhaled in a slow breath, watching me closely. "Interesting. Being out among the humans has given you gumption. I must say, I'm glad to see it. I always thought you were too passive for a queen. Tell you what, I'll give you one 'freebie,' as the humans say, because I'm feeling generous: you might not know that it takes time to build up enough power for my device. I need around three hundred units of power this time. It is a small amount, really. I've tried several other power sources over the years, but never found anything that was quite powerful enough—but for you, three hundred units should be easy. And I've perfected the siphoning, but it will still take about twenty minutes to charge."

"Three hundred power units all at once? But why? What could possibly be your motivation to make that big of an explosion? Especially now?"

---

3   It was not at all fair that he knew my weaknesses like this: youngthings and fruit.

My curiosity was leaking out, and I wished it had not when he smiled smugly and shook his head. "No. That is all you get. If you want to know why, I can tell you—I can even tell you where my item is, and how to keep it from exploding. But you must switch on the power, first. Then you will have twenty minutes to come up with a way to stop me. Seem fair?"

He always made everything seem too good, too logical. Perhaps this was part of why Penny had always been drawn in.

And why I never had: logic never held much draw for me.

I stuck out my tongue and blew a raspberry at him.[4] "I would have that and more if I *do not* activate the royal power."

He laughed. "That is true, but with far less information. It's up to you, Your Majesty. But without more information, you're likely to end up giving me what I need in ten days anyway. We all know that despite your previous recklessness, you could never hurt your people on purpose. Ten days is a long time of pointless discomfort for you if it will end in the same result."

I lowered my head, trying to get my angry breathing under control.

"Take as much time as you like to decide. Just um . . . keep it under ten days, hm?"

The casual way he said this made my ears itch. I turned my chair, not looking at either of them.

He was right. I did not have many choices. But ten days

---

4   This is one gesture we do exactly the same with the same meaning. I think it might be universal.

was a long time: the previous ten days—meeting Greg, investigating Woods, thinking I'd lost Penny—that had been a lifetime for me. Maybe by the end of these ten days, I would find a way to overpower Woods. Maybe by then Penny would come around. Maybe he would be so annoyed by my obstinance, he would just let me go. If this was a competition to see who was the most stubborn, I liked my chances. I clamped my mouth shut and shook my head, still facing away.

Woods sighed again. "You disappoint me." From the corner of my eye, I saw him take a step in my direction.

And that's when someone knocked on the door.

"Aria?" Greg's voice said from the other side. "You in there?"

[30] My throat clenched in fear. *No.* Greg was no match for Woods. Between Penny and Greg and me, maybe we could incapacitate Woods. *Maybe.* But without Penny? Never. Greg *could not* come in.

Woods turned and glared, his eyes dark, almost as black as they were when he still looked like one of us. Then he stood and charged toward the door.

I gasped. He was going to kill Greg, without a thought, like he would a *snoozefly* who was bothering him, before Greg ever even knew what was happening.

"No!" I yell-whispered, standing and running to the door, pushing Penny out of the way and blocking Woods's path. "No, please. Please do not hurt him." For a moment, his hand frozen on the bolt, he looked like he might kill me instead. When he did not, I swallowed, then continued. "He is your friend."

Woods scoffed. "He's a human." He still did not turn the lock.

"Yes, but . . ." I thought about the times they were together, about the cooking competitions, the playful banter. Even if Woods was that good an actor (and I knew he probably was), could anyone be that close to Greg and not love him? Never. "You have been among the humans for years; you have come to know them. Can you really not count a single one as a friend?" I slid my hand toward the lock. "Let *me* send him away. I will get rid of him. I can do it."

He finally looked me in the eye, his hand still on the silver deadbolt, his expression clearing. "Fine. Have it your way. You activate the royal power, and Greg lives. He is a decent human being. Might even be worth it."

I felt a spike of alarm when Greg knocked and spoke through the door again. "Aria, if you don't answer, I'm going to break in . . . I can hear you talking to someone in there." Woods glared at the door and then me, a dark smile gracing his lips, and started to turn the deadbolt.

"Yes," I whispered, my voice breaking. "Yes. I will do it." And before I could change my mind, I took a deep breath and activated the Sponge.

Woods looked down at a black watch–like device on his wrist, his face a smug mask. "Thank you, Your Majesty," he said in a low voice, bowing. Then he and Penny backed into a corner where Greg would not be able to see them unless he came into the room.

Greg knocked again. I swallowed a sob, taking deep breaths. What had I just done? I did my best to compose my face, and then I unlocked and opened the door a crack.

"Greg," I said. "Leave."

Greg's eyes were wide. "Are you okay? I heard voices. I got ahold of [Ash?], and he said you were on your way back to your Compound. But I don't know. I had a feeling . . . I just wanted to be sure. How did you get away? What's going on?"

"Do not worry about any of that. You must leave. *Now.*"

"But, just let me in for a minute?"

"No, Greg." I blocked the gap with my body. "I told you, you need to leave. When we made our deal, you said you were nothing if not obedient. And I am telling you to go. *Now go.*"

He narrowed his eyes and tried to scan the room over my head. Then he looked back at me, and gulped. "No."

"No?"

"No."

Oh so *now* he decided not to obey?[1] "But you said you would go when I asked!" It came out like a whine.

"Look, I just . . ." He leaned against the doorframe, "I know I already said sorry, and I am. You were right. You never lied, and I did. I'm sorry that I lied to you about [Ash?], Aria. And that I lied about some of the reasons I was helping you. I wasn't really cut out for spy work, obviously. And, I may have purposefully hindered the investigation once or twice—not because [Ash?] wanted me to, but because I didn't want it to end. I didn't want you to leave. And then when I found out the truth, I was upset you were an alien because I'd hoped that you and I might . . . well anyway, I don't even care anymore that you're not human, for some reason." He flushed and leaned closer. "What I really . . . what I wanted to ask you now is if you could ever, if we could ever . . ."

"No, Greg!" I yelled.

He froze but then tried to push his way into the room. "Can I just come in, please?"

"No!" I was going to have to commit to this, or he would be inside before I could stop him. And we were already running out of time. I took a deep breath. "Greg, I do not want you!"

He backed up in shock.

<hr>

1   Do not let his earlier activity fool you. He is not nearly as obedient as he seems.

"Look, you are very nice, and thank you for all your help, but you are only an average, boring, unimportant human, and I am the queen of Brooshaloo. We can never be." I flared my shiny sparkly bioluminescence, and it flowed out of me, making me look bright and silver and alien and regal and intimidating all at once. "Now be a good little human thing and go away." I felt the pain of these lies almost immediately, and I cringed.

For a moment Greg just stared at me. Then his shock turned to suspicion, his eyes and mouth pinched. He stepped closer.

It should have worked. That kind of thing always worked in your movies. He should have been hurt enough to walk away. Even *I* felt the pain of my words. But I'd never been able to lie to Greg, and there was no doubt everything coming out of my mouth was absolute *nellybooboo*. My breath constricted. The one time lies could save him, and I still could not do it.

I sighed, a quick, clipped breath. "*Mushla berry froobo cantabellnicker!*[2] Please, Greg. We cannot talk now. Just go to the FBI. Find Woods. He has started charging the bomb, and we do not have time. I felt it. Please, you go stop him, and I will do what I can from here. Then, if we are still alive afterwards, we can talk. If we are still alive, I will see you in thirty minutes." We would not be. But at least most of what I'd just said was the truth. And Greg would believe me and be far away when the bomb went off.

I shut the door in Greg's face, then leaned against the

---

2   Translated, this says, "Everything is a big stupid mess." It is a foul phrase in my language, but I did not bother censoring my language at this point.

cool metal, breathing in and out, waiting to see if he would knock again. He did not. I heard the steps as he walked away. Then I turned around and looked at Woods, who bowed again, looking amused. Penny was pacing.

Woods checked his wrist again. "Well done. I'm still not quite sure how you activated the power. It seems there are secrets about our royalty even we, your closest advisers, did not know."

I pointed at him. "You were never my closest adviser, Woods Breaker of Worlds!"[3]

He sat again and leaned back, crossing his legs. "Maybe not to you, but to the Crown."

"I *am* the Crown," I said furiously.

"My mistake," he said, smiling pleasantly in a way that made me want to have him executed again.

I found I preferred my anger over the devastation I had felt a few moments before, so I hung on to it. "Now," I growled, "you said you would answer my questions. Tell me where it is and how to turn it off."

Woods nodded, still smiling. "It's right here in this cooler."

He patted a big black cooler I had been too upset to notice under his chair. It had what looked like a complicated timer on the top by the latch, with a red light and a series of dials.

"And how do I deactivate it?" I clenched my jaw, trying to see a way to grab the whole thing out from under him.

"You can't."

---

3   For those of you dying to know what he did to warrant this title, too bad: I am not going to tell you here. Maybe I will tell you later.

I cried out in objection, but he held up a hand to ward me off. "But you *can* stop it from exploding," he continued. "Simply keep the cooler closed. I had the other three devices set to open on their own, but this one is so much larger; I didn't want to take any chances. So I plan to open it myself. Keeping it closed is a temporary solution for you, but there it is. I had no need to design a permanent method of stopping it."

A temporary solution seemed better than no solution at all. Perhaps I could take the whole thing back to the Compound? Surely my scientists and advisers would think of a permanent way to keep this from exploding before it killed anyone. The problem was, I could not think how to get the cooler away from Woods in the first place. Perhaps I could simply grab it and run . . . without either of them catching me?

I slumped down into the wooden chair across from him again to try to get a better view and think this through.

"No more questions for me?" he asked, his legs crossed, one foot bouncing.

Would more answers help? I was not sure, but the questions came anyway. "How do you look so different, so human? Your face . . . you have looked like this for seven years? Is it possible you have been stealing power from me for that long for the facebender, somehow?"

He laughed, in a fantastic mood now. "This is your question? Yes, I've been like this for seven years, but not with *our* technology. Humans have this technology as well."

"They do?"

"It's called plastic surgery. It does an even better job,

actually, since it changes everything drastically—my nose and face shape and eyes. I got it seven years ago. It was a gift from the humans. Along with my life after you had me killed."

I glanced at Penny. How long had she known he was alive? The few months after Woods was executed were terrible for her.[4] Had it all been an act?

Woods went on. "As soon as I died, the humans took it upon themselves to take me for their own purposes. They revived me somehow, did some tests and experiments, gave me plastic surgery, altered my physiology to better survive Earth's atmosphere, and conditioned me to be an agent for them. I went along with their conditioning since it got me out of the Compound and inserted into the FBI, with my cover as a chef." He seemed to be enjoying telling his story now, reminiscing. "I do love human food science, so similar to chemistry, and it gave me access to a lab. And my human abductors already had some of our technology—I don't know if it was stolen or if you gave it to them—but they didn't know how to use any of it. I managed to take a thingamabob and snatcher and facebender without their knowledge, and I became an agent for myself, too."

"Did you not steal a translator? Your English is perfect!"[5]

"English isn't all that difficult. You should give Swahili a try—now *there's* a language. Most Earth languages are

---

4   If you think she is grumpy now, you should have seen her then. She is
    the inspiration for the phrase translated as grumpety grumpface in my
    culture.

5   I know this should not have been important, but I guess I was a bit jealous.
    If I ever turned off my royal translator, any words I happened to remember
    in an Earth language would have been unrecognizable.

simple for the intelligent mind,[6] especially when I didn't have to waste time giving all my energy over to the *Keeper*. Did you know humans have to sleep every day, even though they aren't charging any royal power devices? I had a lot of extra time on my hands while the humans were sleeping."

Everything he said was meant to bait me and I knew it, but I felt only the urgency of stopping the explosion. I needed to keep him distracted answering questions and telling stories until I figured out a plan. "But I saw you, and you looked like yourself. Twice! I *talked* to you."

"Yes. That was fun. When I siphoned the power units at the gala, I reserved a few in order to change my appearance with the facebender at a moment's notice. I wanted you to know it was me, to keep you close by for a bit while I performed a few more tests. It's been so long since I was my true self that I don't know if I got my face right. How was it?"

I scowled. "And how did you know I would be here in DC? And would stay after that first night?"

"Your Royal Everything Device has a very unique frequency, and I created a tracker." He dipped his head in false modesty. "When I saw you were coming here to Washington DC, I decided to take advantage of your proximity. I didn't know you would be drawn in by a human and want to stay, of course. That was just luck. It certainly sped up my timeline. One more reason to be indebted to Greg, I suppose. Isn't that funny how things work out?" He put his hands behind his

----

6   Yes, I recognize this as a dig against my own intelligence. I did not notice at the time, but let us not talk about that.

head in a relaxed gesture, and my eyes bounced over to Penny. She looked miserable.

"How long?" I asked her simply.

She shook her head and stepped forward, her eyes pleading. "He came to me when you gravitated me out of jail. He explained everything, told me who he was. I swear I didn't know before that. But I understand everything now. He didn't mean to hurt anyone seven years ago. He still doesn't. Truthfully, Aria. He wouldn't do that."

Penny's expression made my heart ache. I had grave doubts about what Woods would or would not do, considering what he'd threatened to do already. I glared at him. "Oh, *really*."

He considered for a moment. "While I may not be as protective of humans as I am of our people, Penny knows me better than anyone. I didn't mean to hurt the humans, believe me. You might have noticed that while I had to use the locations where you had recently activated the gravitator, I didn't set anything off until those areas were virtually empty of humans. And while the explosions were grand and flashy, they didn't do much damage. Only one person was killed in that first explosion. Who knows if it was even from my device? He could have tripped while walking down a nearby street."[7]

I scoffed. "But the third one, the police station, was

---

7   I am sorry to say that this is what he thought of humanity, even after living so long among you. But he also thought I was an idiot as well, which is untrue, so maybe it is untrue about you as well. I do not actually know you, so I cannot judge.

destroyed. Dozens of humans were put into the hospital. Greg said five died."

He frowned, as if puzzling it out. "The last one was a bit grander than I expected. I was still working out the kinks. It was the purpose of the tests, after all: to get the bugs and kinks out."

"You keep saying tests. Tests for what? I thought you were just trying to break the Accord to get us evicted? What is it you are trying to do?!"

"Ah, and now we get to the important question, the one you should have asked right away." He leaned forward. "I'm trying to finish what I started so many years ago, before we even landed on this Earth. I am following your *Royal Command* to terraform the planet."

[31] I will admit, invasion and terraforming had been our plan before the Arrival on Earth. Do not act too surprised, it is what you expected of us all along. Your planet is (was) great as is (was), of course, but not ideal for us. Your incompatible atmosphere required us to consistently use up power units to create air more conducive to our health.

But Royal Command? Had I *commanded* Woods to terraform Earth? He had been the lead adviser on the re-airing project. And I had been so young, so unacquainted with the power of the Sacred Sponge. But if I had commanded[1] him . . .

It explained more things than I was eager to admit. It explained his compulsion to make it happen, the reason why, even after our Arrival on the planet and after we'd rejected the terraforming idea (when we discovered it would kill too many of you humans), he'd still moved forward with his part of it, resulting in dangerous and treasonous experiments seven

---

1 Some of you smarty pants/skirts/kilts have already thought of some solution here that I did not at the time. Something that would have solved everything, perhaps? For this I commend you. Even now, I cannot think of the right solution, but if you have, feel free to send me a message detailing it. I may never get your message, and it will not do either of us any good, now, but it might make you feel better. However, in case your solution involves using the Royal Command, such as, "Well then command him again! Command him to stop, or Penny to stop him!" I cannot. Remember that it works only a few times a year anyway. But also, you should know that Royal Commands have a built-in and airtight, "no take backs" rule which allows for absolutely no runarounds or loopholes on fixing a previous command. One more reason I do not like to use my Royal Commands in the first place.

years ago that ultimately led to the accident[2] and his own execution. Had I caused all of that through my own ignorance? And every explosion since? I squeezed my eyes shut.

"But . . ." I said aloud in a whisper.

"Don't take it too hard, Your Majesty. I would continue with this directive even if I was not biologically forced. And we don't even need to do a full terraform, just change the air to be more like Booshlaboo so our people can breathe. Can't you see, if you leave our people in the Compound, you are slowly killing them?"

I opened my eyes and shook my head vigorously. "Full terraform or not, your air explosion would surely kill humans. And it is not so dire as you suggest for us. My scientists tell me we still have time. Yes, our people are tired, and the energy they give has become weaker. But we likely will not completely run out of energy for another hundred years."

"What is a hundred years in the life of our people? Our young stay in stasis because we lack space. Our people are losing their sparkle, dulling from silver to gray while underground. We must get out of there. We mustn't put the humans' lives above our own any longer. We *must* survive."

---

2   I do not really want to talk about it. And also, it is none of your business. And I do not want to talk about it. Now you are making me repeat myself. But since I know you cannot hold back your irritation and such irritation will make you unable to read further, I will simply say it involved an experiment with a two dimension pocket world in which 300 pocket people and also three of our own people died. It also broke the pocket planet like a dinner plate. It was not the first pocket planet he'd destroyed (the first was one dimensional), but he apologized so profusely the first time, all he got was a slap on the proverbial wrist. Feel any better? I did not think so.

I scoffed but my heart was not in it. "So, you *do* want to hurt the humans."

"It isn't about hurting anyone, it's about helping us all." He stood up, his eyes dark holes. "But yes, if I have to choose, I choose us. I don't know when you gave up on your people, Your Majesty, but if we don't save our people, nobody will. It's us, or them."

The phrasing was something he'd taken from the humans, I suspected, but "us or them" were almost the same words he'd yelled when they took him away to be executed seven years before. At the time, I had only wondered about it for a few minutes before moving on to other matters. But now I let my mind wallow in the thought, my palms over my eyes.

I was little more than a youth when we arrived on Earth, so I did not understand the nuances of an invasion. There was much of your planet that was unlivable for you, and we assumed that terraforming would only affect those parts you did not want or need. When we chose to discard the whole project, I had intended to continue researching, to find a solution that would work for us all. We knew our current conditions were not sustainable, but we grew complacent.[3]

I opened my eyes and looked at Penny, but Penny was not looking at either of us anymore, hanging her head to one side and staring off at nothing. I knew she had been thinking all of these same things about saving our people, but after Woods's execution, she'd stopped saying them out loud, using

---

3   We also had to give away any technology we did not hide from you, so perhaps we would not have made much progress anyway.

her energy instead to keep me out of trouble. Or maybe she still said these things, and I'd stopped listening.

I looked back at Woods. "You are right."

"Yes?" He narrowed his eyes.

"You are right, about every bit of it. I was tired of the responsibilities of the Crown, of all of the pressure and decisions. Instead of trying to find a different solution, I let our people continually give and use up their power simply to keep us alive, all while I went on jaunts around the planet without any thought to the cost. You are right about me. This is my fault. And now it is time for me to take responsibility."

I jumped at him, reaching toward the device on his wrist, and got my fingers around it.

He moved almost quicker than I could track, crushing my wrist and fingers in his fist. I cried out, and he shoved me down into the chair, tying me to it with some rope he produced from a desk, his otherwise smooth hair hanging in his face as he wrapped more rope around me. I sat helpless, gasping and unable to fight back, my left hand on fire.

Penny paced behind him again, pulling at her tentacles. "Woods, you promised." There was a hitch in her voice.

"I know, I know." He turned back to me. "Was that really the plan you came up with, Your Majesty? Use brute force to get my snatcher away from me? You could never beat me that way: I'm a scientist!"

Perhaps I should have tried other plans first, but my mind was a blank now. The pain in my hand flared and I whimpered.

Woods stood, glancing back at Penny and then at me

again. "Well, I did tell you I could and would tie you up. You forced my hand, and I always keep my commitments."

I tried to swallow the sob threatening to break the surface, but some of it came out. His words were another jab at me, just as sharp and painful as the throbbing in my hand. But he was right. He did keep his commitments. And he did as commanded. Everything he'd said since I arrived was true, and much of what he'd said before.

"I wanted to keep my commitments too," I whispered, gasping. "I wanted to be better. But I failed. Just as I always do. I am so, so sorry. For all of this." I hung my head. My sentiments were real. But it was too little, and it was too late.

Neither Penny nor Woods responded. They did not need to. Our people were dying, smothered by a home too small and deep underground, by a hundred thousand Accord stipulations that kept them there, and by a queen too selfish to do anything about it. And now, judging by the damage done by the last bomb and how many units he was using to power this one, not only would the explosion wipe out any breathable air for the humans, it would likely destroy Washington DC and blow a crater right here in the Earth. And I just sat there, tied up, unable to stop the destruction even if I'd wanted to.

Did I want to?

Perhaps it was better this way. I never could have allowed a course of action that would kill humans, so perhaps going over my head was the only option: the only way to save us. Did I not want to save us? Even if it meant killing humans? Could I really continue to poison my people, dulling their vibrancy to gray, leaving the youngthings in stasis? What kind of queen was I to do such a thing?

So what was it to be? Us or them?

"Us *and* them." I found myself saying aloud, my voice barely a breath.

"What?" asked Woods.

I looked up. "If it is between us or them, I choose them. *And* us." My voice was stronger now.

He scoffed and sat down. "And if you must choose between the two?"

I shook my head. "I will not let my people become murderers, Woods. I have already let *you*, perhaps even *forced* you, to become a murderer through my own ignorance and complacency. That is unacceptable, as your queen." Despite the desperation of the moment, or maybe even because of it, I felt my confidence growing. Not confidence that everything would turn out as I hoped, because it probably would not. Confidence that I was right. "I will not let my people wage war against the 'general population, ignorant to our presence.' Not against the people that keep us and feed us and clothe us, even as they oppress us. We are not murderers. We are not oppressors. We will find another way."

He looked at me for a while, head tipped, and sighed. "And if there isn't another way?"

"Then in a hundred years, we die as peaceful a people as when we left Boovashoo."

He nodded and stood up, all business now. "Penny, gag her, won't you? I'm tired of the games and the questions. Sorry Aria, but this is too important. I know I said you could ask anything, but I grow weary, and time grows short."

Penny turned and stepped over to me, her head still hanging. I'd had plenty of words for Woods, for all the good it had done, but none for Penny. Penny was my friend. *My only* friend. I had no words for her. And I could not fight her, even if I was not tied up. Even if I wanted to. And I *did not* want to.

Penny reached behind me and undid the ropes binding me. I looked up in surprise.

"What did you do?" barked Woods.

She shook out the rope and dropped it to the floor. "I won't gag Aria, Woods." She stood beside me, her hand clenched white on the chair. "She's right. Aria, our queen, is right. I let myself be convinced by what you said, and I still believe you are right too, but this is not the way. It was not the way seven years ago, and it is still not the way now."

"You're choosing *them* too?" His voice was acid.

She breathed out. "I'm not choosing them, I'm choosing *us*, and I know this isn't the way. You have to see that."

"Do I?" he spat, and struck her across the face with the back of his hand.

I'd never seen anyone even come in range of striking Penny before, and the few people who got close suffered for it. Penny can destroy people with little more than a glance their way.

Now, she crumpled to the floor, out cold.

[32] "I guess I will save our people on my own," Woods said, slicking his human hair back with one hand, looking shaken. He busied himself with the cooler, twisting dials and checking his snatcher every few seconds.

"You hurt Penny," I said, my voice quiet. I was untied, but no less helpless with Penny lying beside me on the floor. "You said you would never do that. Thrice."

He looked down at Penny, and the bright blue mark where he had slapped her stood out neon against her silver skin.

He looked regretful for the first time. "So I did. I didn't intend to hurt her. I do care for her." He looked back at his dials with a snap. "But she is alive, and she and you will continue to live as long as you cooperate. My device will only take a few more minutes to charge up, and the three of us can gravitate back to the Compound in Alaska before it goes off. We will be safe there until everything settles."

My hand he'd smashed was starting to throb with sharp stabs of pain. "But, once you kill the humans, I could never allow you to live among us again."

He waved this away. "I am so completely changed, I don't know that I could live among you regardless. So be it."

Then, he was willing to stay here, die here among the humans. He'd been willing to die for our people all along. The truth of that was clear on his face. It was commendable. More than I'd been willing to do.

If only I could reason with him.

"Help me move Penny up onto the bed," I insisted, and he nodded, strangely docile now, his energy spent. There was not much time left: the twenty minutes his device needed to charge were almost up, along with any options I might have had to stop him, and we both knew it.

We moved Penny to lie on the bed and I sat next to her, stroking her cheek, confirming she was still breathing. "I have always been so impressed by your intellect, Woods. It is too bad we could not have worked together for the last seven years on a solution that would satisfy us all."

"Yes. If only you hadn't killed me," he said, putting the big black cooler onto his lap and sitting on the bed on the other side of Penny.

"You are right. I should not have ruled for your execution, I should have talked to you then as I am now. I did not know what I had done."

He did not respond, watching me stroke Penny's cheek.

"Please, Woods, will you not reconsider using your brilliance to help us find a better solution? Our people are suffering, yes, but I think we can work *with* the humans. I believe, with your help, we still have time. As you mention often, I am not scientifically minded, but you are. And you even have an in with the humans, with their FBI. Can you not foresee anything that could change the conditions, create an aboveground complex that could be expanded, with breathable air, that would not destroy our host planet?"

He remained expressionless, fiddling with the latch on the cooler, his eyes on Penny's prostrate form.

"Would you not consider waiting? Your obedience to my Royal Command is fulfilled. You could come to the Compound with me, discuss this with the rest of our brilliant minds. You could come home. You would be adviser to the Crown again, no longer Breaker of Worlds, but Builder of Worlds once more."

His face was relaxing. I held my breath as he slowly took his hand off the cooler's latch. He glanced up at me, his expression uncertain.

The doorknob to the room rattled, and then with a bang, the door swung open.

Greg burst into the room, then froze, looking at me, at Woods who looked like [Ash?], at Penny unconscious in a lump on the bed. Then back at me. Woods and I froze too.

"Uh. . . basket of dragon fruit?"[1] I said.

---

1   This is the other code phrase Greg came up with when he thought I was a spy. To signify trouble. The code word we should have chosen for trouble is "Greg," but I suppose that would have been confusing when I needed to address him.

[33] The light on the cooler flashed.

Charging was complete.

Woods' eyes snapped to mine, his expression fire, the temporary spell broken. "Don't feel too bad, Your Majesty," he said in English. "It was a good attempt, but it never would have worked." And then he hit the latch with a *bam*.

A gunmetal-colored ball the size of a cantaloupe floated into the air.

Immediately the kishwellium began to sublime with the metallic smell of ozone, gigantic bubbles blooming out of it in waves.

I looked at Greg. This was it. Would there be enough time to tell him what he really meant to me? To say sorry? To say goodbye?

I reached out to him, but then ran to the ball, unhinged my jaw, and swallowed the thing down whole.[1]

---

1   By the way, despite its comparable size, this did not taste like a cantaloupe.

[34]   Woods cried out and lunged at me as the explosive settled down into my abdomen, but Greg tackled him to the ground.

"[Ash?], what are you doing?" Greg yelled.

"I'm arresting her! Get off, Greg!" He pushed Greg off him and jumped to his feet, twisting Greg's arm behind his back. "Are you really ready to go to jail for some alien girl?"

"No," I squeaked in English, surprised my voice still worked. "Woods, do not hurt him!"

Greg's eyes widened, and at that moment Penny awoke. With a war cry, she kicked Greg behind the knee, pulling him out of Woods's grasp and forcing him to the floor.

"Penny!" I cried, but then she tugged Woods around into a headlock.

"What are—" Woods started, followed by a stream of choked off Booshy curse words. I watched as Penny shoved Woods into a chair. She was back to her fierce self, but the pain in her eyes when she looked up at me was clear.

"I am so sorry, Your Majesty," she mouthed as she tied Woods down.

I nodded at her, my arms around my middle.

My swallowing the device was only a temporary fix, I could tell that almost immediately. It had settled down into place at the center of the Sacred Sponge, and the Sponge was absorbing the energy.

But something was wrong. The power felt like poison inside me. I could feel the Sponge expanding, the power of the bomb inside of me twisting and growing.[1]

"Penny! Where is the Royal Everything Device?" I cried. She frowned, confused, but pulled the device from her pocket and handed it to me.

I clicked it into place around my neck. A quick glance at the gauge readings confirmed that the *thing* was growing, the force of the explosive multiplying with each second. I'd just made everything much, much worse.

I did the only thing I could think to do. My people still needed me, but I had to eject this thing somewhere it could not hurt anyone. If I was quick enough, I could just gravitate right back here again. It was a risk, but I did not have time to deliberate. I activated the Sacred Sponge, closed my eyes, took a deep breath and held it, and then gravitated myself out. Out of the room, out of the country, out of the atmosphere.

Or I *tried* to gravitate away. Instead, nothing happened at all. I opened my eyes to see them all watching me: Penny perched over Woods, Greg sitting on the floor. I was still in the condo.

I tried again. I activated the Sponge, and then with as much purpose as I could muster, directed the power units into the gravitator. I willed myself up and away. For a moment, I felt like it had worked—but like a snap of a rubber band, I was

---

1   Even though I never learned much about how the Sacred Sponge worked, I had been its keeper for the last ten years. I had become as aware of it as if it were a body-part, like a limb or a nostril.

back again, stumbling to the floor in the condo two meters away from where I'd started.

Woods threw his head back and started laughing.

"What did you do?!" I pointed a finger at him, climbing to my feet.

His laughter died down to a chuckle. "*Planetary Gravitational Field Lock.* Easy feature to add, so all my devices have it built in. Now, it appears, so do you." He chuckled. "You won't be able to leave Earth's atmosphere as long as my device is inside you, Your Majesty, no matter how hard you try."

I glared at him as he started laughing again.

"Aria . . ." started Penny, obviously worried about what I might do.

"Take Woods back to the Compound for processing," I told her through gritted teeth.

She grabbed Woods by the arm, her jaw clenched, and I reached out and gravitated her away. Greg stood up, his eyes glued to the spot where Penny and Woods had just disappeared.

I was stuck here. On Earth, with a growing bomb inside me. And eventually, it *would* blow. I could feel it. More than just poisoning the air and leaving a crater, I suspected the Sponge itself was turning into a super-amplified version of Woods's bomb, able to destroy everything.

I had *definitely* made things worse.

Time was short.[2] And I was about to give birth to a planet killer.

____

2   Time is *always* short. And annoying. And sticky. Like a child.

"What do you want? You're fired, Greg. Go home." Senator Gwyn Kilcher stood at the door to her apartment in DC, tapping her foot.

Stepping around Greg, I lowered my hood and removed my sunglasses, revealing myself in all my tentacled, silver-skinned, black-eyed glory. Unlike at the masquerade, there would be no bowing, cowering, or letting Greg take the lead talking to the senator this time.

"Hello Gwyn, so nice to see you again. I am Aria, Seventh Daughter of Morr, Keeper of the Sacred Sponge, Heir to the Fallen Branches of Bough, Final Monarch of the Thirteenth Planet of LifeStar. I have swallowed a gigantic planet-killing bomb. Any chance we can come in?"

She looked me up and down, a look of resignation on her face. "Sure."

Greg closed the door behind us, and the senator offered us a seat as if we were regular guests.

"You're the girl from the masquerade, aren't you?" she asked. I nodded and she sighed. "Would you like anything to drink, or should we get right back to the threats, *Your Majesty?*"

"The bomb is not just a threat. Not from me, that is. But it is real. We have a matter of hours before I must let this thing out or it will kill me and most of the planet." I took a deep breath. "You said you are paid by the UN. Any chance by UN you meant UNOOSA?"

"Yes, actually." She perched gracefully in her chair, but she was leaning forward, rolling her hair into a tight bun, no nonsense.

"Good. We need government help, but we do not have time for leaders to sit around and debate. If any humans are to survive, then we need to mobilize now . . . Sorry," I added.

She stood. "And what, Honored Keeper, about *your* people?"

"Well, they are probably in danger from the blast too—and even if not, they can no longer stay where they are." I had a flash of belated surprise. "Did you say 'Honored Keeper'? How do you know to call me this?"

She cursed. "That just slipped out. I suppose there's no point in being coy now, anyway. I'm actually the newest member of the UNOOSA committee in charge of the Booshlaboo refugees. And I apologize, but our linguists figured out your language years ago, and we have been observing you ever since."

I flushed. "So, they know I have been leaving the Compound. Why did not the peacekeepers ever stop me from leaving?" I could not help asking though I knew we did not have time. My entire torso was starting to sting, even with the Sacred Sponge taking the brunt of the abuse from the explosive.

"Yes, they did know about your annual breakouts, but you were doing such mundane things—going swing dancing, to soccer games, kindergarten graduations—so we decided it was just research and to leave you to it. After all, we were researching you as well, so it seemed fair. We didn't know you had a human boyfriend."

"Oh, no, we are not . . ." I looked at Greg and instead of objecting, he smiled at me. I gulped in response and then started coughing.

Greg's expression was much like the first time we met. Mischievous and smoldering. But unlike the first time, there was depth to his expression. Sadness.

"Greg—" I started when my coughing was under control.

Gwyn waved her hands between us, cutting me off. "Look, whatever this is, I don't actually care. Tell me about the bomb and what you need from me."

I spent a few minutes summarizing Woods's role, *my* role, in the recent explosions, explaining his motivations and what the bomb would likely do once I ejected it, i.e. suffocate everyone and blow everything to bits.

I looked down at my Everything Device. It was difficult to predict exactly how much time we had, but based on the readings and the rate at which the power units in the Sponge were climbing, Greg and I had calculated a rough estimate. "I do not think we have more than ninety-six Earth-hours before this bomb explodes, and your planet breaks." We would need every second of that time, but the longer I waited to eject the Sponge and the bomb, the bigger the resulting explosion would be. Was I dooming the entire planet Earth by waiting? I swallowed, but said none of this.

Gwyn nodded, pursing her lips. "Four days is nowhere near enough time to involve UNOOSA, even if we had a solid plan. They would have to take it to the entire UN. That would eat into time we don't have."

"Well then," I took a deep breath and grasped my hands

together, wincing at the pain where Woods had crushed my finger. "I think it is time for plan B."

"Plan B?" asked Gwyn.

"Yes. Or C? Z. Whichever letter means I just came up with it but it is our last hope. Firstly, I need to contact my people for some technology. Then I will need access to some of your visual recording equipment and satellites."

It was a good plan, and with minimal argument from Greg and some key input from the senator, I made a list and then we put everything into motion.

Step one: it was time to invade for real.

[35]   In our first Arrival eight years before, we'd made ourselves look like you expected us to look: bug-eyed, hairless, and green. We kept our best technology hidden, and only contacted a few humans, letting them take control.

This time around, for a true invasion, I presented myself as I am.

I always expected my differences to disgust you, frighten you. But your reaction was closer to awe. I looked like a glowing silvery angel,[1] displayed immediate superior technology, and I spoke in every language to every screen, on every personal and trusted communication device in the world, simultaneously.

Eight years before, my researchers had said this type of invasion would never work, but it turns out we were wrong about a lot of things back then. After all your looting and screaming in the streets, our more-aggressive invasion went off perfectly. This time around, instead of being looked down on as refugees by the humans, we were revered as deliverers.

On every screen in the world, I told you that an enemy alien force had planted a giant explosive device on your planet. I recommended that all eight billion of you evacuate to

---

1   One of your angels, that is. Our angels are burn red and black black, with seven sharp spikes coming out of their chins.

your nearest capital city, and that authorities would be there to direct you once you arrived.

Some of that was a lie. And I am very sorry for that. Our plan was good, but only half-formed, at this point, and there'd been no time to develop it further before evacuation began.

Almost two Earth-days later, Gwyn, Greg and I sat in a large room inside the White House, with a few other aides and what remained of the UN[2] arguing with each other at a table nearby. They had already mobilized the peacekeepers to assist in the evacuation, and everything was in motion.

For all the good it would do.

Step two of our plan, the part that would actually save you, the very reason we'd sent you to your capital cities in the first place, had hit a series of roadblocks. Without step two, all this effort was just busy work to keep you occupied and unaware of your impending doom.

Step two was Gwyn's idea, originally. You see, even though Woods had never known in all his years at the FBI what UNOOSA was doing with the kishwellium or why they had been transporting it all over the world in those black refrigeration trucks, Gwyn *did*, and now so did Greg and I.

From the day of our Arrival eight years before, UNOOSA had been working on a contingency evacuation plan of their own. After a few years of secret observation and testing, they'd finally learned to combine kishwellium with copper

---

2   Most of them were now too busy mobilizing themselves into secret government bunkers.

and recreate the gravitator circuit. And ever since then, they'd been using that kishwellium to build rudimentary gravitators all over the world, in the capitals of every state and country.

So, all we had to do was utilize the human evacuation plan already in place: gravitate everyone to where the bomb could not reach them. Except that UNOOSA had yet to build the orbiting ships in space to evacuate onto. And also, even if there *were* somewhere to go, there was the teeny tiny little problem that the humans had no way to power the gravitators in the first place.

Harold Royal Calculator and a human scientist named Max were currently presenting their plan for step three (ejecting the Sponge-encased bomb), but it was not going well, I thought.

"So, we've found a place to eject the bomb," said Max as he held up an intricate world map. "It's right in the middle of the South Pacific Ocean: the oceanic pole of inaccessibility. It's called Point Nemo. For almost a hundred years, global space programs have been crashing satellites and retired craft, even entire *space stations* right into Point Nemo when their orbits start to decay. This is because it's the farthest possible point from land and has virtually no plant or animal life, so there is very little impact. It's literally been nicknamed the spacecraft cemetery. If we can send the bomb deep enough in the ocean at Point Nemo, it should create the smallest amount of damage."

Harold Royal Calculator used his portable translator to whisper something in Max's ear, and Max nodded, continuing. "Of course, since we don't know exactly what the bomb is constructed of, we can't say any of this with any certainty.[3] Nuclear material, for instance, has serious repercussions if exploded in salt water, but we are assuming this device isn't radioactive. Is it?"

"Not that I know of," I said, trying to ignore the stab of pain in my chest that punctuated this. My people's technology had already healed the pain in my hand from where Woods had crushed it, but the technology could do nothing for the pain inside of me.

Max smoothed his lab coat, nodding. "Then based on our calculations, this is our best bet. It should allow a small section of land to remain safe and livable."

"And where will this small section of livable land be?" asked Gwyn sternly, leaning forward in her gray leather seat.

The two whispered to each other again, even though they clearly knew the answer.

Max cleared his throat. "Kazakhstan."

Gwyn laughed. "Are you truly suggesting we evacuate the entire human race, eight billion people, to *Kazakhstan*?"

Harold stepped forward, pointing at the map. "There may also be a sliver of livable land nearby in Russia, China, and Mongolia."

Gwyn scoffed. "Great."

I spoke up. "Harold, Max, you must see that this could never work. The space and resources are not the only issue; we are having enough trouble evacuating the humans the

---

3   They'd asked Woods for this information, but considering he was facing execution again, he was not forthcoming.

small distance to their capitals. There is simply not have the time to move everyone to Asia."

Max looked down. "We aren't proposing we send *every-one*." He gulped. "Just governments, and other select persons who it is in the human race's best interest should survive."

Gwyn, Greg, and I stared at the pair of scientists in shock.

Gwyn swore. "You mean the rich and powerful." She stood up. "If you have to choose such a small part of the Earth, such a small amount of people to survive, why not choose the United States? DC? Why not just save all the rich white men?" Her expression was angrier than I'd ever seen her.

Harold, not understanding Gwyn's tone, shook his head. "That was never an option. If we put down the bomb any-where closer to land, or *Clap* forbid, *on* land, I do not believe any of your planet's people would survive at all." He blinked a few times and stepped back.

Gwyn sat back down, her movements slow and deliberate. "Even those in bunkers underground?"

Harold and Max squinted at each other, then back at her. "We do not know. Perhaps," said Max.

We let this devastating information sink in.

Finally, Gwyn nodded, "Thank you. That's all for now."

The two shuffled away.

Greg stood up and started pacing. "This cannot be our best option! Only the rich and powerful? We're talking like ten percent of the population at most! There has to be a way to get the gravitators working so we can evacuate *everyone* to Kazakhstan . . . But, even if we did have a way to power them, would there be enough time left to gravitate everyone at this point? How many people can each gravitator send at once, and how long does it take?"

"Theoretically, thousands of people could be sent at a time," Gwyn said, rubbing her eyes. Neither of them had gotten much sleep, but Gwyn never looked less than perfection. "And transporting is practically instantaneous. But none of that matters because we've tried everything, every battery, nuclear reactors . . . we even connected a gravitator directly into a city's power grid: it wiped out the power in a ten mile radius, and still only transported ten people ten feet. We designed the gravitators for large quantities of people, but we had no idea how much energy would be required."

I rolled my neck. There just was not enough time. Even if we had another *year*, the humans were unlikely to come up with an energy source powerful enough. My people's power source was completely unique. Using the Sacred Sponge to power the human gravitators had of course occurred to me, but I'd spoken to Stone and knew it would not work. Was there another option we had not thought of? It felt like there was, but I could not quite grasp hold of it.

"Aria," Greg said softly, sitting down next to me. "What if *your* people power them?"

Apparently, he had been thinking along the same lines I had. It being the end of the world and all, I had divulged my secret and told Greg and Gwyn about the power of the Sacred Sponge.

I shook my head. "I am sorry, but it will not work, Greg. The power in the Sacred Sponge is growing, but . . ." I attempted to put my feelings into words, "the power is all wrong. I tried to access it, and it . . . burned me. I thought my people could add more *good* power on top of it, but they are spent. They are tired. The Compound has not been good for them. We are lucky to be able to power a two person gravitator, let alone one for thousands. And I am told that if we tried, it would not work, and it would kill them."

"We've been talking about this for too long," Gwyn sighed. "I hate to say it and sound like I'm on the side of those two *scientists*, but I don't see that we have any other options. Let's just fill the bunkers, basements, whatever we can. Let's hand it off to the leaders of the UN," she motioned to the other group in the room, "and try to get as many people to Kazakhstan as possible. That includes me and you, Greg."

She looked away from us, and I saw her wipe her hand across a wet cheek. None of us were happy about this decision, even if she was probably right. Greg put his head in his hands.

I stood up, my arm around my middle, and Greg raised his head to look at me. "Aria, how are you doing? Can you hold out for step three?"

I nodded. Ejecting the bomb was still two days away, but the pain was already becoming distracting and it was likely to get a lot worse.

Two whole Earth-days. There had to be something we could do.

On the edges of my perception, something kept niggling at me—an idea that had been floating around my head for days, but never quite in focus. What was it? I opened my eyes and watched Greg who sat on the other side of Gwyn, his head hanging.

I thought back to the first time he touched my hand, of

our stolen kisses. They had been electric. Rejuvenating. As all kisses should be. But was there something more? The idea finally fell into place with a gentle, tired *sigh*, climbing through the fog and confusion and reclining there like a giant parasitic *earblade*.

Gwyn leaned back and yawned next to me. I reached over, laid my hand on Gwyn's arm, and looked into her eyes. I looked into her soul, searching not for zest, but for wakefulness. Perhaps it would work, perhaps not. Perhaps she would be too tired even for me to test it. I closed my eyes again.

There *was* something. Some type of energy within her. Like wakefulness, but it felt different. Sharper. More awkward. Like trying to caress someone's cheek, but missing to caress a cheese grater instead. I reached for it.

The zing of energy came so strongly the Sponge expanded to double its size, filled with light even considering the bomb poisoning it. I coughed and my bioluminescence flared purple and then gold. I suddenly felt lighter than I had in days.

"Holy cow," Greg whispered, staring at me with wide eyes.

Well, one more thing my scientists were wrong about: humans could power the Sponge.

And there was so *much* power. And so potent. Would all the humans be like this? Perhaps it was all that time you spent above ground, living and loving each other, building your lives. My people had almost forgotten what that felt like.

"What was that?" Gwyn asked, her eyes closing.

Greg was looking at me slack-jawed. "What'd you do to Gwyn?" he asked.

I patted Gwyn's shoulder as she fell asleep, then hopped up. "She will wake very soon, do not worry. I only stole a second of wakefulness. But I now know what to do," I said with conviction, even though I still had one big concern. "I know how to implement step two. And we have to hurry."

[36] And so, we offered you all a free alien abduction, no questions asked.[1] We sent another message-blast, telling you that we'd tried and failed to stop the bomb, and the world was coming to an end. We sent out the addresses of each gravitator and told you that if you wanted to live, you should converge on those locations and then a very nice alien queen would come and pick you up.

Most of you humans took us up on it. It was not an ideal solution, but it was the only one we had. Kazakhstan would soon be full to the brim with more people than it could support. The overcrowding, mass illness, and starvation would be devastating to the population, and I also suspected that the explosion might be too big to leave *anyone* alive, even there in Kazakhstan. But at least your chances of survival were significantly higher than if you stayed where you were. Gwyn left right away to evacuate the rest of the UN and start preparations in the middle east to receive you.

Hundreds of thousands of humans gathered at each gravitator site in North and South America, Europe, Africa, and Australia: two hundred abduction points filled with frightened people, anxious for me to arrive.

The gravitator platform in DC lay hidden in plain sight as

---

[1] What kinds of questions would I ask? I can think of several: Have you ever been abducted before? What is your five-year plan for this abduction? Who is your favorite Alien queen, etc.

an art feature behind the White House. Gwyn had mentioned that the gravitators they built were big enough to move thousands of people at once, but I had not been prepared for the scope of it. I stood on a fifteen-meter copper circle in the ground, its two delicate copper arches crisscrossed above our heads and a maze of electronics flashed faintly under our feet. It was built like a sort of giant gazebo. A hundred thousand men, women and children stood gathered in and around it.

I pulled Greg from where he waited off to one side, had him stand across from me in the middle of the platform, and grasped his hands in mine. I instructed all those nearby to lay their hands on my or Greg's shoulders, then to send a message on to the thousands gathered behind: *Squeeze together as tight as possible, linking hands or touching the shoulders of those in front of you.* Not everyone fit on the platform, but as long as we were linked, it would not matter.[2]

There was a fair amount of murmuring, and even some tight, fearful giggling at this, but we could hear the message rippling through the throng of humans around us. And already, I could feel the power building inside me, bright around the pain of the bomb, so eager to explode.

But would it be enough? There were at least a hundred thousand humans here. More than my entire race put together by far. Which brought me to my big, final concern, and it involved Greg.

I tried to catch his eye, but he may have been distracted

---

2   Of course, the people-pile-hug works best, but I realized that much physical contact might be a hard sell for humans.

by the many other people bumping up against him or by the many hands on his shoulders.

"Greg?"

"What?" he responded, finally looking at me.

"I need to ask you something important."

"Okay."

I took a breath and held it, then let it out. There was no time for delicacy or embarrassment right now. Billions of people's lives were on the line. "Do you love me?"

His eyes bulged. "Do I . . ."

I pushed on. "There are a lot of humans here, humans with voracity, will to live, wakefulness. It might be enough. But I need to be honest, this power-absorption works with my people mostly because they love me. Love is, of course, the most powerful force in the universe."

"Aria . . ." Greg's eyes shifted around to the strangers watching us curiously over our shoulders, and I pulled him closer, keeping his attention on me.

"If you do not love me, I think we can still save these people, Greg. I love *you*, and that might be sufficient," I said simply. "But I still need to know. Do you love me?"

He looked at me then, contemplating me, his head tipped to the side, but there was smolder behind the gray eyes, some of the laughter returning. "What about all that stuff you said about me being an unimportant, average, boring human? And you, a queen?"

I nodded. "Yes, you are. And yes, I am. And you are per-fect and amazing. I love you. Do you love me too?"

His gaze traveled over my face, over our clasped hands,

and then settled looking deep into my own. He smiled his half smile. "Yes. I love you," he breathed.

"You do?" I cried, louder than was probably necessary, pulling him to me so others behind him had to step forward in a ripple.

He chuckled, low and quiet, and nodded.

"Great," I said, clearing my throat and nodding, "Yes. Okay then. This should work fine." I was still nodding, unsure how to stop. "Oh, I think—yes, I think just for safety, we should kiss, then. Kiss me, Greg."

He laughed, a light, joyful sound I wanted to hear again and again. "You bet, Your Majesty."

An older human male behind Greg patted Greg's shoulder, making Greg freeze in the act of leaning in.

"You got this, son," said the human with a squeeze.

Greg looked sideways at him. "Uh . . . Thanks, man."

And because Greg is nothing if not obedient, he kissed me then without any more hesitation. A perfect kiss. A kiss to save the world.

As soon as I activated the Sponge, I knew. I knew this hundred thousand people-pile we'd created and sealed with Greg's kiss would work. And there would be enough power to send a hundred thousand people hundreds of thousands of miles.

Booger bubble!

It was enough to send the humans *light-years.*

And so I did. I sent you 4.24 light-years away. Had we promised you an alien abduction or not?

Greg and I repeated this process again and again, jumping to the next gravitator location and then to the next and to the next, where we sent millions and then billions of people off planet, each gravitation powered by an epic kiss more powerful than the last.

Over the next forty hours, we abducted humans until all the gravitator locations were empty.

When we finished at the last location, the Alaskan gravitator just outside the Compound,[3] and had finished sending all the remaining peacekeepers away, I looked at Greg, at his pillow lips and curl of hair on his forehead and smoldering half smile. He leaned in and kissed me again.

And with that kiss, I used the gravitator to send Greg away too before I could think too much about it, before he could argue, before he could talk me out of it. And I stayed behind.

I sent him to Shubarkuduk to the same government bunker as Gwyn.[4] I sent him so he would live. So that he might eventually eat delicious fresh fruit, go dancing, go to kindergarten graduations every day for the rest of his life if he wanted to: the rest of his life without me. He would hate me forever for this, but it was the only way to save him.

Then I stood there in the center of the platform, looking around at the lovely docile pines, at the peculiar blue sky, at

---

3   Those sneaky humans built a gravitator right outside our door and we never knew it! I suppose they hoped to remove all the peacekeeper guards quickly in case we suddenly rose up and became violent.

4   Perhaps I should have sent him off-planet. But if you knew Greg, you would understand. Never was there a human more human than he, and he was meant to be on Earth.

the mountain top where the Compound stood, my people safe in their metal box deep underground. Soon, they would not need me or my power units anymore. They would be free.

"Goodbye," I said aloud even though neither my people nor the pine trees could hear me, and then I gravitated myself to Point Nemo with only seconds to spare, immediately plunging deep into the salty ocean.

It was too late to eject the Sponge now. It had been too late for hours. I only hoped the time spent gravitating those last few humans would not make things worse, would not mean the destruction of the entire planet. And I hoped that by not ejecting the Sponge, perhaps my body itself would absorb some of the blast? I would not know either way. But thinking back to every one of those world-saving kisses, confused humans looking on, it seemed worth it.

The moment arrived. As I sank slowly downward, there was an intense flare of pain and heat from my belly button, and a flash of colorful light coming out of my extremities, bubbles bursting out of me in waves within the dark water.

I felt a strange sense of peaceful euphoria as I watched the shooting colors, and then everything went bright white and then black.

$[37]$ Of course I did not die. You already know this. I am the one writing this report to you. But for a time, I was very sure I would. I was very sure I *had*. But then I awoke floating on some space junk in the middle of the ocean. Somehow, I'd survived. Naked, skin raw, all devices gone, Sacred Sponge gone, aching all over, and the furthest from land I could possibly be—but still alive.

I do not know how I survived. I am convinced that the Sponge managed to protect me, somehow, perhaps ejecting itself before it exploded. And maybe the personal shield on the Everything Device then protected me from the brunt of the blast before it disintegrated as well. This seems as good an explanation as any.

And I am very sorry to have misled you—both when I first gravitated you away and again throughout this report—but the planet also survived. My words were not an outright lie: we do still call this event the end of the world, even though the planet is still technically intact. But aside from the devastating earthquakes and massive tsunamis and volcano eruptions, and the loss of power and homes and lives across the globe, the damage was actually quite minimal. Nearly all human-made infrastructure is gone except in the middle east, but the plants and animals seem to be recovering and adapting quite nicely. This is good news, is it not?

It took weeks, maybe months, for Penny to retrieve me from Point Nemo. I spent the time exploring an almost completely intact space station that was bobbing along under-water.[1] I admit that, though I had been ready to die for you, I was grateful I had not died and more grateful to be given clothing, even if it was only a sheet toga.

Hopefully, you were grateful to be alive where you were, as well. Not on your own planet anymore, but alive.

You are welcome.

I chose to send you to the space station planet MageStorm[2] because, besides the easy proximity (less than five light-years!), the artificial air there is comparable to Earth, though with less smog. Is less smog a positive or negative for you?

Also I sent you there because, as a very popular waypoint for space travel in the galaxy, the people on MageStorm are accustomed to enormous groups arriving en masse, so I did not think your arrival would cause too much of an upset for them. It is only temporary, but you have many options from there.

I do think those on MageStorm might have been surprised when all of you arrived in piles and asleep. You were likely only somewhat-less surprised when you awoke to a bustling metropolis, a metal planet fifteen times bigger than Earth, in perpetual night, and filled with aliens of every shape and size. Four billion humans, and you are only—how do you phrase it? A drop in the bucket. Or two.

---

1   I was very glad, now, to have received that royal training course on long-term underwater survival, even though it had seemed boring at the time.

2   Which is in the vicinity of the star you call Proxima Centauri. I hope you already know this, since knowing one's position in the cosmos is helpful for a traveler among the stars such as yourself.

The Human Survivors, I hear you call yourselves. Seems a little dramatic for such a large number of you, but I suppose you can name yourselves anything you want. I did explode your planet, after all, and though I did not completely destroy it and I saved your lives, it was still the end of the world, for you. Which is sad. Your feelings are valid.

You'll be pleased to know Earth is faring fairly well now, considering. I understand we missed a spectacular light show when the explosion went off. I am told that from a distance, it looked like a giant colorful zit bloomed and then popped out of the side of the planet, shooting out gas like a glitter bomb.[3]

The air in many parts of the world is permanently changed, but I understand it will only be another ten years before places like Africa and Europe will also be somewhat livable for you again. Maybe some of you will decide to return. The trip will take you ten years on most freighters—if you can convince any transport freighters to come this direction—so you should arrive just in time.

Around a billion people survived back here on Earth, waiting patiently underground for seven days in Kazakhstan, and our expeditions are finding more survivors every day all over the globe. It is true that many people died, and with current conditions, many here are still dying, for which I am sorry. However, I have noticed that at many human meetings I've attended, the talk and complaints are less about the deaths and destruction and more about the lack of Wi-Fi and something you call Netflix. I myself do miss many aspects of your western culture, as was, especially new Hollywood

---

3   My favorite kind.

movies. But once we are able to rebuild more, we should at least be able to watch some of the *old* movies, which *I* prefer anyway.

While I do live half the time with my people in Antarctica (in structures *above* ground), they generally govern themselves now. No Sponge means no Keeper, and in the absence of this official hierarchy, we decided to try a democracy again, with me as little more than a figurehead.[4]

In fact, Penny is running for one of our leadership positions. I voted for her. The person running against her is Barry Hickenbottom, and as a human, and one who wears boxers in public, he is unlikely to win, but maybe they will give him an honorary position like mine? And although she will not admit it, I suspect Penny is seeing someone new. A human. I will try not to be too smug when she finally tells me. A bit of distance from me seems to be good for her.

When I am not with my people, I live among the humans, off and on. Gwyn,[5] for example, has become my favorite shopping buddy, shopping being what it is now. And Greg and I are able to go out on recovery expeditions to search for survivors, art, working technology, undamaged sticky notes, etc. Most of our Booshy technology was also destroyed, so either Greg or I must always have some kind of human air filtering mask everywhere we go, but Booshy scientists are

---

4   We have not tried that since Harmer the Barrel-Waisted broke the sacred hammer a millennia ago. But I still have high hopes.

5   I know I told you in a previous footnote she was dead. Well, I lied. But if you ever return here and see her again, could you please pretend not to notice? I think she would appreciate it. She is enjoying the anonymity of death.

working with the human scientists to create something more sustainable that also will not get in the way of kissing. It is a serious problem.

Since almost nobody knows my people caused the explosion, the humans here respect and revere us "good aliens," some of them even worshipping us as gods. It's a little awkward, but the situation is better than when we were your refugees, no offense intended.[6] We are trying to be worthy of human regard as well as pay back the generosity we receive by helping to return your planet to what it once was. We are working to rebuild the structures, and the technology, and we keep nothing back from the humans here anymore. I think if you return, you will find your planet much changed for the better. Do not thank us: it is the least we could do after destroying it and sending you away.

So, I am sure that many of you reading are asking why I bothered to write this very long apology (I know this because both Penny and Greg have asked me many times while I wrote it). As far as you understood until reading this, the bad aliens destroyed the Earth but then died with it,[7] and the good aliens saved you and sent you somewhere safe. So why tell you that most of what you believed is a lie only to anger you and then apologize for it?

Well, firstly, lies are bad, and apologies are good. Apologizing is what good people do, *by the way, Greg.*

---

6   The humans even negotiated giving us Antarctica, officially and permanently, for our own use and development. If any of you lived there before the end of the world and want it back, we can thumb wrestle you for it if you ever come to claim it.

7   Which is actually true. Rest in peace, Woods.

I want to make good choices, even if they are hard. And it was not easy to write this, believe me. Since I no longer have the Sacred Sponge, I can no longer power the translator to speak your languages automatically. So, one of your humans, Ms. Pozo, is helping me as a ghost writer/translator/editor. She is a bit weird, but I chose her because she is very good at what she does.[8] The process has not been smooth. Still, I think it is what you would call "the right thing to do."

Even though I've come to realize that humans have just as complicated a relationship with truth as we do, it was still *your* example that convinced me we never should have lied and then told the truth only to lie again. And even though Greg has repeatedly tried to dissuade me from doing this, it was being with him that convinced me to write this apology report in the first place: you do not tell lies to people you might come to love.

So, sorry humans. Especially Greg. For lying and now for telling the truth. And I love you. Especially Greg, again.

The other reason I am writing this long apology is because MageStorm is not truly meant for long-term living, but as a stop between destinations.[9] And I have recently learned that plans are underway for you Human Survivors to relocate to a new planet. One with sunshine. It is called Fathma.

---

8   Meaning she is available, cheap, and does whatever I say.

9   Living on MageStorm is very like living on a spaceship, actually, and trust me when I say living in space might seem fun at first but gets old fast. Which is why my people did not stay on MageStorm more than a few years either.

So, for those of you planning on relocating rather than returning to Earth, I wanted to send you our well wishes. The planet is already inhabited, but the inhabitants only live in the frozen sections, which leaves all the hundreds of thousands of private islands with white beaches and un-sentient delicious plant life up for the taking. The big yellow sun and un-frigid air seemed disappointing to my people, but maybe you will enjoy it. Humans are hard to predict.

Still, you will be guests there, dependent on the generosity of others. Which means you will soon find yourselves alien ~~invaders~~ refugees too. And as someone who has recently been an alien refugee, I think I can offer some advice.

1. Be yourself. You might assume that being yourself would make a bad impression, and be tempted to try being someone/something else very unlike yourself, then when that does not work, going back to being yourself again. But considering the result for us, I suggest having your identity crisis *before* arriving on the nice, new, intact planet in the first place. You should get on that right away.

2. I suggest abandoning any silly, meaningless last name you possess and coming up with a title for yourself instead. Reinvent and rediscover yourself[10] anew in this brand new place. You could be Bill Handy with a Fishing Pole, Jane Cannot Cook but Cleans Windows,

---

10   I know I just said to be yourself, and I still stand by that. Maybe you can be yourself and reinvent yourself at the same time. Be your new reinvented self.

or John Not a Port-a-Potty. Also, I should probably mention this naming convention is a requirement on this particular planet, so this is less of a suggestion and more of a law.

3. Try not to have unrealistic expectations of your abilities. Just because you do not have any intention of blowing up a very nice planet and hurting lots of very nice people's feelings does not mean you might not accidentally do it anyway.

4. If you meet someone named Greg, no matter how innocuous he might seem, nod politely, and then simply walk the other way.[11]

Oh, and when you arrive at Fathma, you should perhaps be aware that my uncle is technically the leader there in the Frozen Mountains, as one of the Fallen Branches of Bough. And since I am technically heir to the Fallen Branches of Bough, I would prefer he not know I blew up your planet and that I am here? He already thinks me irresponsible after that whole debacle with the painting I made of his nose when I was nine, and he is *soooo* annoying when he is mad. Why do you think we did not settle there in the first place? We applied and were denied, just like everywhere else. My uncle loathes family reunions. But I am sure he will be much more welcoming to you, as poor helpless refugees, than he was to us, his annoying relations. And if not, you can always turn around and come back here. Just give us a heads-up as soon

---

11   Sorry, Greg. But you know what you did. Also, can you pick up some canned beans for dinner tonight?

as possible so we can try to clear out some more of the rubble for you.[12]

Anyway, sorry again, but all you can do is your best, right? Good luck! ☺

Aria

Seventh Daughter of Morr, Keeper Destroyer of the Sacred Sponge and a Very Nice Planet, Final Monarch of the Thirteenth Planet of LifeStar, Reluctant Heir to the Fallen Branches of Bough, Apologizer Extraordinaire.[13]

---

12   The sooner you send word, the better, since it may be a few years before any mail gets to us. Letters are always notoriously slow once you get past the Faraday belt.

13   I no longer share this full title, for a few obvious reasons. Mainly because it is just way too long. And I prefer my new last name of Jones.

Greg's Flapjack Recipe

1 ½ cup buttermilk

2 cups of flour

4 tablespoons white sugar

1 ¾ tablespoons baking powder

½ teaspoon of salt

2 eggs

4 tablespoons salted butter, melted

A dash of vanilla

A dash of club soda

Extra butter for frying

Instructions:

Mix the wet and dry ingredients separately (whisk the wet ingredients to a froth), and then add wet ingredients to a well in the dry, mixing until there are no more clumps. Add buttermilk or flour until desired consistency.

If you have time, let the batter breathe for about a half hour before frying. If you are in a hurry (because you are trying to help a beautiful alien prevent death and destruction or something), you can forgo this step.

Heat a skillet over medium heat, and melt a slab of butter for frying. Pour pancakes to desired size, and fry each side until edges are dry, about 2 to 3 minutes each.

Eat with fresh cream and the fruit of your choice (Aria prefers sliced strawberries with a dusting of powdered sugar).

Aria's Flat Fried Food Thing*

Liquid substance

½ cup Night Foley oil

½ cup squeezed Junju tree sap

½ cup water

½ teaspoon Starbelt crystals

Solid substance

5 – 6 cups Delta bun crumbles

½ – ¾ cup Delta dandruff

½ – ¾ cup Numbum dust

Instructions:

Combine liquid substance in a large pan.

Liquid Substance Substitutions: If Night Foley Oil is unavailable because one of the moons is in retrograde, use any vegetable oil of your choice. You may substitute honey for the tree sap, as Junju trees are often migrating, making the sap hard to extract. And salt is a slightly less colorful and less bitter substitute for the Starbelt crystals.

Bring to a very slow simmer (careful as it will boil over), and let simmer for five minutes, then let cool. Add spices as desired. Make sure to tent the mixture as it cools in case any stray spores remain.

Combine solid substances in a large pot or bowl. Keep in mind that our harvesting of Deltas is what probably led to their eventual uprising and kicking us off Booshlaboo,† so it can only be done during hibernation. Substitutions may be better.

Solid Substance Substitutions: Harvested Delta is vaguely similar to your oats, so rolled oats could substitute for the bun crumbles, and oat bran for dandruff. There is nothing like Numbums on Earth (as was), but wheat germ or toasted quinoa would probably work.

Mix the solids and liquids into one bowl or pot until thoroughly moistened. Spread into a shallow baking pan and bake at 150 degrees C for up to one and one-half of your hours. If you desire a crumble consistency instead of a cake consistency (which is actually what I would suggest because it is too hard for your soft teeth to bite into otherwise), stir occasionally so the browning will be even. It is done when it is your favorite shade of brown.

Eat with fresh cream and the fruit of your choice (I prefer sliced strawberries with a dusting of powdered sugar).

---

* Note that on Booshlaboo, we do not have bread or cake because we do not technically have usable grains, but this is a recipe that is somewhat close to Greg's flapjack recipe—or at least as close as a non-bread, non-cake can be—and has been handed down in my family for generations of royalty.

† This might surprise you since you may have gotten the impression that the plant life was trying to kill us, not kick us off Booshlaboo. Well, it was actually both. They kicked us off for refusing to be killed.

Acknowledgments

Most of this book is completely unrecognizable compared to the first draft, and there have been many people who stuck their noses in along the way, so thank you. First and foremost, thank you to my family who continually showed patience and support for my writing even when I stopped paying attention to anything else. Many of my jokes came from my family because they are way funnier than I am. You guys are my reason for writing, my reason for living, and I love you.

And thanks to my ANWA writing group. When I brought my first chapter of Sorry, Humans, I was absolutely positive you were all going to hate it, but instead you were so complimentary and showed so much support, I decided maybe to keep writing it. I *had* to dedicate this book to my husband (If you've seen how pretty he is, you understand), but truthfully I wrote most of this book for you guys. Thanks for being who you are.

And thank you to Splinter Press. I came on staff thinking I was the only editor, but what took me years of schooling and experience to learn apparently comes naturally to you people. You are amazing in the most annoying way. Thanks so much for making this book what it is and having patience with me during the process.

A big thanks to my readers and proofreaders for pushing through when the book wasn't very fun to read. Specifically, thanks to Brooke Hampton, Tifani Clark, Jessie Olson, Heather Randall,

Becky Saldivar, Keven Prusak, Regan Wolfe, Janelle Youngstrom, Michelle Hutchins, Dedra Tregaskis, Joyce Gunther, Tanya Knudsen, and Trina Pettus.

And thanks to you readers for picking up this book and reading it. I hope you had as much fun reading it as I did writing it. And, if you didn't, please forgive me. I hope we can still be friends.

Faralee Pozo is the senior editor of Splinter Press. She's also worked as a freelance editor for several years, editing and formatting books for authors and companies worldwide. *Sorry, Humans (Especially Greg)* is Faralee's debut novel.

In her spare time, she plays tabletop games with her family, reads, and tries to avoid cooking.

Join my newsletter

Get early access to stories
and exclusive content

Scan with
your camera
to join

www.ingramcontent.com/pod-product-compliance
Lightning Source LLC
Chambersburg PA
CBHW020249010826
48973CB00006B/1721